PRAISE FOR *BEFORE*

"A haunting dystopian thriller. . . .Fans of *The Handmaid's Tale* won't want to miss this one." —*Publishers Weekly* (starred review)

"Stands on its own as a novel that will have readers contemplating rebellion and revolt, sex and power, and the many ways women's bodies are sacrificed for the good of society." —*Booklist*

"An overdue enlargement of the cultural conversation that [*The Handmaid's Tale*] continues to provoke." —*Kirkus Reviews*

"Shah's novel is both explicitly connected to Atwood's marvel [*The Handmaid's Tale*] and working to expand it by imagining what a secular, Middle Eastern Gilead might look like…. One of the best books of the second half of 2018." —The Millions

"Provocative." —Syfy.com, One of the Best Books of Summer 2018

"Essential." —Barnes & Noble Blog

"Stands out among all the other dystopian future books of its kind." —*Seattle Book Review*

"A timely novel of women's resistance and determination. By setting her book in a future Middle East and South Asia, Bina Shah has given us a welcome addition to the feminist dystopian thriller that expands the genre beyond a white-centric gaze. Women's stories and women's voices—in all our diversity—are important and Bina Shah's thriller is a necessary reminder." —Mona Eltahawy, author of *Headscarves and Hymens: Why the Middle East Needs a Sexual Revolution*

"The 21st century answer to *The Handmaid's Tale*… Gripping, smart and dystopian in the most terrifying way, which is to say that it seems so very possible." —Molly Crabapple, author of *Drawing Blood*

"The most subtly disturbing of dystopias, richly textured and appallingly intimate, Before She Sleeps has hints of Huxley and Atwood but is uniquely Bina Shah." —Nick Harkaway, author of *Gnomon and The Gone-Away World*

"The world building is superb… a powerful and interesting metaphor for us to listen to today." —Audible.com Best New Releases, September 2018

"A moving tale about a frightening future that could all too easily come to pass." —Tor.com

ALSO BY BINA SHAH

Animal Medicine
Where They Dream in Blue
The 786 Cybercafe
Blessings
Slum Child
A Season for Martyrs

BEFORE
SHE SLEEPS

A NOVEL

BINA SHAH

DELPHINIUM BOOKS

BEFORE SHE SLEEPS

Copyright © 2019 by Bina Shah

A hardcover edition of this book was published
by Dephinium in June 2018

First Delphinium Paperback Edition June 2019

Library of Congress Cataloguing-in-Publication Data is available on
request.

ISBN 978-1-88-328580-7

19 20 21 22 23 LSC 10 9 8 7 6 5 4 3 2 1

Cover and interior design by Greg Mortimer

For her

PART 1

RELUCTANCE

FROM *THE OFFICIAL GREEN CITY HANDBOOK FOR FEMALE CITIZENS*

No citizen is permitted to write or maintain a personal journal or diary.

This rule applies to all citizens, but for Green City's girls and women, understanding is even more important than compliance. We must focus completely on the task of survival, which means we must focus on the present and the future. Trying to salvage the past is an act of self-indulgence that can lead to selfishness; you must avoid this at all costs. Only when each individual girl exchanges selfishness for selflessness, and sacrifices self-involvement for the care of others, can Green City achieve its destiny as a place of ingenuity, industry, and prosperity. You will be its foot soldiers, working hard to fulfill your role as the mothers of the new nation.

SABINE

I make it a rule to always leave the Client's house in the darkest part of the morning, the half hour before dawn, when the night's at its thickest and the Agency Officers are at their slowest. This is the time of day I fear the most, out of all the hours in the day that pass me by like flies crawling in front of my face. The Client, a man whom I only know as Joseph—none of us uses last names in this business—nods impatiently at all the rules as I set them down; he's done this many times before, and not always with me. To my relief, he behaves himself, wrapping his arms around me and contentedly sighing every few moments, not attempting anything more intrusive than those chaste embraces.

Within a half hour, I can tell by his regular breathing that he's fallen asleep. I never sleep when I'm with a Client. Insomnia is a lifetime's curse without a night's reprieve, even though it's precisely what makes me so good at what I do. I slip away from the bed, find the armchair in the room and sink down in it. I match my breathing to mimic Joseph's as he shifts from left to right and back again. Normally I don't think, or daydream; I just sit there waiting for morning, knowing that the slightest tension in my body would be enough to wake him from his slumber. I don't want that.

But toward the early morning, when the alarm on my wrist begins to glow, and I come close for a last embrace, Joseph tightens his arms around me again.

Although it's not allowed, sometimes I bend the rules and allow a Client a moment or two of comfort before extricating myself gracefully and heading for the door. Lin always tells us to be wary about who plays by the rules and who pushes the boundaries. Joseph's expensive watch on the nightstand, his plush bedroom slippers by the door, the black silk sheets on the bed, and the low glowing lights sunk into recesses at regular intervals across the floor, making a chiaroscuro of the ceiling, all tell me that this is a man to push boundaries wherever he can.

"Joseph, I've had a lovely time with you. But now I have to leave." I turn around to smile at him, the smile that manages to smooth things over with anyone. I've spent hours staring into the mirror, perfecting that smile. It doesn't come naturally.

Joseph raises himself up on one arm. His body was once powerful but now it's on its way to fast decline: heavy, untoned shoulders, a neck that wrinkles and crepes around his throat, white hairs outnumbering the black ones still dotting his chest. "Stay. I can afford to keep you all day if that's what you want."

I grimace, my back to him. "I'm sorry, Joseph. The rules are the rules. I have to be out of here before dawn."

"But why?"

"You *know* why," I say, momentarily nonplussed. We all know what's at stake if we're caught: the Agency has made sure to publicize all crimes well in the Flashes on the display, the Bulletins, even through door-to-door visits, something almost unheard of in this time where almost everything is done remotely and anonymously. All the more ominous when an Agency car is parked outside someone's house and two Officers, with their immaculate uniforms and unreadable faces, are educating someone inside about the repercussions of associating with illegals like me.

Joseph rests his hand lightly on my forearm. "I know people. Nothing is going to happen to you or me. If you knew who I am —"

"It's too dangerous for me to know who you are. Or for me to stay any longer than necessary. Now would you please let me get dressed?"

Joseph sighs. But he doesn't give up. He follows me to the bathroom, standing in the doorway, turning his head away as

I coat my skin in gold silicon powder, then put on my clothes. He studies my face as I cover my body with as much cloth in as little time as possible. He follows me to the door of his apartment, his forefinger lingering on the security button, circling it, taunting me with his nonchalance. "Are you sure you're not going to change your mind?"

The sun's starting to rise, the sky shifting from black to smoky gray. In a few more minutes the blanket of night will start to lift from the horizon and the next Agency patrol will be on the street. Our cars are programmed to keep a two-hundred-yard distance from the patrols, and to abort the pickup if a patrol is on the same street as a Client's house. My car will simply never arrive. Stranded, I'll be spotted and my presence immediately messaged to the Officers. I'll be arrested and taken in and my life, as I know it, will be over.

"Joseph, let me go. Please."

My fear is an animal I can't hide—I've never been able to completely control my expressions—but for some reason my vulnerability assuages something in Joseph.

"All right. But keep a night free for me sometime next week."

I nod, wishing I never had to see Joseph again. His eyes search mine for some sign of disappointment that I have to leave. My gaze is fixed steady on him, and his finger depresses the security button. The door slides open silently. I step in, exchanging the calculated danger of his apartment, and the greed that furnishes it, for the open territory of the illegal and the hunted.

I move down the stairs, pause, then creep to the doorway of the luxury apartment building where Joseph lives. My footsteps echo like gunshots in the giant marble-floored hall.

The robotic doorman hums quietly at the left of the entrance. It's just a computerized desk, where residents punch in for security and to collect messages, or to leave their own messages to complain about a malfunctioning cooling unit or request an extra display to be installed in the second bedroom, but Joseph likes to pretend it's human, and makes fun of it for being stupid.

I'm grateful for the desk's stupidity. The gold powder that I'm coated in will prevent the security systems from picking up my DNA on the scanners. The video camera won't get activated and I can't be identified as I walk into or out of any building in Green City. As for the other humans: most of the residents are asleep this early in the day. If anyone does see me, they'll keep their head down and pretend they can't see me either, like the doorman. No matter how many good-citizenship sessions they attend, now matter how much of the Handbook they've memorized, nobody really wants to report me—the filling out of voluminous forms, the interrogations: it's just not worth the trouble.

My eyes scan the road for the unmarked car, and with a spasm of horror I see a dark blue Agency car with hologram plates sliding down the street toward the building. My heart starts to pound. I pull my head back in. For a moment I'm afraid I'm going to lose all sense of reality. I tremble as I stand in the doorway, counting slowly backward from a hundred.

The Agency car stops directly opposite Joseph's building. I flatten myself against the wall as the two Officers emerge and stand at the side of the road. I'm ready to run back to Joseph's apartment and beg for his protection. My own car will have sensed the Agency car and gone straight back to the Panah. My only hope is Joseph's generosity.

If the Officers come into the building, they'll easily see me from across the hall with its cavernous ceiling and absence of greenery; the large hall is as open as an airplane hangar. I might be able to duck down behind the doorman and crouch into the space beneath the counter. If they only glance into the hallway to look for suspicious activity, there's a chance they won't catch me. They might be tired, their senses and instincts not working at their best. They will conduct only a perfunctory search, and I can hide, then signal for a new pickup from a different location.

My body lowers, instinctively assuming the stance of a sprinter. I'm a good short-distance runner, but I lack the stamina to go long distances. A sudden burst of energy is all I need now to get under the desk. In my peripheral vision I can see the Officers kneeling down, examining the ground for traces of something. I hate the very sight of them, their close-cropped heads and their authoritative, well-developed shoulders. Why have they sent Officers to do what a security squad could take care of? Where's their electronic equipment, the sniffer bots, the handheld scanners that can trace a drop of blood in a ton of dust?

One of the Officers shouts out to the other, and reaches out in front of him to pick up something small that glints and sparkles in the morning sun. I realize that this is no murder investigation. It's not even a sweep for illegals. The Officers don't look like they are on active Agency duty. They've spotted something valuable that someone dropped as they walked by—a gemstone, perhaps, or a currency stick. They're not exercising their official powers. It's good old-fashioned greed that's made them stop, get out of their car, and acquire the trinket to keep it for themselves. I almost laugh out loud in relief.

They get back in their car and drive away. I bend over, trying to regain my calm. My mouth tastes bitter and I reach into my purse for a mint strip that contains a small calming agent embedded in the freshness crystals. My skyrocketing pulse immediately comes back down to earth. As I stand up, the unmarked black car sweeps in to pause in front of the building.

The Panah is waiting for me.

I slip inside the car. The doors lock automatically and

the car glides away from the pavement, a big black swan that folds its wings around me and carries me back to the Panah. Embraced by the warmth of the heating and enveloped in the softness of the leather seats, I allow myself to close my eyes. I never have to worry about the Agency Officers when I'm inside; they have their instructions never to stop a car with darkened windows or the special silver detailing on the back, which triggers a DO NOT OBSTRUCT message to their handheld devices as we pass them by. I usually never speak to the driver, but right now I have a desperate need for friendly contact. "What happened? Did you see them?"

"Good morning," the driver replies at last. Well, he's not really a human, just a computerized voice and chip system, behind a customized panel, since this is a self-driving car. That keeps all of us safe, in case someone stops the car when it's on its way to me. It can't talk much beyond its basic command set, and it's been programmed to emit false destination signals to Agency Officers. "My system detected a potential threat," continues the driver, "but threat level is now low and I am authorized to continue your ride."

My fingers reach for the flask of tea that Lin always puts in the car. The physical manifestation of her warmth and her care takes the edge off my exhaustion at the end of a long working night. I take a few grateful swallows, then sink back against the seat and close my eyes for a moment.

I want only to see darkness, but instead, my mind conjures up the image that Rupa, Lin, and I saw on this morning's info bulletin: a dead woman, lying on the floor of a nondescript house somewhere in Green City, her body picked out from the shadows by a ray of bright, unforgiving sunshine.

The info bulletin's quick, urgent female voice issued from the display, a large screen on a low table in the middle of the Panah's biggest room. "It is reported today, I repeat, today that a Wife has committed suicide in her home in Qanna neighborhood. She was found by her third Husband, who reported the event to the Agency. The Agency immediately sealed off the area, but our sources tell us that the Wife committed suicide in a most criminal manner."

My stomach clenched at the sight of the woman, arms and legs splayed in grotesque angles, blood pooling around her body, trapping her like an insect in a circle of red amber. Rupa clutched my arm, Lin stiffened by my side. They knew how difficult it was for me to hear this kind of news.

The tinny, officious voice went on, each word a hammer to our hearts. "Nurya Salem had five Husbands and was due to be married again to a sixth at the end of the month. It is suspected that she was opposed to the marriage, although this cannot be confirmed. Her children, five girls and two boys, have not been told about her actions. They will be taken to a care facility, informed of their mother's death, and treated for trauma before being returned to the house where the Wife lived with her Husbands. This particular family will be reassigned a Wife by the end of the month, along with compensation for the tragedy endured by them, by order of the Perpetuation Bureau."

Diyah was saying a prayer in the corner of the room as Lin switched off the display. Even Rupa bowed her head, watching me from the corner of her eye to make sure I was all right. There were no whispered prayers on my lips. Why should I weep for them?

The picture of a tree-filled settlement, green leaves skittering in a gentle breeze, now filled the display, to calm and soothe us. But the woman's corpse still lay heavy on our minds, her blood smearing us with complicity and despair. It's understood that while the Officials try to make life in Green City look smooth and placid, sometimes violence or lust or greed breaks through the artificial calm. Crime illustrates what we humans are fully capable of when our manmade defenses against our lower selves prove too much to bear. They'll even use suicide to their advantage. By showing us the woman's body in such a cruel way, the Bureau wants us to see what happens when human nature isn't contained. It wants us to know we aren't strong enough to contain it by ourselves. That we need their help, their guidance. Otherwise, we're lost. However, we are not Wives, because we aren't of Green City: we do not consent to their conspiracy, first to decimate us, then to distribute those of us who remain among themselves as if we were cattle, or food.

When I open my eyes again, we're already far away from Joseph's compound, sailing swiftly for home. I watch the growing dawn through the darkened windows of my car. The sun has vaulted past the horizon now, the city's ambitious skyline shot through with threads of a lighter gray. The edges and spaces between the skyscrapers are already starting to bleed red. But the city isn't singing yet. On a busy day, with its myriad radio frequencies and optic lines, the buzzing of the high-efficiency cars cutting smoothly across fiberglass roads and planes vibrating through the sky, Green City is a chorus of sound and sight. Only the crackle of neon punctuates the hush in those last ghostly minutes when night fades and gives way to a new day in Green City. When I come out of my underground life to the surface, my eyes are weak as a mole's. I'm dazzled by all the sunlight, limitless space: infinite possibility.

It's hard to believe that only a hundred years ago there was nothing here but sand. Can you imagine a city pushing itself out of the ground, a nation giving birth to itself? First modest houses, low walls, long dusty roads, the infant city encircled by desert, reminding it of where it came from. Then more ambitious buildings, bigger houses, children overtaking their fathers, suburban settlements cratered far and wide, pushing the desert back further and further. And now the desert is a mirage where our ancestors once lived. We have defeated the desert and replaced it with this paean to human achievement.

This city, among whose numbers I used to count myself, was once known as Mazun, an ancient name meaning "clouds laden with rain," even though deserts rarely see rain. The heat used to be unbearable every day of the year, and most summer nights you felt as though you couldn't breathe when you stepped outside. So the Leaders ordered the planting of thousands of trees and cared for them as if they were made of gold. "Plant Your Future," the scheme was called. They requisitioned millions of gallons of cultivated water so that the trees would grow faster than normal, and in twenty years dry desert gave way to lushness and fertility. Seduced by such beauty, the clouds massed over the city, but still needed coaxing to release their treasure. The scientists seed them regularly with biospores whenever they need rain, some of which is falling now on the wide boulevard, misting the windows of the car.

This is how Mazun came to be known as Green City. The Leaders didn't mind; in fact, they encouraged the new name, knowing everyone would feel prosperous and content as the citizens of a green and pleasant land. They wanted to sever the ties with the past, and to be known as the creators of this oasis, powerful deities who could change even the weather through their will. The Green City ecosystem, a trademarked brand, is all about preserving the seasons and cycles, or at least the illusion of them.

But we have had to pay a heavy price for the new version of normality.

Sipping Lin's tea, speeding safely away from Joseph's building, at certain moments in the back of this cold steel carriage, my femininity is no longer my weakness. Then again, women like me are never meant to feel safe. We steal our freedom when and where we can. And I, the provider of peaceful sleep to these men who pay for something they can never own, am destined to spend yet another sleepless night in my bed at the Panah. I never sleep; I keep vigil over my Clients, the men, while they dream. I give them protection and shelter against their nightmares, their loneliness, their melancholy. I'm their sentinel, and in return they pretend to the authorities that I don't exist. Because if the authorities knew about me, or the Panah, we would die.

I am Morpheus, Insomnia is my ever-faithful lover. Maybe we're crazy, or we're criminals, like wretched Nurya Salem. But we know exactly what we are doing, and at what cost to ourselves.

Lin always waits up for me, no matter how late it gets. When I return, I always go straight to her room, and we sit together, while she smokes an e-spliff. I love Lin's room, the walls painted dark red, the old Moroccan carpets on the floor, her antique wooden chest, sides carved with a filigreed design, underneath the most intricate wall hanging. A brass lamp mirrors the same design, sending richly woven mosaics of light on her walls when, lighted, it turns and twists above our heads, throwing stars onto our bodies.

Her bed is made of the same wood as the chest and draped with a rich, rust-colored bedspread. Another brass lamp stands on a nightstand next to the bed, casting a warm glow in the room, and cushions with mirrored covers are scattered on the floor. They belonged to Lin's aunt Ilona Serfati, who smuggled it all in when she, along with her best friend, Fairuza Dastani, founded the Panah. Those names are legend to all of us. We never get tired of hearing how the two of them came to this place, built it with their own hands, and kept it all a secret under the Agency's nose. We see their brilliance in the artificial garden they built, the Charbagh, with its flowers, shrubs, hanging vines. Their vision illuminates the sophisticated lighting system they set up to mimic the days and seasons. Their rebellion thrills us, gives us courage when we don't think we can make it through another night or stand to see another Client.

Ilona has been gone for twenty years, but her treasures make Lin's room feel rich and warm. They remind Lin that she comes from somewhere, from someone. It's a good thing she had Ilona to help her grow up. I know all too well what it feels like to be motherless, although I'm luckier than Lin. At least I had my mother for twelve years, though the line that truncates my life into before mother and after mother is as painful as a blade on my skin. I can't imagine what it's like to grow up orphaned.

I'm the only one Lin lets inside her room. I'm glad. I'd be jealous of anyone else she'd allow into this inner sanctum. We all respect Lin, want to be in her favor, but I am the one chosen to be her confidante, for reasons that she's never told me.

She rolls her eyes and half smiles when I lie down on her bed, covered in silicon, shining like a golden child. Lin has to perform miracles with both Clients and our benefactors in order to procure the gold. It's smuggled from the mines of Gedrosia, a country rich in minerals and ore. They send it to her in small tins, hidden underneath other cosmetics, and she mixes it with silicon for us. Clients always complain that it leaves a shimmering residue in their beds, but they're only half upset about it. My Clients are always fascinated with it, stroking their fingers against my shimmering skin. Some even say it's an aphrodisiac, but I think they like that it's real gold dust: we signal to them that we are even more precious than gold.

Lin knows the ins and outs of our bodies, our secret birthmarks and tattoos, the days of our cycle, how often we wash our hair. We're racehorses she sends off into the night and takes back into her safekeeping in the morning.

Every time Lin sees the dark circles under my eyes, she shakes her head. Sometimes she says she can smell insomnia coming off me in gray, depressing waves.

"Come on, Sabine, there's always something you can try. They're coming up with new drugs all the time."

"No, Lin. Believe me, if there were a magic pill to cure me, I'd take it in a heartbeat. Nothing affects me, not even this," I say, pointing at the spliff. It's true: I'd like nothing better than to shut my eyes and drift away, surrender myself to unconsciousness even for a few short hours, with her watching over me. But there's no cure for the insomnia, chemical or natural, temporary or permanent. I know Lin thinks I'm being foolish. But Lin's a sound sleeper; she never understands that my mind can't rest, that my thoughts chase each other like snakes swallowing their own tails, in a dark chemical wave. I often wonder about my father: I wonder if he misses me, if he wishes we could see each other again. Does he realize the cost of his greed to get me married quickly? Is he sorry? Am *I* sorry that I came here? You can go into your household as a reluctant bride—that's only a minor infraction—but there's no way to bow down to Green City when there's rebellion in your heart. I had no choice, but five years on, I'm still not at peace with my decision. Maybe insomnia's my punishment for my reluctance.

"Joseph always tries to get me drunk. He says it'll make me sleep."

"Aren't you ever tempted?" Lin asks me. I know this is a test, so I feign ignorance.

"What? By the alcohol?"

"Of course," says Lin. "What did you think I meant?"

"It's against the rules. . ." I intone. "No intoxicants, no drugs, no alcohol."

"Thank God for your unshakable integrity," Lin says, with

a straight face, looking at the e-spliff in her hand. "Imagine if I were having this conversation with Rupa."

I smile. "Rupa's only human. And so am I." That's as close as I can get to admitting to Lin that I have tasted the drink Joseph has offered me. "You're so hard on her sometimes."

"I have to be. She's younger and she's difficult."

I have felt the sharp side of Rupa's tongue as much as the others have here, but then I know things about her that the others don't. So I feel sorry for her, and often defend her when Lin remarks drily on how Rupa's being "difficult." It's not easy when you've come to the Panah from the outside. Lin doesn't remember because she's always called it home.

Whereas Rupa bridles at any decree, I actually like the rules Ilona and Fairuza made for us here all those years ago: not because they make me feel safe, but because they give me a space within which to contain myself. Otherwise I would dissolve, boundaryless, into the air surrounding me. I've always needed structure to push up against; it defines me and gives me shape. That's probably the consequence of growing up in Green City: we're told what to do, how to behave, even what to think, from the day we're born. I'm not yet used to thinking for myself. The rules of the Panah provide a halfway house between the strictures of Green City and the complete freedom that exists in places I can't even imagine.

FROM THE VOICE NOTES
OF ILONA SERFATI

Today, I kidnapped my own niece.

How ridiculous that sounds! But as the head of the Panah I can't exactly walk into my cousin's house any time I please. And it's only been a few months since she died—this most recent wave of the Virus is particularly vicious; there have hardly been any survivors this time around. People are terrified; they jump if you so much as mention it. So I'll have to save my outrage for another time.

My poor cousin, my precious Hanna. We lived together in one compound as children; I looked after her when she was a baby, I was a second mother to her. I got her ready for school, gave her a bath in the evening, made sure she ate well and that her uniform was clean and laundered for the next day. Such things count for nothing in Green City; the only loyalty a woman's supposed to have is to her Husbands. The only reason we're allowed to grieve her death is because it's the loss of another precious woman from this corrupt society. The ones who die should consider themselves lucky to be done with it for good.

I am amused at my own ingenuity, I'll admit. I dressed myself as a male social worker, with all the appropriate clothing, genetic switch chips and prostheses in place—obtained from the black market at great cost. When I got to Hanna's house, the windows and doors were already turned black to mark it as a house of mourning.

I don't know which of Hanna's Husbands opened the door to my insistent knocking. I said that I'd been sent there from the Bureau, and that Lin needed psychological testing to make sure the death of her mother hadn't affected her physically or mentally. He stared at me as if I were an alien from space, announcing my intention to conquer the entire planet. But he didn't question me, preoccupied by his own loss.

By the time they realized that Lin was gone, it was too late. They don't even know where to look for her.

In six months—let the dust settle—I'll send a message to them that the Bureau has decided Lin needs to be placed with a family that has a Wife already, so that Lin has an appropriate female role model. She's only seven, but they'll have to accept the Bureau's directives, like all good citizens of Green City. They won't even think to investigate.

I wonder if they'll miss her. None of them knows whose daughter she is, and three fathers aren't much better than one, in my experience. Lin doesn't ask for them, she only cries for her mother, and that too, only at night. I soothe her as best as I can, and tell her stories of what her mother was like when she was her age. Her previous life will eventually fade away, and that will be a great relief to all. I'll mother her as I mothered her own mother; we women know how to do this without having to be taught.

She'll grow up in the Panah, and she'll take over when I die. I wish it didn't have to be this way, but I need a successor and I'm not getting any younger. And this way, young Lin will be spared from having to become anyone's Wife. I owe her mother that much.

SABINE

The hour I'd turned up on Lin's doorstep, tired, frightened, and penniless, was the hour my childhood ended. I'd fled my father's house, terrified that he would call the Agency to chase after me and turn me in. By fleeing, my crime worsened from reluctance to rebellion. And it wasn't unintentional: a girl couldn't leave her father's home and disappear in Green City without a great amount of forethought, manipulation, and deceit.

There were few of us girls left in my Green City neighborhood when I was small. Those of us who did exist — maybe ten or twelve, certainly not more than twenty — weren't encouraged to befriend one another. They didn't want us to talk, to question our roles in life, or dream of another life for ourselves. We would, at the very least, school each other in reluctance. Still, we looked up the Bureau records from the safety of our homes and found out all about each other — girls and women in Green City were required to have public profiles that men could peruse before applying for a Wife.

Sometimes we would catch each other's eyes when we were out with our parents or guardians. We'd walk in the Galleria on hot days, browsing the shops teeming with luxurious clothes from Kolachi, tulipwood furniture made in Chabahar, precious jewelry from Gedrosia. On pleasant days we'd visit the large open-air rainforest parks to see the exotic sloths and porcupines, the rare whales and giant turtles that had been cloned back into existence. Or we'd go to the Corniche, aimlessly wandering amid the food stalls and fountains. We turned our eyes to the blue waters of the Gulf, we pretended to admire the crystalline kites soaring above it in the breeze, excited little boys controlling them with wireless remotes on the ground. We were really searching for each other. That spark of recognition as we stared into each other's eyes, that furtive smile, the twitch of fingers to wave hello or goodbye, would signal that girl as a friend— and an ally.

We connected with each other in ways that our parents and the Agency didn't know about. At least, that's what we always told each other. We couldn't use our parent-connected devices at home, couldn't use the Network to find each other, so we resorted to things that had become almost obsolete: scrawled notes dropped in places only girls would search, inside jewelry boxes at certain stores, underneath a pile of dresses, tucked among a row of hairbrushes. The chances of our notes being found by others were low, because there were so few of us—but still, we tried.

We dealt in optimism. On those notes, we wouldn't write messages, but we left codes for online TalkBots, automated computer-based messaging services, like mailboxes, that hold messages on a server that can't be traced, messages that are automatically erased if left unresponded to for longer than a few minutes, messages we hoped other girls of our age would find and reply to. We sent messages in bottles to each other, even though we all lived on the same island.

"I live in Sur. I like chocolate and horror stories."

"I have three brothers. I'm from Green City Central."

"I live in a village in the Wahiba. My favorite color is lavender."

"My mother died when I was a little girl."

We didn't tell each other our names. Instead, we used nicknames—flowers, like Rose, Jasmine, Honeysuckle; gems, like Ruby or Opal; birds, like Sparrow and Dove. We grew a little community that existed nowhere but in our own heads, arranging bits and bytes into patterns that relayed our thoughts, hopes, and dreams to each other.

We could have been punished for reluctance but it was an irresistible game to see how we could connect to each other, and how much we could get away with. How much freedom we could create for ourselves underneath the stifling, watchful eyes of our parents, and the future that awaited each one of us at the end of our girlhood.

It was one of these girls, unromantically named Chicken, who told me about the Panah. At first I laughed at her for spreading a silly rumor. With a name like Chicken, what else could it have been but the crazed invention of an overexcited girl? But she insisted that her father was a high-up official in the Agency; she'd somehow come across one of his classified bulletins mentioning rumors of an underground community where rebellious women existed outside the system, traitors to Green City and the largesse of its Leaders.

Ignoring my disbelief, Chicken soon told me even more details: that there were virtual tunnels on the Deep Web. The Agency tried to surveil them and shut them down, but they were architected to shift from one anonymous and undiscoverable server to another. With the right codes, Chicken said, she could not only reach out and make contact with those women, but she could tell them about herself and send them her profile, and they might select her to join them. If that happened, then a girl could escape her fate, and disappear like a cloud in the sky. Or a snowdrift that would simply melt away with the warming sun. One hour there, the next, gone. A strange feeling, to think of oneself as "disappeared."

But then, wasn't that just what had happened to all those girls and all those women in Green City who should have been alive, but weren't? The missing girls, aborted out of existence, killed by the Virus, buried alive in marriages they didn't want? I was one of the lucky ones who had survived the first two, but I didn't know if I would survive the third.

"Would you ever do it?" I wrote Chicken, when she sent me what she said was the code for a tunnel access point.

"Maybe I would try, " she wrote back.

"Wouldn't you be afraid to get caught?"

"I would be more scared if I didn't try."

We knew that when we were women, we would be forced into marriage at least twice but more likely three and four times. Chicken herself was a product of one of those multiple marriages, and sadly had no idea—and was never told—which of her mother's four Husbands was her father. She said all the fathers treated her well, spoiled her, and brought her gifts. But how her mother felt—we never spoke about that. Her silences on the subject said more than her words ever could.

It was a capital crime to hit or abuse a woman: women in Green City were precious resources, to be treasured and protected, looked after and provided for, in return for their bodies given to the cause of repopulation. The fertility drugs took their toll on the women's health; women started giving birth to triplets and quadruplets because of the high doses, and the high-risk pregnancies wore them out quickly. So they were discouraged from taking up too much activity outside the house, in fresh air. Work was considered beneath them and domestics did a lot of the household chores.

The women I saw moving around the City were always accompanied by two or three of their Husbands. They were dressed well, and their husbands were attentive to them, bringing them presents from the shops in the Galleria. No matter whether a woman was rich or poor, when she became a Wife her status rose, and the Green City government doubled the family allowance each time she gave birth. Her womb was the ticket from poverty straight into the comfort of the middle class for her as well as all her Husbands. And yet, those Wives I saw were bowed down, shrunken, and meek, unmoved by the generosity of their Husbands and the state.

The times when I caught their eyes, I saw them fix me with steely looks of recognition, as if they were saying to me, *I was once young and carefree like you. Treasure these days, girl, they don't last.*

When I got to the Panah, I was unused to the sight of women's bodies not swollen and distorted by pregnancy. It seemed wrong, at first, as if something was missing. It took me months to realize that a woman's stomach wasn't always convex; that its default state was not always filled with another being.

Over the next several months Chicken sent me secret codes for flags that would let the Panah know I was looking for them. "I'm not interested," I messaged her angrily more than once. "You use them!"

"You didn't believe me. Now you have to. Go on, send them a message and see what happens. Then you'll know I'm telling the truth. Or are you too scared?"

"It's not a game, okay? If I get caught, you know what would happen to me."

"You can't get caught. The flags are randomly generated, they disappear every five minutes. Nobody can catch you if you don't want to be found."

"Why don't you do it then if you're so smart?"

"Maybe I will. Then we could go to the Panah together."

I grew nervous then, and terminated the session. It was one thing to talk about it, but another to actually plot a disappearance and an escape. It was more than rebellion; it would be classified as revolt. I wanted no part of it.

Soon after that, my father told me he was going to fast-track me into the Perpetuation scheme. I would have to leave school early and become a Wife.

I begged and pleaded with him to reconsider, but he was obdurate. After my mother died, when I was twelve, my father, not rich enough to be assigned a Wife immediately, had applied nevertheless for a chance to bring in a Wife from the divided north. The women from the north were blue-eyed and fair-skinned, with blonde or red hair, different from our dark hair and olive skin. The Levantine Wars in the early twenty-first century had destroyed their countries, but not their beauty. My father was refused by the Bureau for reasons he never told me. He spent the next four years alone, but responsible for me. I assumed there was money to be made in fast-tracking a daughter: hefty Bureau rewards for providing a young woman to the Scheme at the peak of her health and beauty. Or perhaps his reward would be another Wife, an even trade.

I was burning to tell my father I wouldn't be sold like a slave. But I kept my silence after I'd gotten over the initial shock. Something in me told me to go deep inside myself, to squeeze out every last bit of patience and cleverness that I had, and to rescue myself if my father was not going to help me.

I don't believe in life after death; it wasn't my mother's voice guiding me from beyond the grave, no. I've said I'm not a Religious—the three religions that had merged into one still have their followers, but we regard them as eccentrics now that science has become our way of life. As long as the Religious don't try to proselytize or influence Green City affairs in any way, they're allowed to practice their strange rituals, believe in their god, a weak, watered-down version of what they'd had before. They're too insignificant to be counted anyway.

Had I remained with my father, I would have been sent to the Girls' Markaz, the large hostels outside Green City: a weird mix of finishing school, indoctrination camp, and fairy castle. Everything, or so we heard, is painted pink. After completing their secondary education, boys attend university, while girls go to the Markaz to learn how to become good Wives. The girls are given classes in Household Technology, Health, and Reproductive Sciences. Most girls are thrilled to begin the process of their elevation in society and barely pay attention to the classes, distracted by the idea of their impending first marriages. Others, like me, pretend enthusiasm while secretly feeling nothing but a sense of impending doom.

Two days before I was due to leave for the Markaz, I sent out a secret flag to the Panah across the Deep Web, using the code that Chicken had sent me. And with it, a desperate letter, addressed to whoever ran the Panah:

"My name is Sabine. I'm sixteen, almost seventeen. My mother killed herself when I was only twelve. She didn't want to be married to anyone but my father. I don't want to be married to anyone. I don't want to be Wife to three or four or five men. I'm terrified. I know you don't know me, but I'm begging you to help me. I will do whatever you tell me to do, if you can help me escape."

I attached a picture of myself in my school uniform, and sent the message quickly, before I could change my mind.

Then I waited.

The whole time, I couldn't sit down, couldn't eat, couldn't sleep. I paced in my room like someone gone mad, and kept checking and checking to see if there was a response. Each time it came up a blank: *No Answer. No Answer. No Answer.* It felt like a judgment upon me. What if the code had gone obsolete? What if Chicken had just made it all up? What if there was no Panah? I began to think that the waiting was a form of torture devised by the Bureau to drive us mad, a fitting punishment for just daring to think I could escape.

Sixteen hours later, a response chimed out from the Deep Web. I ran to my device and punched in the access code with shaky fingers. The message quickly unfurled itself: it told me where to go, when to go, how to get there.

I told my father I had to go to the Girls' Markaz early for medical tests. I was about to name all the examinations—fertility checks, uterine and ovarian and breast cancer gene testing, was I sexually innocent or experienced (they could

n my pockets to give my nervous fingers something to do. I
edged into the parking lot they'd told me to find, the one with
the broken sign and the barrier stuck halfway open. A recent
thunderstorm must have short-circuited the power, and they
hadn't got around to fixing it yet.

The black car was waiting for me in a corner.

I'd been told not to talk to anyone on my way to the Panah,
but I couldn't help myself. As I climbed into the back, I
muttered nervously, "Are you. . . did they send you. . . am I
doing this right?"

The automated driver responded in a nasal voice: "Welcome. Please buckle your seat belt. Your safety is important to
me." So: a self-driving car—I'd never sat in one before—but I
was disappointed that I wouldn't have a real hand to hold on
my journey into the underworld.

We drove north out of the city for an hour. I tried not to
fall asleep, to watch every landmark, to even commit the stars
to memory, but when the bright buzzing buildings gave way
to silence and sand, I drifted away. Fear had worn me out. I
woke up again only when we slowed down, and I saw gates
sliding open to let us in a compound with a warehouse at the
far end. I figured we must be somewhere on the edge of the
Free Trade Zone, to the north of Green City.

When the car door opened automatically, I blurted out,
"Where are we? What am I supposed to do now?"

Again, the driver didn't answer me. The car was clearly
preprogrammed; it just waited blankly until I got out; the
door slid closed, and it smoothly drove away. Even before the
gates shut I began to turn around frantically, looking for a
sign, some lights, noise, anything to tell me I wasn't alone.
Tears welled in my eyes and my heart banged in my chest.
Like a rabbit, I'd die of fear if someone didn't—

"Hello, Sabine."

The voice rang clearly across the compound. I whipped

do virginity restoration procedures in half a day),
didn't want to hear any details; he just waved me a
his view, he had already sorted out what to do with m
a problem solved, a folded shirt neatly put away in a
But my father had a habit of leaving loose ends untied
incomplete, doors unlocked. It was this carelessn
allowed me to escape.

I was instructed by the Panah to take the Metr
Corniche on Green Day, the yearly celebration of t
the Leaders signed the South West Treaty and crea
alliance between Green City and the other territories.
blend in with the heaving crowds until I got to the C
and I should walk eastward for three kilometers. Th
sun would draw the crowds westward to watch the fir

I would need currency sticks, jewelry, any valual
I could bring with me in order to open certain g
under normal circumstances remained closed, greas
that prided themselves on staying dry. My father ha
made me feel that what was his belonged to me.
always made me feel obligated to him for earning
and supporting me with it. Never mind that the Bur
rewarded him with all sorts of grants and benefits fo
a healthy girl. He kept all the money, spent the mini
me, said he was saving "the rest" for "my future."

Well, I thought, *my future is now. And I'm takir
rightfully mine.* I stole what I could from my father
his jacket pockets. I even stole his gold watch, a pres
his father.

I climbed onto the Metro, got off at the Cornich
east when all the others went west. They didn't n
not even the Officers guarding the Corniche; ever
too drunk with excitement and patriotism to keep cl
on a girl scurrying along like an insect. I walked an
shivering the whole way, feeling the currency and t

my head up to see where it was coming from. She was a distant shadow, but, as she walked toward me, she pushed her veil off her head and let me look at her. I wiped my tears with the back of my hand while my eyes raked over her face, as if its contours could slake my loneliness. She was older than me, with high prominent cheekbones, a long nose, and a high forehead; that was all I could make out of her in the gloom.

Her voice was low, matter-of-fact. "So. Now that you're here, what shall we do with you?"

I let out a sharp gasp. Was it all some horrible mistake? Was it all a trap to capture me and send me to the Agency? Was I under arrest already?

But then she gave me a wry smile, and then she stretched out her arms. I took one careful step to her, and then another. What made me leave Green City was the same thing that made her live in this forsaken place. What else, in the end, truly binds us together, besides the desire for each other to be free?

A few months after my eighteenth birthday, Lin said I was finally ready for an assignation. Over the last year, she'd schooled me in all the security protocols for arrivals and departures. She'd taught me the necessary etiquettes in apparel and hygiene—shower when you get to the Client's house, never sleep the whole night in a Client's bed, don't allow him to take all his clothes off either—and admissible signs of affection: a hug was acceptable, a chaste kiss—lips closed—permissible on rare occasions; a real kiss very risky, and to be avoided.

But more than this, she'd taught me the reason we were able to play the game we did, and survive. Unlike Wives, whose presence in their lives is little more than a bureaucratic arrangement, women of the Panah remind the men of the mothers whose arms they sank into as infants; the sisters who nurtured them as they grew; the girlfriends and companions they sought to impress and please. Men's physical appetites are huge, but their emotional appetites are without end. No regime can change that.

So instead of selling our bodies, we spend the night with certain men, special men, the most powerful of them, who remember the old days before the Gender Emergency. We give them an experience they themselves destroyed long ago: we let them soothe themselves to sleep in our presence. They want this more than anything else in the world, but we're the only ones who can give it to them because there are so few of us left: free women, unattached to anyone else, our loyalties belonging to no one but the Panah. One Wife shared by four or five of them isn't enough, can never be enough. Nor can prostitute bots, with crevices and grooves and hollows to be filled by them, fill the holes in their hearts in return.

We let them believe that possessing one woman, just for a short while, is still possible in Green City, even though that kind of life went extinct the moment the bombs went off in the Final War.

That first assignation, a few minutes before eleven o'clock in the evening, the feeling came over me that I was slowly leaving my body, that my consciousness was slipping out of its confines of flesh and bone.

Lin chose my clothes, a silken robe that she'd taken from her own closet and lent me for the night. She washed and dried my hair herself, and styled it into an easy tumble down my back. She lined my eyes with kohl and smudged it with the tip of her little finger.

"You're there for companionship, not sex. Don't trespass the limits and you'll be fine," Lin said, inspecting her handiwork, looking pleased with the results. I didn't recognize myself when I looked at my face in the mirror.

"Companionship, not sex," I muttered back. "No going near the limits." But I still couldn't believe that I'd be safe, that nothing would happen to me, despite all her reassurances. My legs shook, my stomach tightened, my throat grew a lump that refused to budge no matter how hard I swallowed. "How will he stop himself? I don't think I can do this, Lin."

"You can. Don't be frightened. Remember, Sabine. No matter what they say, or how strongly they claim to control us, how weak they say we are, they still need us. Not our bodies, or our sex, but our love and care, our human warmth, our physical presence. These men won't risk losing what you offer them."

Lin placed the veil over my head and adjusted it like a frame around my face until everything pleased her. "You look like a painting," she said. "Beautiful." But I felt like a human sacrifice.

She rode with me to the Client's house even though it was against Panah protocol. "Remember, we only survive because of the rules we've made, Sabine," she said, holding my hand. "They suit us more than the Clients, and they don't like it. But they have to obey them, or else we don't go to them. Why do you think my Clients are all faithful customers? When they let us in their lives just once, they realize how they've been lied to as well. And they hate it. Calling us to them is their rebellion. Going to them is ours."

Lin assured me that my first Client was known for his integrity, that he was an old patron and had behaved impeccably at every assignation. I still couldn't shake the terror that he'd break the rules and rape me. And indeed, as he and I climbed into the bed, I spent the first hour with one foot on the floor, in case I needed to flee. But he was as Lin promised: courteous, gentlemanly, kind. He slept peacefully all night while I sat wide awake beside him, holding his hand. It was like being with a grandfather who'd had a wild youth but wanted to cap his life with a sedate, chaste courtship. When I left in the morning, he kissed me on the forehead and sent me back to the Panah.

A thousand nights later, now a consummate professional, it is fully I who regard myself in the mirror before leaving the Panah for a Client's house. Sometimes I'm seized by sorrow at the position we're all in, how fragile our inner safeguards against the betrayals that can happen to us in so many ways, internal and external. But as long as Lin's waiting for me at the end of the night, I can live with the fault lines that run beneath my life.

FROM THE VOICE NOTES
OF ILONA SERFATI

I haven't got much time; I'm an old woman now. The elegant kaftans I wear don't hide my shrinking bones, my withering flesh. It's been ages since I dyed my hair; I can't remember the last time I cared whether it looked white or not. I hardly have any eyebrows left, although I paint them on every morning in a nod to my vanity, the only thing about me that's still young. But I want Lin to stay innocent just a little while longer.

These new rules the Bureau just released today, they'd make me laugh if they weren't so disturbing. Regulating the minutes a Wife spends with her Husband: How will they measure that? Will they have a man from the Agency in the bedroom, stopwatch in hand?

"With each new baby, a new hope for Green City and South West Asia." Indeed. Do they think they can regulate us into multiplying? Well, of course they think that. Why else would they send around these ridiculous rules, thought up by the madmen in the Perpetuation Bureau? What human, man or woman, can obey them? More important, which woman can choose to disobey?

Has it really only been fifty years since the nuclear winter? I remember watching the news with my parents, the countries turning black on the satellite maps, from the remains of India and Pakistan westward over the former countries of Afghanistan, Iran—Tehran also hit in the small warhead strikes—and the Gulf Peninsula. Only fifty warheads had been detonated, fifty kilotons each, small in the schemes of military planners. Somehow they miscalculated their effects: five megatons of carbon were released into the air, and the black carbon rain killed millions in those unfortunate lands.

Within days, people's lungs collapsed—we saw them on the bulletins, turning blue and gasping for breath. Children of survivors had severely underdeveloped respiratory systems, and suffocated to death almost as soon as they were born. The atmosphere was choking them to death, in revenge for what they had done to it.

That's why they constructed the bunkers, like this one, deep underneath the ground. I spent some time underground in a different one, near my childhood home, while we waited for the dust to settle, hoping the fallout wouldn't come our way. It seemed like a game to me then, something concocted by my parents, like a holiday, or an adventure.

When we emerged like ants out of our subterranean sanctuaries, we learned that huge swathes of those blighted countries had become wastelands, poisoned by radiation, ozone loss, and toxic frost. Green City, Gwadar, Chabahar, Kolachi had been spared because our cities hugged the coastline, and our monsoon winds, stronger because of all the disturbance in the oceans after the blasts, blew the nuclear dust east and southward.

The remaining nuclear arsenals were dismantled and the bunkers demolished. In school we learned about new treaties formed, old boundaries between nation-states eliminated. The survivors aligned themselves not in federations, but in abbreviated trading corridors and economic zones, including the Sub-West Asia Region, of which they chose Green City to be the capital. I was hardly ten or twelve, but I still remember the celebrations, the fireworks exploding in the night as if all the stars had been set on fire. We went around waving flags all day, painting our faces the colors of the new territory's quadricolor: black, red, indigo, and white.

What an achievement, to be the leaders of the new territory. We were told it was a great responsibility, but that we had been blessed, too. Surely we'd have some years of

peace and tranquility now, to establish the new systems. . .
Yet hardly months after the declaration, the conflicts of the
east spread their tentacles all the way up into Green City,
plunging us into chaos and uncertainty all the same, because
of the Gender Emergency. Our Leaders took charge by
taking drastic measures, establishing the Agency and then
the Perpetuation Bureau in quick succession. From a blessed
dominion we had turned into a police state, almost overnight.

Nobody dared disobey the new directives that kept Green
City under control in the Emergency years. Obedience
became a Green City hallmark by the time the Gender
Emergency had come about. Already half a generation had
been lost to war, terror, and disease; women were now the
endangered species. The Perpetuation Bureau acted fast;
before they knew what had happened, the remaining women
in Green City found themselves put on an eerie pedestal to
bring an entire nation back to life. At least that's how it was
presented to us; in reality, refusal to obey the new rules would
result in an accusation of reluctance or revolt, a swift trial,
and elimination. The Leaders did not mind sacrificing a few
women in order to make the rest of us compliant.

The gamble worked; within five years, no woman voiced
opposition when she was directed to marry once, twice,
thrice, as many times as the Bureau told her to.

Just when it seemed that women had no choices left,
Fairuza and I decided to speak with our feet and escape. But
the borders were sealed and there was nowhere to go.

Except down.

Thanks to my notes, Lin knows how we hid here in those
early days, terrified of discovery and denunciation. We need
to record our own history and tell our stories, if only to each
other. We need to know that we can survive, even if we are
outcasts and criminals. And I am the keeper of the Panah's
history, the guardian of its secrets, as Lin will be after me.

Sometimes I curse all the legal, legitimate citizens of Green City who spend their lives in the prison of their so-called peace and security. If they knew of our existence, they'd revile us as Rebels. And it's the Wives who would shout for our execution the loudest. We pay for their complacency, for the complicity of both men and women in a system that is as unjust as it is unnatural.

But even in our own imprisonment, we gain something that a woman of Green City can never have. It's different for each woman, but I see all of them as stars in the same constellation—of choice, of autonomy, of freedom.

Happiness, though. Is happiness part of that constellation, too? If Lin asks me that question, I won't know how to answer her.

Lin arrived at Reuben Faro's villa past midnight, as usual. The clouds hung low over the sky, the air a stifling, humid soup that pressed down on her chest and made it hard to draw breath easily.

She shivered as she heard the far-off keening of some animal, a feral dog like the ones that used to roam the streets during the Emergency days, when buildings had burned and corpses lay on the street for days. The dogs had run wild then, feeding on the bodies, until order had been reestablished. Then extermination crews patrolled the streets, gathering the bodies to be sent to the incinerators, and shooting the dogs.

Lin varied the times that she came to the gated enclave far away from Reuben's official residence, where he'd been allocated a house like all the other Agency heads. He wasn't technically supposed to own another property, but all of them did in one way or another. Reuben's villa was in the name of his mother, claimed by the outbreak of the Virus that had killed so many of the women in Green City. He never spoke to Lin about her, or of his sister, who had died a few days later.

The muscles in Lin's arms and shoulders unclenched the moment she got out of the car. She felt a whispered blessing of benevolence as she passed through the villa gates, open all day and night in the tradition of hospitality customary to the richer, safer neighborhoods of Green City. A riot of bougainvillea graced the walls, jasmine flowers perfumed the air, a mosaic fountain in the corner of the entrance trickled a small amount of water between its columns.

Reuben Faro, one of the most important men in Green City, was waiting for her in the doorway. He took her veil, hung it up on the stand by the door, and pulled her into his arms, embracing her tight.

She leaned into his body. She was fascinated by his deep

chest, strong shoulders, the white hair at his temples, his thick legs, the steady pulse at his wrists and the backs of his knees. He had a peculiar scent she liked, leather, cloves, and old-fashioned cigarette smoke. It had been thirty years since the last cigarette had been manufactured in Green City—where did he get his cigarettes from? There was still rough tobacco around that could be hand-rolled into a cigarette but his were beautifully made, thin and elegant, tipped with fine filters. Reuben had only smiled silently when she quizzed him, spotting the cartons on his bureau, but then he allowed her to smoke one, and the exquisite aroma made her feel giddy.

And his beard, trimmed close to the skin—she'd thought it would scratch the first night she'd spent with him, but it was soft, unexpectedly silken on her skin. He was rubbing it on her shoulder now, raising goose bumps on her arms.

"You're very relaxed about security for someone in your position," said Lin.

"I can afford to be confident." Reuben led her by the hand to his bedroom, turning off the lights as he went. Lin saw the half-empty glass of whiskey on the table by the window in the living room, four or five displays scattered all around his chair. He was always working, working, even when he came home at night after working in his office all day. Lin had often been woken in the middle of the night by an important message chiming on his device; he'd never once refused to see what it said. Security plans for Green City's national day celebrations, a new policy directive for handling illegal migrants, the overseeing of border guards: his responsibilities were vast and varied. He'd proven his capability and loyalty to Green City over and over again, rising quickly in the hierarchy of leadership. His reputation for being a man willing to do anything to preserve security in Green City had not gone unrewarded by its guardians.

Lin kicked off her shoes in the hallway as she followed

him. "Confidence is dangerous." As the head of the Panah, she could never refuse the heavy weight of responsibility strapped to her back, day and night. She had that in common with Reuben, at least.

"It's also lonely," said Reuben, reaching for her. "Come here. I've been thinking about you all day."

"It's not safe," said Lin, her face serious.

Reuben raised an eyebrow.

"You say you know my body. . . Haven't you been keeping track of the days?"

Lin enjoyed the games they played; increasing the tension between restraint and capitulation heightened their mutual desire. They were both masters at teasing and taunting, at threatening to take away what they offered to one another, lest too easy a conquest make either of them complacent. Neither of them was young enough—Lin was forty-two, Reuben fourteen years older—to be excited by the illicitness of their relationship; there had always been an inevitability in their coming together. The dangers the outside world presented paled compared to the endless dangers they could invent for each other.

Reuben's mouth twisted in a smile, and he held her hand tighter, stroking her palm with his fingers until shivers ran up and down her arms and legs. "I can smell it."

She trembled in anticipation and stepped towards him. He was already loosening the tie from his neck, undoing the buttons at his wrists and collar. She reached him in time to help him pull his shirt off. His shirts were always crisp and white, even at the end of the day—she suspected he kept three or four in his office and changed them whenever one became wrinkled or stained.

She leaned over him and ran her hands over the smooth muscles of his back, feeling the knots and tension underneath his skin. She removed his shoes and socks, while he groaned softly. When she slid her hands around his waist, he looked up at her, feigning surprise. "Oh, hello. I thought you said it wasn't safe."

"It is," she said, and kissed him firmly on the mouth. Something told her that she was not meant to be a mother; her body would not provide fertile ground for a child to take hold and disrupt her life. Still, she'd taken her precautions, thanks to the herbs in the Panah garden: steeped neem leaves, wild carrot seed, gingerroot. Maybe she should feed them to the others, to be safe. It was ridiculous that with the most advanced medical science available, she should have to rely on the old methods, but she had no choice.

Reuben took her in his arms, and turned out the light. He could be a tender lover, but tonight was not a night for tenderness.

Afterward, as the feral dog keened again outside, long and low, Lin lay there in Reuben's tight embrace, drowsy and relaxed, but not wanting to sleep. Finally she slipped away and went to the bathroom to wash herself. In the mirror, she saw her reddened skin, her disheveled hair. She smiled ruefully. She'd taken pleasure in the encounter, too. When she'd been younger, it was hard to focus on her own body, easier to concentrate on the man insistent on slaking his thirst in it. Now she knew what to ask for, and how to receive it. If that made her a hypocrite, she didn't care. She deserved some leeway in return for the risks she took for all of them.

Reuben was already asleep when she returned to the bed. She slithered under the covers, fitted herself against his body, her back to his chest. He moved and murmured, put his arm around her. They slept.

At 3 a.m., Lin opened her eyes. Reuben was sitting up in bed, staring out the window at the moon. It filled the entire room with a cool pale light, illuminating Reuben's face like a painting under a spotlight. Lin could see his eyes settle on her with a strange gleam. He watched her without speaking.

"What is it?" she asked him.

"Lin, do you love me?"

"No," she mumbled, sleepily. His shoulders slumped, and for a moment, dark shadows cratered his face, making him look as though he was closer to death than life.

"Probably for the best. It isn't in our contract." His tone was jaunty, yet touched with an unfamiliar remorse. Lin opened her eyes, reached out to touch his back. He tensed, half moved away from the touch, then leaned back into it and sighed. Her fingernails raked his skin, enough to stimulate, not enough to hurt.

"We don't have a contract," she said softly.

"Never put anything in writing," said Reuben. "It's safer that way." He caught her hand in his and turned it over to kiss her palm, then put it down and moved out of her reach.

He continued to stare out the window, leaving Lin the privacy to puzzle over his sudden melancholy. She shouldn't have given an uncensored answer to his unexpected question. She knew he loved her. That love was the hidden currency that kept the Panah going. Skilled as Lin was in the art of making herself indispensable to Reuben, or any man, she had forbidden herself the emotion. And yet the need for it still existed in her, too. It was hard to admit, but she felt flickerings of it within herself.

He was her lover, but should she think of him also as her friend? She had known him for ten years now; she did not fear him. She had calculated the risks of being with him the first day they'd met, and accepted them unflinchingly. Their relationship had been transactional at first; she'd told herself she was giving him her body in return for safety and security for the Panah.

But over the years she'd been able to calculate what kind of man he was. Reuben was the only person who understood what it was like to be the solitary figure at the top. How isolation could cut like a blade into your soul, how lonely it was to pass the long hours working and being up late into the night. Reuben knew the pride she felt at being who she was. Even though officially she represented everything he had sworn to root out and eliminate from Green City, she liked to think he respected her, the way two equally strong enemies could form a firm friendship off the battlefield. This bed was their armistice. In it, she offered Reuben a different pleasure, one more satisfying than the chaste kisses and caresses offered by the rest of the women at the Panah.

But Reuben was no ordinary Client, and she was no ordinary woman. The usual trade of secret for secret, the mutual agreement to maintain the subterfuge, didn't apply to him. He was too powerful, too big to worry if he was caught with an ordinary woman of the Panah. Nor was he a type of man like the rest of the Panah's clients: wondrous and grateful at finding a temporary illusion of fidelity.

As a head of the Agency, Reuben took a huge risk by consorting with Lin. After all, his job was to catch people like her and run them to ground, eliminate from society the malignancy they represented, so that Green City could thrive in the coming generations. Caught with her, he'd be stripped of his rank and titles, disgraced, and executed publicly to serve as a lesson to the rest of society.

Lin knew *she* was the hook for him: in being with her, he was defying the authority of the Agency and the Bureau. And in her moments of deepest honesty with herself, Lin knew that she, too, was hooked on the power of being with him. Running the risk was the thing that made him feel most like a man, and she was the only woman in the world with whom he could test the limits of his inviolability. Defying the rules was the ultimate turn-on for them both.

At five in the morning, before dawn broke, Lin got out of

bed and dressed quickly. The space in the bed next to her was empty, a pocket of cold air in its place. No matter how early she woke, Reuben was always up before her. A remnant of military training? No, he'd never mentioned serving in the army. If not, then it was the natural wakefulness of a man who found it hard to relinquish his grip on the world he controlled for more than a few hours' sleep at a time.

She knew she would find him in the garden, in the company of his beloved roses. He was sitting on a small wooden bench among the flowers, wrapped in a robe, sipping a cup of tea and examining a rose in his hand. She saw him holding the rose in front of him incredulously, as if barely able to believe its beauty.

He spoke without turning around. "Leaving so soon?"

"How did you know I was there?"

"Your perfume gave you away."

She smiled. "That's the rose, not me."

"Exquisite as you both are, it's not the same. And my sense of smell is the finest of all my abilities. Come and sit down next to me before the car comes. You look beautiful in this garden. How long do we have?"

"I can't tell you that." She sat down next to him, the veil thrown back on her head, not yet obscuring her face.

"I could get you out of there, you know," he said to her, still looking at the rose. "It wouldn't be hard for me to get you in the system. Assign you exclusively to me." A searching glance at her. "Would you do it if I asked you?"

"How would you do it?" she said, disbelievingly.

"I might have to kill a few people." Again the elusive smile appeared. His warmth reached out to her like a caress.

"And what about the rest of them? My women?"

"Ah. . ." Reuben's voice trailed off. He touched his nose delicately to the flower and inhaled deeply. "I could make arrangements for them, too. They'd have to go through a mock confession and trial, but I'd make sure nothing happened to them. They'd be taken care of afterward."

"To be Wives for six Husbands apiece?"

"What more can I do?"

Lin turned away from Reuben. "Why are you talking like this, Reuben? Why now? Don't you think we have a perfect arrangement? Do you really want to complicate things?" She softened her eyes and tilted her head to look up at him, keeping the bitterness out of her voice. Wearing her tone lightly, jokingly, like a loose set of clothes.

"I suppose you're right," said Reuben, closing his eyes and inhaling the scent of the rose once more. "Oh. Before you go. I have something for you." He took her hand in his and pressed a small vial into her palm.

The moment was over, the tension snapped like a wire breaking underneath too much weight. Lin didn't know if she was relieved or disappointed. "What's this?"

"For all those *nuits blanches*. You looked so tired last time. I thought this might help."

"Taxes," said Lin, shaking her head. "You know how it is. I deal on the black market to avoid paying them, but instead I have to pay four times the normal prices. I'm up late, working out the accounts. Why didn't you tell me being a criminal was so costly?"

Reuben laughed. "I'm sorry. We're shutting down the cryptocurrency channels. Makes your life harder, I know. Try this."

"I sleep well, most nights."

"Doing what you do? I don't think so. Look, it's harmless, nonaddictive; they've just developed it in the lab and the initial trials were promising. Why don't you see for yourself?"

Lin remembered just then that there was someone else in the Panah who suffered from sleepless nights. "No side effects? Are you sure?"

"No morning-after drowsiness, no hangover. I don't pay all

the best scientists in the territories for nothing. Just one thing: don't mix it with alcohol."

"That's hard enough to come by."

"Just in case. The volunteers in the trials were fine, but they were men. Your body might react differently."

"What's it called?"

"They were going to call it something fancy—Ebrietas, I think. Who knows what it means. . ."

She put the vial in her pocket and kissed him lightly goodbye, knowing, as she walked away, that she would always need him. Reuben was security, but he might be her undoing one day.

The car ride home was usually where Lin emptied her mind of everything she had undergone in the last ten hours, steeling herself for life back in the Panah. Lin realized she was shaken by Reuben's offer to take her out of that life. He'd never talked like this before. Did he really mean it? What if she said yes, abandoned the Panah and the women inside it, for a life of real power by Reuben's side?

Lin touched the vial in her pocket, thinking absently. Some of the women had more of a problem with the adjustment between life above and under ground: they struggled with erratic sleep cycles, erratic appetites, and depression for six months to a year after entering the Panah. Lin remained unaffected, practically born into this twilight life. But it just might help Sabine. Lin could slip a small amount of the drug into the tea she prepared for Sabine to drink on her way home from her assignations, so that she would be at least more relaxed, if not fully asleep, when she went to bed. Otherwise she'd be restless all night, the adrenaline and cortisol coursing through her body, robbing her of the downtime her body needed to restore itself. There was no need to worry about alcohol with Sabine; she hated the stuff, said it smelled like gasoline. If it worked, then Lin would tell her about the drug. Sabine's gratitude would outweigh her annoyance at being helped without knowing. And surely the drug was safe; Reuben was a man of his word.

Lin wondered if Sabine really wanted to give up her sleepless nights. She wore her insomnia like penitence; guilt over her mother's suicide lingered like poison in her blood. Lin still remembered the impassioned plea that Sabine had sent, years before, her fear and terror at being trapped in a system that had made her mother kill herself. Sabine's teenaged face in the photo, beautiful but painfully thin, the school uniform barely hiding the comeliness of her adolescent body, evoked a ferocious pang in Lin's heart. She, who had never known her own mother, felt as though she were looking at her own ghost. She'd decided instantly to take in the motherless girl.

Sabine's sorrow should have faded away over the years she'd spent in the Panah, and that hadn't happened. You wouldn't survive if you couldn't accept where you were, if you kept clinging to the past like a life jacket. You had to somehow override the memories, otherwise they'd seep into your dreams and torture you in your sleep.

Maybe the drug would even help Sabine to overcome the remnants of her sorrowful past. "What harm could it possibly do?" Lin said to herself, out loud.

"Please buckle your seatbelt. Your safety is important to me," replied the car.

Lin chuckled, then closed her eyes and let Green City shrink away as the Panah loomed larger and larger. The night lost its immediacy, becoming the memory of an oasis she had once visited in the middle of a long journey. She even let go of her fear of the future: her power over it did not lie in her hands; there was only the quickly fading near past and the approaching present, time running on the wheels of the car gliding beneath her through Green City's quickening streets.

The car approached the abandoned warehouse. Reuben

ensured that its location never appeared on any of the Green City maps—by what kind of technology, she didn't know. Lin waited until the car had driven away and counted sixty seconds after the warehouse door slid shut behind her. Then she went to the old-fashioned elevator and put her thumb onto the button. A slight vibration informed her that her thumbprint had been accepted. The door slid open, revealing a long black well. The elevator car had been torn out of the shaft long ago; only a small steel pipe snaked along its back wall. It was to this that Lin clung and let herself down, inch by slow inch. Her feet found the small indentations that had been etched into the wall with painstaking deliberation by Fairuza Dastani. The escape shaft had served thirty years of Panah women. There had been other entrances, once upon a time, but they'd been blocked up to prevent infiltration or defection. This shaft was the only remaining way into and out of the Panah.

At the bottom of the shaft, in near-total darkness, she let go of the pipe and dropped the last two feet down to the ground, her veil billowing around her like a parachute. Only after she'd pressed her eyes into the iris scanner and the door opened to let her in did she dare remove the veil, roll it into a ball, and stuff it into her pocket.

Everyone else was asleep, or about to return from their assignations. Soon it would be time for Sabine's pickup. Lin padded to the kitchen to prepare the mixture of cardamom, honey, turmeric, fennel, black pepper, and cloves. She opened the vial Reuben had given her and slipped one tiny pill into the tea, then stirred it well. She'd send the flask out with the pickup car, then go to her room and wait until Sabine came home. They might share an e-spliff before going to bed, giggling like schoolgirls over silly things, sweet relief from the heaviness of their existence.

She walked along the hallway, but miscalculated a step, stumbled and dropped the flask. As she bent down to retrieve it, her fingers touched another scrap of something on the floor. She picked up the flask and the other object, holding it up in the dim light. A memory slip, small enough to hide under your fingernail. She didn't use them much, but maybe it was one that had gone astray.

She took it back to her room and placed it under the infrared, throwing its pages onto the display in magnification. She started at a random page in the middle. It took a moment for her eyes to adjust to the words written by hand instead of typed text. She drew back in surprise, then bent in again for a closer look. If books were antiques, then handwriting was downright obsolete—voice-to-device and even thought-to-device had replaced pens and pencils long ago. But someone had filled the memory slip with pages and pages of painstaking notes in this cramped and urgent script. First, a list:

THE DANGERS

> *Virus*
> *Pregnancy (how would we deal with childbirth if. . .*
> *   something went wrong?)*
> *No doctors (dying is better than being discovered)*
> *Agency will punish us for Revolt*

Then, beneath it:

> *I know Lin's got a secret. Maybe she's got a man but she doesn't want the rest of us to have one because she's jealous of us for being younger, prettier.*
> *   None of the others are brave enough to defy her, but I did, and now I know. And I'm glad. He was so good to me. So kind and gentle. And when it was over, he kept touching my nose pin and telling me how beautiful it made me look. Like a Gedrosian princess.*

As the fragments started to create an unwelcome picture, Lin had to hold on to the table to steady herself. She skipped ahead a few pages, steeled herself to read again:

> Lin *hates my nose pin. She thinks it makes me look cheap, like a prostitute. She makes me take it off outside the Panah, but I put it back on when I'm with a Client. Just because I can.*

The erratic words, the jerky sentences almost hissed off the page. Lin was stunned by the repetition of her name, written darker and underlined to emphasize the writer's resentment. She read the passages over and over again, until the tightening in her chest subsided into a dull, constricting ache, making it hard to breathe.

There was only one woman in the Panah who wore a nose pin. And Lin, who had never been afraid of her, now found herself stunned at what she had discovered.

RUPA

Ma told me once that there are two types of envy. The first is when someone has something that you want, and you wish you could have it, too. The second is when they have something you want, and you wish they didn't have it. But there is a third type of envy, a black feeling in your heart when you have something, and you actively work to take it away from anyone else who might get it. That's the kind of envy Lin has for us. She makes sure the happiness she knows is something we can never have, because she keeps it from us deliberately.

The others exist in a perpetual state of gratitude towards Lin for saving us from the fate of being Wives. They've swallowed all the restrictions and the secrecy without question. The rules have become a part of their bodies, clinging as leeches do to their flesh.

What if I had wanted to live on the outside, like a normal woman? What if I wanted to be a Wife, to bear a Husband a child? My choice was robbed from me. Once I set foot inside the Panah, I became a criminal. I could never go back. They are not *my* rules. I never made them, I never agreed to them. I never got to say what I wanted.

The Panah holds hardly half a dozen of us, and there are as many as forty or fifty Clients who want us, so we often end up on assignations with the same men. Of course Sabine is Joseph's favorite, but when she isn't available, he asks for me instead.

I know how to be grateful when I go to Joseph's house and enjoy his generosity. Sabine is wrong about Joseph; where she sees a tiresome, greedy man, I see a man I can admire, strong and confident, powerful and accomplished. He's good to me, as he would be to anyone who understands and respects his place in the world. His wealth and power are secondary to his character, which Sabine isn't wise enough to see.

I truly cannot understand Sabine's reluctance to be in Joseph's company. He is thoughtful, kind, and never holds back on treating the woman with him to all the fine things in his life: the best food, silk sheets, and most of all, the best wine. Instead of treating me like a child in a woman's body, he confides in me as an adult would confide in another adult, tells me about the difficulties and stresses of his job, his troubles with other supervisors at the Bureau, the late nights he spends attending receptions and dinners for visiting dignitaries. And I in turn give him advice, like offering Sabine his best wine so that she will soften toward him.

When he asks me what I do when I am not with him, I am reluctant to tell him about my mundane days in the Panah—the boredom, the quibbles and the pettiness of the other girls. That we spend so much time together underground, it gets on our nerves and we take it out on each other. Silly fights erupting over who has eaten whose special food, or who has used up all the hot water for a bath. And everyone trying to curry Lin's favor, so that she will send them outside on more assignations. When else do we get the chance to be above ground, in the company of such sophisticated men?

I get on well with Diyah, for the most part. She and I play cards in my room, an old-fashioned game that Ma taught me, which she'd learned from her mother. I'd once described it to Diyah and a few days later she presented me with a pack of playing cards that she'd made with her own hands, cutting out paper and drawing pictures and writing numbers on all fifty-two of them. I nearly cried when she gave them to me. We spent many peaceful evenings laughing together and playing cards, just the two of us. She'd often beat me, but she was too good-natured to crow or gloat.

Diyah can tell the future, too, or so she says, from the leaves in a teacup.

"Show me, show me!" I beg her. "Tell me what you can

see for me." I grab her hands and kiss them over and over again. "Please, Diyah, sweet Diyah, pretty Diyah. . ."

"Not now." She laughs, pulling her hands away. "I can only do it when I'm in the mood."

"That's what Joseph says," I tell her with a straight face. "But he's never in the mood." I wink at Diyah and she glances back at me with an odd look in her eyes.

"Rupa. . ."

"Don't worry." I look down at my cards so that Diyah can't see my face. "I'm safer with Joseph than I would be with my own family."

SABINE

It's the third night in this month that Joseph's called me. Usually he isn't so greedy, but lately he can't seem to get enough of me. I enter his apartment, take off my veil, drop it on the chair near the door. The last few visits, I've been bringing my flask of Lin's tea with me, sipping it on the way here instead of saving it for the ride home. I know it's just a habit, but it's been helping me to feel more relaxed when I come to see Joseph. I must remember to ask Lin to make more for me when I get back to the Panah.

He locks the door, then greets me with his usual kiss on the cheek, and an embrace that lasts a little longer than it should. I pull back but let my hips press against his. Even with a Client I don't like, there's a protocol to be observed, a dance with steps that need to be followed in the correct order to end up in just the right place.

I do make fun of Joseph with Lin, but it isn't unpleasant being with him. Living in the Panah among women provides one kind of safety, but spending time with a man who'll risk his own stature and life to have you in his home is a different feeling altogether. Gratifying. Satisfying. Pleasurable in a perverse way. The leaders set the tone of morality for the rest of the citizens; they call their city Green, but the only color they've chosen for its women is white, a purity that only exists on paper. In truth, the color of Green City women is red: red for the blood that they bleed every month when they've failed in their duty to add another child to their tallies; red for the blood on which those precious fetuses are fed and nurtured for nine months; red for the blood that's spilled when they're born.

Whenever I go to see Joseph, he prepares a gourmet meal for me that I'm usually reluctant to eat. He tries to feed me a bite of this or a morsel of that. He sees himself as a bon vivant; feeding me well is just another way of impressing himself.

I take a few sips from his wine glass when he offers, but I usually refuse my own.

Tonight, he insists on pouring out a glass of something fizzy for me. "Sabine, you have to try this. It's black champagne, from Venezuela. In South America."

"I know where Venezuela is," I say and he laughs at my bristly response. I take the glass from him, secretly admiring the way the crystal is cut into so many flawless facets, each one reflecting a small rainbow of light from the chandelier overhead.

Joseph watches my face carefully, to see if I'm annoyed. Men like Joseph don't like uncertainty; it makes them act in strange ways. Maybe treating a young woman as if she is a pupil eager to be schooled in the ways of the world is merely second nature to him. A kind of chivalry that appeals to his vanity.

I take one delicate sip from the glass. The beauty of the liquid just barely touches my tongue before exploding into full flavor.

I put down the glass quickly. "What is this?"

The lines around his eyes crease into starbursts as he smiles. "I told you. Black champagne. It has minerals extracted from volcanic rock that are infused into the soil the grapes are grown in. The grapes take on the color and the sheen of the minerals; that's why it has that oily look. See?"

He holds up his own glass to the light and I see it then; the black giving way to a mercury silver that changes tone as he tilts his wrist this way and that. Then he laughs softly, the sound grating against my ears.

"What?"

"I know you didn't actually drink it."

"I did!"

The lines deepen around his eyes, and for a moment he is

no longer an urbane, powerful sophisticate, but almost like a simple fisherman, face weathered by sea and sun. "Your face. You look like an innocent little girl. No, no, Sabine. Don't take it the wrong way. It's lovely. I haven't seen anyone look like that in a long time."

Joseph's use of the word *innocent* makes me cringe. Maybe he means naïve, or unworldly, or even foolish. I would call it cautious. But maybe I should be less uptight. Why shouldn't I enjoy a glass of rare champagne, poured out for me in an expensive goblet by a man as sophisticated as Joseph?

He dresses immaculately, beautifully, for our nights together: a jacket and tie, which he later exchanges for a silken dressing gown and a pair of silk pajamas. After dinner, he likes to put on old music, smoke cigars, drink brandy while I watch him fuss with the bottles and the music player. He doesn't need me to talk to him; he just wants me to admire him being masculine and masterful. These most powerful men, Lin tells us, have hard lives, difficult decisions to make, and without women in their lives, they grow bitter, old, and dissatisfied with themselves and their place in Green City's upper echelons. "Even a man who's achieved everything, fulfilled every ambition, won't really be happy, feel truly at ease with himself without a woman."

I take another sip and glance back at Joseph, realizing that he can be surprisingly kind when he isn't trying to put his hands in places they don't belong. I know he's fond of me, with an affection that borders on possessiveness, something that Lin observes might be adoration but not necessarily love. Sometimes his attentions are lustful, at others, avuncular. We talk together and he takes comfort from my presence. Maybe this is enough for him. Maybe he's too tired to want more.

Joseph's own Wife died from the Virus, but because he was older, they didn't give him a new Wife: they save that privilege for the younger men, the ones who can father healthy children. That's why most of our Clients are the older men of Green City, like Joseph.

I don't like the idea of being the sandpaper to smooth a man's rough edges, but it's better than being an entire nation's incubator.

When the smoldering end of his cigar fades out, and the last song winds down to its stuttering conclusion, Joseph moves around the room, turning out lights and putting away his shoes, his brandy snifter, his books and files. This sudden burst of activity calms his nerves, I can tell. All his worldliness, his knowledge about politics and history and fine wines can't disguise his fear that he might be rejected by a young woman because he's growing older and less virile by the year.

As I watch him shift around the room in a semblance of busy-ness, I stretch my arms and legs. The room is conditioned to a comfortable temperature, and a pleasant scent of smoky incense rises in the air. My anger from the last time I was here, when Joseph almost ruined my morning departure protocol, has faded with time. I pick up the wine glass and drain it, and smile at him brightly. "See? All gone."

"Very good," murmurs Joseph. The tension between us breathes, expanding and contracting. Our eyes lock, and something flickers in the light, making his gray irises look full, like clouds filled with heavy rain. My head is already feeling distant from my body: the drink's having an effect, faster than I'd imagined. I feel a tightening somewhere between my stomach and my thighs, and I have to tense the muscles of my hips to keep myself from sinking down.

I stare at Joseph with new eyes: he's a little blurry and I have to strain to focus. I'm not like Rupa, always imagining that a Client's falling in love with me. But all of a sudden it's as if nerves and channels that I didn't even know existed in me are starting to open and bloom. I can sense his heat, his need. He looks back at me with eyes shaped like question marks, curious and all-seeing. My mouth opens and I breathe hard, then lick my lips because they've become so dry.

Finally, I break Joseph's gaze, walk to the window, and look out at the skyline, all perpendicular lines: the sharp ruler-straightness of roads and horizon, crossed by the verticals of dozens of skyscrapers arranged in groups as if pushed together by a giant toddler putting all his toys into order, reaching up to the clouds. Cold, stark shapes are silhouetted against the sky: rooftops shaped like triangles, like diamonds, thousands of lights twinkling from the windows, blotting out the stars. An architectural rainbow: the indigo of the ground and buildings, the violet of the deepening night, greens and blues of darkened glass, then the oranges and reds of illuminated signs, and atop the light, a fading yellow canopy reflecting cumulus and desert dust.

Here and there it looks as if a rooftop is melting, then falling. The lights are turning into stars, erasing the barriers between construction and creation. I have to blink hard to keep it all straight, and I'm annoyed at myself for getting tipsy so quickly. I'm such a naïf, in more ways than one.

I glance down at my hands; they've grown so pale from lack of sunlight. My fingers look lonely; they long for companionship. Once I traveled everywhere with my parents, holding their hands as they guided me in and out of buildings whose names I hadn't needed to know. Now I spend my life in this indoor existence, going from the Panah to one rich man's bed after another.

My head has too much noise in it, I buzz like high-tension wires with all the words and sentences that built up during the day. In the Panah, we pass the days by talking; at night, my Clients talk to me. So many words, words, words. I want to run out screaming with my hands pressed to my ears with the strain of never-ending chatter. Utter silence, just for one hour—I want that more than currency or clothes or carats.

Joseph is making impatient sounds now, somewhere halfway between a groan and a growl. I turn around again to see him opening the door to his bedroom. He turns down the covers to the bed, a new, sleek, chrome and platinum offering. It glints under the low lights of the bedroom.

He works methodically to make the bed comfortable, to his liking, and then he arranges himself on it and pats the space next to him, a wolf inviting me to lie down beside him. I pad across the heated floor, my nose filled with the scent of cologne and leather and brandy. Dizzy, I'm glad to be able to lie down. The whole world is slowly wheeling around me.

I look up at Joseph, who's gazing down caringly at me. I begin to panic. There's a thickening in my chest and throat. I need to stand up. I need to. . .

"Sabine? Sabine?"

I blink. Joseph is staring at me from the bed. "Why are you just standing there like that? Come here. Are you all right?"

Who is this man with his arms stretched out toward me? Why am I standing in a room with chilled air and a heated floor? And why am I shaking?

"Lie down," says Joseph. "It's all right." He wraps his arms around me but his embrace is gentle, the way a father would cradle a daughter, protective and warm. My heart is still galloping. I close my eyes and breathe out slowly.

"There, there," he whispers. "You're all right. You're safe with me."

"I'm fine, Joseph," I say, making my voice bright.

"Ssshh, ssshh." Joseph enjoys playing the role of my protector.

I give up the struggle. Joseph feels my limbs unlock, and he grows even more tender towards me. His kisses on my forehead are gentle, the timbre of his voice deepens. There is a courtliness to his embrace, as if he's rediscovered his own nobility in my weakness.

I wonder if Joseph ever wants to know what goes on in my mind, or if he is only concerned with how I make him feel.

I rest my head on Joseph's shoulder. I've always fantasized about being able to sleep easily, a butterfly floating into the air, wings fluttering in gentle currents. Instead, I'm taking a run to the edge of a canyon and leaping high into the air, to hurtle down towards a great blackness where nothing exists, and nothing can ever grow.

FROM THE VOICE NOTES OF ILONA SARFATI

The Charbagh is my favorite part of the Panah. It's best at night, when the others are out with their Clients, and the garden goes into nighttime illumination mode. I like to sit on a bench at the far side of the garden with a cup of tea warming my hands.

Fairuza's a brilliant biochemist. She's used all her skills to nurture this garden, divided into four quarters, lined by waterways, a small fountain bubbling in its center. Its murmurations delight us, the quiet whispering of the grasses and plants, the bushes and pygmy trees releasing natural, not synthesized, oxygen. Panels on the ceilings absorb and process it into soft artificial sunlight that lights up the garden year-round. If there's a god, may he bless Fairuza's Persian ancestors for coming up with the idea of a garden meant to re-create paradise on earth. It gives us some measure of beauty in our underground colony. When I was in school, I learned about ants, the workers, sexless drones marching in and out serving a glossy and beautiful queen. Here, Fairuza and I are the queens but we toil for a purpose totally at odds with the way nature works.

Fairuza found the old map in the Geoscience archives and together we discovered this bunker. We had a small window of opportunity to come here, before they widened the restrictions on international movement to include domestic territories as well. We both chose the name *Panah*, a Persian word that means "sanctuary." Our refuge is made of reinforced concrete and radioactive-proof metals. It keeps us hidden from the men and their scanners above ground. And with luck we'll be able to go on living here for generations to come.

Gifted as she was, Fairuza could do nothing about the Virus, which morphed from a rare strain of HPV into a fast-spreading cervical cancer epidemic. Men could be carriers, but it was women who were felled, quickly and inclusively. Most died within four to six months of catching it. This is the reason the Perpetuation Bureau stresses fidelity within marriage; a woman's protected from the Virus when sexually restricted to her legal spouses, who are always tested before a marriage is allowed to take place in Green City.

While the Officials tried to put a stop to the men roaming the city in packs, assaulting and gang-raping any woman they could find, in those chaotic days of Restoration and the new rule, we worked day and night to refurbish our rooms here. We faked our own deaths, gave up all our belongings, cut off ties with our families. We even burned our clothes to destroy any remnants of our DNA that could be used against us. A hard thing to do in your mid-twenties, but we had to.

I was a communication specialist for the government of Green City; I was good with words. So naturally I wrote the first message to the handpicked Officials we invited to be our first Clients:

"We represent a commodity no longer available in Green City. It's not just economics; it's also science, of a sort: the alchemy that takes place between a man and woman, far more compelling than any drug for its powers to soothe, heal, rejuvenate a spirit broken by the stresses and strains of the day."

At first we went out on assignations ourselves only with most high-powered Officials: Agency high-ups, Perpetuation Bureau managers, generals in the army. We chose our Clients carefully: men placed highly enough to protect us and keep our activities hidden from the Agency or the Bureau.

In the early days, we looked for how outwardly loyal the would-be Client was to Green City. If a man ranked high enough in the hierarchy of Agents, Officials, and Leaders, yet engaged in behavior that contravened Green City's strict codes—keeping a woman all to himself, for his own pleasure, instead of sacrificing his desires for the greater good of the society and its reconstruction—his involvement with the Panah would be classed as rebellion. Only the ones who expressed doubts in the new order, who wrote of missing the old days, suited our needs and passed our test.

Soon we had enough business to consider expanding the Panah, with caution. We couldn't take just any woman to join us. She had to be double- and triple-recommended by our own contacts. Any assets she could bring to the Panah were a bonus—liquefied property, good contacts, and, above all, an unswerving commitment to our secrecy. The vetting methods were rigid because one weak link would bring us all down. The Perpetuation Bureau would easily sacrifice a few errant women to teach the rest a lesson. Green City would use our deaths to illustrate the futility of revolt.

Fairuza died of the Virus five years after we came to the Panah, leaving me alone to run it. The Virus lay dormant in her system, choosing to emerge when there was no way we could get help, even to soothe the pain at the end of her days. It was a terrible death she suffered, and it left me reeling. That's why I went looking for Lin. Any girl could have carried on here, but I want someone of my own blood to close my eyes after I'm gone.

Sometimes I wonder if the Perpetuation Bureau actually knows of our existence and allows us to continue. What if they're keeping us tight in a web that they can destroy at any time? I like to torture myself with the idea when I'm in a dark mood. They come often these days. Lin does her best to snap me out of them, but she's still a child. Sometimes it's more comforting to think of destruction than survival. I don't know why.

But the Panah has been in existence for the last thirty years, so perhaps our allies have never betrayed us and maybe they never will. The Panah will exist as long as there's a need for it, as long as men need woman—which means forever. It may be a life in the shadows, but at least no Bureau tells us whom to marry, whom to open our legs for. Nobody can experiment on our ovaries and wombs, pump us full of fertility drugs, monitor our menstrual cycles and ovulation patterns. Our bodies are not incubators that will "boost the numbers of women up to appropriate levels." Above ground, we are only women, but here in the Panah, we are humans again.

Every day my mind kept turning to the problem of making Joseph want me more than he wanted Sabine. At first it was a game, but something changed between us once I realized I was genuinely attracted to him. Then I became frustrated with his lack of interest in me, knowing that he desired only Sabine. I pressed myself to him in bed, I wound my arms around him and let my fingers stray. But he kept our embraces chaste, our nights clean. Once or twice he turned away from me, and I had to laugh to hide how much it hurt me.

One night we were sitting in his spacious living room, looking out at the city lights blinking on and off. Faint music played somewhere in the city square, designed to calm the residents down and prepare them for a peaceful night's sleep. The fountains combined colors with rhythms to soothe us into somnolence. Joseph watched me as I sang along to the familiar song, one taught to every schoolchild in Green City, boy or girl. "Don't you know the words?" I asked Joseph.

"The only song I know is the Green City anthem, and that's only because I supposedly wrote it."

Then I tried to kiss him. I leaned close, my lips were only inches away from his mouth, and my breath was sweet with mint, which I'd chewed just after dinner.

He stayed completely still, neither coming towards me nor backing away, and raised an eyebrow.

"You don't like me." I wasn't entirely heartbroken that he didn't want to kiss me, but I wanted to see how close I could get him to disobey the Panah rules. Now the game had expanded, beyond Sabine, to see if my power was greater than even Lin's. And to see if I could get someone as powerful as Joseph to break his own internal rules, endanger his job for my sake.

"I like you. But rules are rules."

I turned away from Joseph. "Don't you get sick of the rules sometimes?"

Joseph grasped my upper arm tightly and pulled me back towards him. "There's nothing less honorable than a man who doesn't honor his contracts, Rupa." He seemed almost angry now. And yet I felt—I knew—that he was being less than honest. He would make love to Sabine if only she'd let him.

"Ow. . . You're hurting me." In truth, I liked his touch: hard and firm, steady and sure, the way a man's should be. The pain reassured me that I did mean something to him.

His fingers immediately eased their grip on my flesh. "I'm sorry."

"I'll have a bruise tomorrow."

Joseph leaned over and, to my surprise, kissed my arm where his fingers had been just a moment ago. His lips on my skin were warm, tender, and I shivered. "There. That will make it feel better." He straightened up and gazed at me. He had bags under his eyes, deep-set and hooded: the eyes of an old man. But I didn't mind. They contained real wisdom; they were shrewd, and they'd seen more than I had in my short lifetime.

"Do you want more coffee?"

"Yes, please."

He got up and went to the kitchen, talking to me as he prepared the coffee. "So how is everyone at the Panah?" I laughed at his offhand manner, as if he were talking about my colleagues in an office, as if I were a man and knew what that was like.

"They're well. As they always are."

"Does anyone ever talk about me?"

"We never talk about Clients."

He brought me a medium-sized blue china cup and sat down opposite me. "Drink up. Before it gets cold. Now tell me what they say about me."

"I just told you, nothing!"

As I sipped the coffee, admiring its strength, I pretended not to notice Joseph watching me intently. I was annoyed for a moment: a man's never happier than when you're talking about him. I knew that Joseph was dying to know what Sabine said about him, what she thought of him. The way he kept giving me little meaningful glances, raising his eyebrows, urging me to say more about her. He could buy her time, her attentions, the superficial signs of affection, but he couldn't buy her love. He needed me because he knew only I could tell him what he wanted to hear. My words had power. I decided right then to barter them for something I'd never asked for before.

"I'll tell you—if you do one thing for me."

"What's that?"

My heart was pounding. "Take me out somewhere—for a meal, for a drink, I don't care. But *outside*. And then I'll tell you everything Sabine says about you."

Joseph let out a yelp of astonishment. "Have you gone out of your mind? *Take you out?*"

"Please, Joseph. I haven't seen proper life in two years. It's killing me. I'm suffocating there. Please, please, Joseph. I promise just this once, and I'll never ask anything of you again."

"You know what happens if you're caught. I'm sorry, but I can't do it. I can't take that risk." He set his coffee cup and empty whiskey glass down on the tray with an angry crack.

"You'd do it for Sabine," I said, unleashing the taunt like a stone at his back as he shifted towards the kitchen. As soon as I said it, I knew I'd made a mistake.

He threw down the tray with a clatter, whirled around, and came up to me in two short strides. "Stop trying to provoke me, Rupa!" Then he dropped his head, breathing heavily to bring himself back under control. When he looked at me again, the rage had gone out of his eyes. He sank down opposite me on the sofa, his face still tight and tense and guarded. "So *now* do you want to know why I want you? Why I ask for you?"

I nodded. I had never quite understood this agreement that was made on our behalf, where we were sent to these men to help them pass the night, without the physical act of lovemaking. I had grown up thinking that was all men wanted from women. Why else did my mother have two Husbands, if not to provide her body to both of them?

"It's very simple." Joseph lit an e-spliff and blew the smoke out in little pauses between the short sentences that he spoke. "I spend my entire day with men. Men serve me. Men work for me. I work for other men. I socialize with them in the evenings. I dine with them at night. And for most of the hours of the day, I like it that way.

"But when it's late, like this, and I'm tired, I want a woman's arms around me. You women don't know—or maybe you do know—what magic there is in your arms. Well, on second thought, of course you know. Otherwise why else would there even be a place like the Panah?"

I glanced down at my arms, surprised. This wasn't the part of my body I'd expected Joseph to be most interested in.

"Oh, there's magic between a woman's legs, of course!" Joseph opened his mouth wide and blew out a smoke ring, a perfect O, just in case I needed more explanation. "But when I lie down next to you at night, and put my head on the pillow next to you, hearing you breathe next to me, hearing your heartbeat when I wake up at night and I know I'm not entirely alone—I can face the next day again without feeling like I want to murder someone."

He pulled me close to him, until we were touching all the way down the length of our bodies. "So you see, my dear. It's you who keeps me human—and alive."

Suddenly frightened, I buried my head in his shoulder. I

knew his words, the lies woven in with the truths, were not meant for me. He was talking about Sabine. Then I realized I could still make this go my way, if I was clever. I took a deep breath and spoke my next words with exquisite gentleness. I straightened up and looked at him.

"Sabine really likes you, Joseph. A great deal. She just doesn't know it. You have to help her realize it."

Joseph rubbed his face, massaging the skin around his eyes with his fingertips. "How?" he muttered into his hands.

I glanced at the bottles of whiskey and wine and vodka on the shelf behind his head. More alcohol than anyone in Green City would ever see in their lifetime. Certainly more than Sabine had ever had in her life. He followed my glance with his eyes.

"Maybe you just need to show her what a *real* man is like."

He scoffed, but from the way his shoulders slumped, I knew my words had found their mark. Weak men all have one thing in common: the slightest hint that you doubt their manhood, and they'll do anything to prove it.

SABINE

Diyah is the only one who knows how lethargic and bad I feel after my sleepless nights. She always tries to distract me with jokes and stories. Today she asks me to join her for lunch in the Panah kitchen, a small space with green-painted walls, wood-framed mirrors, and low sofas that run all along the sides of the room, only a foot and a half off the floor. Our plates of food are balanced on small wooden octagonal tables, carved and inlaid with bronze flowers. A small wall fountain bubbles in a corner of the room, whispering unintelligible secrets.

We usually cook for ourselves in the Panah. Diyah's invitation to share her vegetable-and-lentil broth is a welcome one; I can't resist the idea of someone nurturing me for a change.

It's strange, but over the years I've memorized the recipes in the cookbooks Ilona Serfati left behind. Lin says she was a great cook. I never met her, but from her food, always lighter in spice and oils than the rest, I can tell she was a woman of some discernment. When I found the cookbook, its spidery, ethereal handwriting already fading from the pages, I wanted desperately to save its contents, if not its form. Our mothers, aunts, grandmothers live only in representations of their lives as we, their daughters, try to re-create them.

Lin's agents procure all the food we need, getting it across to us in secret deliveries every two months, but there's always a musty smell and taste to contraband food, duller and less intense than the bold flavors and strong aromas of the gourmet meals that Joseph cooks for me when I go to him. My mouth feels covered in plastic, a film that filters out the intensity and flavor of anything I eat in the Panah. Joseph's meals are seductions in their own right. And I still remember the thrilling taste of that black champagne. . . I haven't told anyone, not even Lin, that I drank it.

I can talk with Diyah about this and that, nothing to do with Clients or the Panah. She's good, chatty company, a fearsome mimic with a roguish smile that she flashes at me behind everyone's back, when I'm trying to be at my most serious. Right now she's telling me about a movie she's seen on her device, an ancient Bollywood film with many spirited song-and-dance routines. She gets up from the table to show me the old-fashioned moves.

"See, she goes like this—" Diyah thrusts her hip up so violently that I hear her joints cracking. "And then she does this!" She drops her hip and pulls an exaggerated sexy face, pushing her lips out in a duck's pout, and rolling her eyes until I scream with laughter. If I laugh enough, I don't think about my meeting with Joseph tonight—our fourth in the last six weeks.

We look to see Rupa standing in the doorway, watching us, her lips twisted in amusement. I glance at her, then quickly look at our food, not wanting her to assume we've been discussing her. Rupa's so moody that you never know if she's going to greet you with a kiss or a slur.

"What are you talking about?" She sits at our table and pours out a bowl of soup from the pot without asking. She begins to eat, every movement sensuous and feminine. The spoon to her full lips, the tip of her tongue snaking out to taste the soup that Diyah's cooked. "Oh, this is too sour,"

Diyah laughs good-naturedly. "Put it back, then."

"No, now I'm eating it."

It's easy to chafe each other in the Panah. Seeing each other for hours and days on end, the closeness breeds an impatience we can't help displaying from time to time, rolling our eyes at each other's stories, finishing each other's sentences. I feel so much for Rupa, who chose me out of all the others to share her secrets with, but there are still moments when she truly irritates me.

"You were talking about something. What was it?"

"A dance," says Diyah, returning to the table and sitting next to Rupa. "I was just showing her an old dance. From Bollywood. My grandmother's time."

Rupa glances at me, flashing a saucy smile. "Sabine's not very good at dancing."

"Oh, please, Rupa." I mop up some of the broth with a piece of flatbread. If my mouth is busy, I won't respond to her, which always turns out better for me.

"I like to dance," Diyah says, "even if I'm no good at it. It's a relief not to have to be good at everything."

"Maybe your Clients would like it," says Rupa.

Diyah tries to sound serious as she admonishes Rupa. "I'm not there to dance for them. They can go downtown and find the dancing bots if that's what they're looking for."

Rupa reaches out for a piece of bread and pops it casually in her mouth. She chews, swallows, finishes. "Girls who dance well are the best at sex. That's what one of my Clients told me."

Diyah clicks her teeth, and my insides tighten unpleasantly, as if someone's reaching in and wringing them like wet washing. Really, this is too much, even for Rupa. "Don't talk like that, Rupa," I say.

Rupa winks at me, expecting a response, the diamond in her nose glinting, her nostrils flaring slightly. She's extraordinarily beautiful with something animal and capricious about her. She's selfish, too, a captive to her own needs and wants.

"You're so prissy, Sabine. You probably would have made a perfect Wife. No frolic, just work. All those procreation charts would probably make you so happy. Look whose ovaries have the most eggs!"

I shake my head, hoping that Diyah will catch my glance.

Rupa's in one of her tempers again today; it's best not to engage her when she's spoiling for an argument. I've never spoken to Diyah about Rupa, but I know that what Rupa went through before coming here has loosened something inside her, unleashed a false bravado in her, a flag she needs to wave at us—challenge and recklessness hiding the fear beneath. And the anger. Always there. Here, in the Panah, and only here, is where she feels safe enough to show it. With us. To us. It's exhausting, but my heart breaks for her all the same. She has a wound that never heals.

"I'm happy where I am, Rupa," I say.

Inexplicably, tears spring to her eyes, two patches of wet dark velvet fringed by thick eyelashes. She cried like this when she told me how she came to the Panah, in the first few days after her arrival. I think I fell in love with her a little bit then, or at least I understood how a Client might desire her in a way very differently than how he sees me. Nobody could resist Rupa in any of her moods. Her girlish tantrums would provoke any man into making wild promises, oaths of devotion, utterances of love. The illusion that she isn't strong enough to resist comes off her in waves. And that's what makes her, in turn, irresistible to those men, no matter how powerful they think themselves in life.

"Happy where you are? What a good little Wife you'd have made. I bet you've memorized the entire Handbook. Do you kiss it goodnight before you go to sleep at night?" I say nothing. She's like an angry child, talking nonsense. I know she doesn't mean it. I must not let her words cut me open.

She's said before that I lack the urges and feelings of a normal woman. They probably all believe it—Mariya, Su-yin, Diyah, maybe even Lin. And maybe Rupa is right. If I have those urges, I've never felt them; they're buried in me. Perhaps I'll never learn how to feel, how to be a woman, how to surrender. Whom do I tell that I never feel anything beneath my waist, though? Apart from the usual aches and pains of menstruation, or the occasional morning when I wake up stinging or hurting, chafed by the cups we use for our flows, I don't really know what sexual desire feels like. That part of me is no more special or different than my arm or my nose. I almost feel, sometimes, as if I just want to erase it. Is that really my fault, though? The way they trained us in Green City, to only think of sex as a means to repopulate a broken city, why would I long for physical contact? The idea of it fills me with misgiving.

I've come close to feeling desired, of course, in a Client's bed at night. But it's not about his face or his body, or how he looks at me. I don't spend as much time preening in front of the mirror as Rupa does, imagining how my breasts or my hair arouses his astonishment. When I'm with a Client, there's a moment where we switch roles: I become powerful and he grows vulnerable. My presence leads to his eventual emotional surrender; it's a far more dangerous transaction for him than me. It's my own decisiveness, not a Client's desire, that turns me on. Rupa, operating on the level of the body only, can't understand it. I've never told her how I feel. Rupa is too volatile to trust with my secrets.

As if she realizes she's gone too far, Rupa suddenly looks thoughtful, maybe even pained. "Sabine," she goes on with surprising tenderness, "I'm sorry. I mean, I actually feel sorry for you. You can't sleep, you can't let go of yourself. And maybe you just can't fall in love." Rupa grows quiet for a moment; her face softens, her hands come up to stroke her own hair unconsciously, naturally. "But don't you ever think about what it could be like, if a Client fell in love with you? Don't you ever think about what it could be like if you could marry and live in Green City normally again?"

Diyah puts her hand on my arm, either as comfort or warning, I can't tell. I shrug it off. "I never think about that,"

I mutter. I can't explain why I become so nervous listening to Rupa. Does she know something about Joseph and the way he acts around me? I've only confided in Lin about his behavior. The last thing I want is for anyone to believe that I provoke his obsession with me on purpose. "Neither should you. It's impossible."

"I'm not ashamed of it," says Rupa. "You can't choose whom you love. I never thought this would be forever, anyway." She waves her hand, taking in the room, Diyah, me, the Panah. Everything Lin's done for her, everything we've been through together means nothing to her compared to the mirage of departure she's designed in her own mind.

"You can't get out of here, unless you leave Green City for good," I say. "There's no way you can float around outside. They'll find out about you, capture you, and you'll be declared—"

"I've got Clients who can fix the records," Rupa interrupts, raising a hand haughtily, like a traffic warden stopping my voice.

I laugh. "Nobody's ranking goes high enough that they can fix the records. Change things, fudge them, hide things here and there, but erase them forever? Not possible."

Rupa fixes her eyes on me. There's a strange light in them, and I wonder for just a second if there's something to all her braggadocio. "Sabine, my Clients are more powerful than you can even imagine."

I push away my broth half finished and stand up from the table. The bowl clatters, soup spilling out on my fingers. I don't flinch, don't grimace, don't let out a sound. I keep my reddened hands at my sides and turn away from her pretty, sulky face. I'm not going to argue with her to provide entertainment on another boring afternoon. Finally she gets up and stalks out of the room. She slams the door when she goes.

I sit back down.

"Maybe she's right. Maybe I'm not normal. Maybe I *am* a freak."

"She's not right about you. Or about love," Diyah's calm, cool voice brings me back to shore. "That you can't choose. You do choose. You choose every day."

"How do we. . ."

"I mean you, Sabine. It would be so easy for all of us to become bitter, to hate what we do, where we are, like Rupa."

"She can't help herself."

"Yes she can. She could be more like you. You wake up every morning and you decide to put your energies and attention into making our little world a little better. You put fresh flowers on the table so that it looks nice. You always have time to listen to us when we have problems. You even laugh at my jokes!"

I'm embarrassed by Diyah's reassurances. All the years I've been in the Panah, I've thought of living here like putting currency into an account. I'm stuck, so I have no choice but to invest more and more of my heart and soul into it. And the more I invest in it, the more difficult it becomes to hate it, or hate anyone else who lives here with me. Rupa resists even now, making an already difficult existence even tougher to bear. She still dreams of escape, while I only dream of survival.

I lower my voice and lean close to Diyah's ear. "It sounds like Rupa's in love with one of her Clients."

"I think it's more than that," whispers Diyah grimly.

We look at each other nervously. We don't dare speak our fear aloud. If Rupa's been having sex with a Client, she's truly lost her mind. Lin would throw her out in an instant. But then if that happened, Rupa would be dangerous. Who knows where she'd go or what she'd do, released from this sanctuary?

"I just can't figure out who she would let. . ." continues Diyah.

"Not an ordinary Client."

"No. Someone really big. She said so. Someone high up. But who?"

Words stop coming into my head for a minute. I don't know what to do with this sudden burst of information from Diyah.

Everyone seems to like telling me their secrets. My sleeplessness sets me apart, like a temple virgin. When you're deprived of your most basic needs, you live on a different plane, as if your atoms are vibrating at a different frequency. Or maybe I draw their secrets to me like magnets because I'm made of darker matter than they are.

Diyah stirs her spoon inside her empty bowl, tapping it to emphasize her words. "If Rupa says she loves a Client, it's because she's chosen to love a Client. Because he's her bridge to another place. She can say she's attracted to him, she wants him, she can't help herself." Her voice is soft, hypnotic, as if she's talking to herself more than me. She seems to stare at something very far away, something only she can see. "Rupa thinks she'll get away from here through love."

"Or sex."

"Sex *is* love, if you do it right. But Sabine, men aren't doors to escape through, or even mirrors to find ourselves in. We're fooling ourselves if we think they can help us."

When Rupa first arrived at the Panah two years ago, she seemed more like a frightened eight-year-old girl than the sixteen-year-old woman she really was. At first, she didn't talk to anyone, just kept to herself. Finally, Lin told me to keep her company, to sit with her on my free nights, when both she and I found we couldn't sleep. Naturally, we forged a bond.

The first thing she confessed to me was how upset she was that Lin had made her take out her nose pin. But Lin had her reasons: a nose pin can set off alarms, trigger sensors.

"I know she's strict, I know it's for my own safety," Rupa

said. "Maybe I am cheap. I don't know. I just loved that nose pin so much. My mother gave it to me. I used to bother her all the time for it, and she gave it to me just before I—"

"You're not cheap," I said, and drew her close for a hug to which she submitted to reluctantly at first. But then she clung to me like a limpet and cried into my shoulder.

"I miss my mother," she whimpered.

They lived together in a small apartment in Qanna— Rupa, her mother, and her mother's two Husbands, whose names she never told me. She only identified them as N and Z, who had both married her mother when Rupa was very young. N was older; he kept to himself, reading his device or listening to news reports late into the night. Z was almost young enough to be an older brother to Rupa. He gave her sweets when her mother wasn't looking and helped her with her homework.

She told me this as she was massaging my head one evening in my room. She'd made up an evil-smelling concoction of sesame and mustard seed, a folk remedy for dry hair passed down through generations in her family, or something like that. She asked everyone if they wanted to try it, but they all groaned at the smell, except for me. Feeling sorry for her, finally I agreed to be her guinea pig. The oil stung like ant bites and I squirmed away from Rupa, but her slim fingers were surprisingly strong, keeping me captive in the chair as she rubbed the oil into my scalp.

"Come on, it's good for you. My mother would hit me with a hairbrush if I complained."

"It's so messy! And it smells like rotten eggs," I grumbled.

"But your hair will shine like glass when you wash it," she said. And she was right. My hair was like moths' wings, silky and smooth, when she'd finished with me. It made me go back to her again and again for the same treatment, which she administered to me, along with the unexpected pleasure of the scalp massage. I stopped complaining and learned to ignore the smell while enjoying the sensation of her fingers pressing at my temples and the nape of my neck.

Slowly, over the next several months, she told me about her flight from Green City. At first she only revealed small details, like the fact that her mother was a Religious. "She believed in god, she taught me to fear him. I was afraid of god, but I never loved him the way I loved my mother."

"You're lucky," I told her. "I can't remember what my mother's face looks like anymore."

Rupa made a sound of sympathy. "You're very beautiful. You must look like her when she was your age. If you want to remember what she looks like, all you have to do is look in the mirror."

Next time, as she began to run warm water all over my scalp, she was like a little mother hen with her critique of my posture. "So tense, Sabine! Look at your shoulders, all cramped and stiff. You can't be pretty if you're stressed all the time."

"Is that your secret?"

"Me? I was so ugly and scrawny when I was little, but my mother prayed for me every night to become pretty."

"It worked!"

"Too well," said Rupa with unconscious candor, and her hands suddenly stopped moving in my hair. I couldn't see her face, but I could hear the darkening in her voice.

"What do you mean?"

"Growing into looking better only took away my peace."

Rupa eventually told me that when she came down to breakfast one morning soon after her fifteenth birthday, her family members stared at her as if she were a stranger sitting in their daughter's chair. And her mother? "She didn't say anything, but she didn't have to. She was so grateful, her eyes said it all. I'd make better marriages than she had, you see."

Rupa confessed to being enchanted by her own loveliness. Her stepfather N treated her the same as before, an appendage of her mother, or a piece of furniture in the room that he'd gotten used to stepping around. Z made his usual jokes with her at the dinner table, slipping her sweets when her mother's back was turned. But when he thought Rupa wasn't looking, he would glance at her furtively, not just at her face, but at her body—legs, hips, breasts. And then he would break away and talk innocently to Rupa's mother. It turned Rupa's cheeks crimson, filled her body with shame.

"I began to get nervous around him. Why did he look at me like that? And he was starting to slink away from me more often, talking less to me than before. My mother noticed, too. She'd always been very strict that I should never let anyone touch me, that sex was only for married women. It's in the religious rules, but I guess the Bureau thinks it makes sense for everyone.

"She told me to go to my room and study, but Z was always watching me, whenever I bent down to take something out of the oven, or reached up high to bring a box down from a cupboard. At first I thought it meant he still liked me, even though it was different than before. At least I wasn't a stone or a shoe."

There were no girls-only schools where Rupa lived, so she went to the regular school in a different neighborhood, the only girl in a class full of boys. She wasn't allowed to take part in the physical activity sessions; she was sent for a few hours every day to special classes on Civic Duties, a class conducted by a Wife of one of the Perpetuation Bureau officials. I'd gone to a class like that, too. We watched endless films about housekeeping and the science of childcare. They thought that by calling us household engineers and domestic scientists, we'd be fooled into thinking our "jobs" were worthy of our intelligence and self-respect. In reality being a Wife was endless drudgery, washing and wiping and feeding and cleaning, spaced between unending pregnancies.

Rupa confessed that once upon a time she thought everything they told her was perfectly normal; she even daydreamed about the Husbands she'd be assigned, the children she'd bear to make Green City strong again. For the few girls of Green City, the ones fortunate enough to turn into women, it's either acquiescence or madness.

Then came the morning when Rupa came out of the shower and saw the bathroom door had been opened a crack. Someone was spying on her, but there was nobody at the door when she looked. When she tried to tell her mother that Z was starting to frighten her, her mother threatened to lock her in her room. She promised never to talk about it again, and Z left her alone for a few months.

Rupa dried my hair gently with a towel, her voice neutral, as she told me that several months later Z started to come into her room at night, after her mother had fallen asleep. His hands would roam all over her body and she'd lie there, terrified and silent under his touch. In the mornings he'd act as if nothing had happened. Every night he came to her room, but Rupa kept silent, fearing a beating from her mother if she revealed something so fundamentally wrong. It was worse that her mother wouldn't believe her, that she willfully closed her eyes to Rupa's torment.

Weeks passed and the molestation continued. Z grew more bold, coming to her room even in the day. At night he seemed more and more determined to edge towards the ultimate goal of taking her virginity. The night he tried to take off all her clothes terrified Rupa out of her silence.

"I thought that getting beaten was still better than letting him do what he wanted. I couldn't bear it, so I finally told my mother that it had been going on for months."

She had forgotten to remove the towel from my shoulders,

she was so caught up in her story. She spoke so softly that I had to lean forward to hear. "I thought my mother would kill me on the spot, but she was quiet. Then she went to her room. I couldn't move. Finally she came out and said I wouldn't go to school that day. N went to work, then Z left as well. I tried to study but couldn't concentrate. I gave up and lay down in my bed, looking at the wall.

"Z came home and my mother gave him his meals in his room. He didn't come to my room for two nights. The third day, my mother took me into the drawing room. 'Sit down, Rupa,' she said. I thought she was ready to talk to me. I thought there would be no secrets between us."

"Did she listen? Did she believe you?"

"She took out her nose pin from her nose, the one I'd always admired, and told me I was finally old enough. At first I didn't understand what she meant by that. . ."

I was mesmerized by her story. I couldn't stop listening to her words. I was gripping the sides of my chair, feeling all the terror that she was speaking about as if it were happening to me, not her.

"She pressed her thumb into my right nostril. She pressed hard with the pin, into my flesh. But I didn't scream, not even once."

"She took me by the arm. I'd always thought of her as tiny and delicate, but she pulled me all the way to the door, even though I tried to hold on to the wall with my fingernails. They broke as my mother tore me away.

"There was a black car waiting for me. I cried, I begged, I apologized, but my mother didn't listen. She pushed me out and locked the door."

The nose pin, which Lin had finally allowed Rupa to wear only in the Panah, winked and flashed, a third eye on her face. It was her mother's brand, marking Rupa as both her offspring and her outcast for the rest of her life.

My mind was reeling, my ears ringing with her words.

Surely there was something I could say to make sense out of all of this for her, for me? "She was keeping you safe," I gabbled. "She thought she was doing it for the best, to protect you from him." It was Z she should have thrown out of the house, not her own daughter. Thoughts of my own mother, of loss and longing, assailed me, and I covered my face with my hands.

Rupa's face was drained of blood and emotion. "It was all my fault." Then, seeing how miserable her story made me, she reached out and hugged me.

After the confrontation with Rupa, I go back to my room to rest before my assignation, but when I lie down on my bed, I start to cry. I'm not normal, but neither is Rupa. None of us is. Green City stole our normality, our childhoods, our futures. What is normality anyway? We live in bizarre circumstances; either we cope, or we crack and shatter like glass. The Panah has taught me that much; I've learned not to mind my own insanity. But Rupa's newfound love doesn't seem to have done anything to heal her or make her happier. It's only honed her dissatisfaction, and she's torn my defenses with her casual cruelty.

My tears defeat me, pouring out of my eyes faster than I can wipe them away. In the end, I let the tears soak into my pillow. The love I wanted to give her is a waste; she's thrown it back at me with both hands. She doesn't want or need the Panah anymore, now that she's found true love. She doesn't need me either, and there's no feeling worse than that.

I spend a lot of my time asleep, resting lightly on the earth that will soon claim me for its own.

We don't bury bodies here in the Panah; we have to incinerate them, using chemicals that reduce our bodies to biological ash in a matter of hours. We thought of everything when we set this place up, even the area in the back of the Panah where our cremations take place. Each woman who dies is buried here, ashes scattered around the trees in the Charbagh. Nurturing and replenishing us with the remains of her existence, her cells and atoms become part of our atmosphere. Fairuza hasn't left us. And soon I'll join her. If I see her after I die, I have only two questions for her:

Was it all worthwhile? Was this suffering better than the other way?

Lin doesn't know, or if she does, she's closing her eyes to the truth. She keeps talking about the New Year, the plans she has for improving the garden, the lighting system, whether or not we'll get another girl in the Panah. Sometimes I want to grab her by the shoulders and ask: "Don't you understand the situation? By this time next year I won't be here." She averts her eyes from mine, and doesn't let me talk, the wretched girl.

I'm not worried about her. I've trained her well. She runs the place already, she's like a little dictator with the other girls. I've told her to be softer with them, to follow the rules but remember they're human, they all have broken hearts. Not because they came here, but because they're girls from Green City.

SABINE

I wake up in Joseph's house, and the morning light hits my eyes like a fist to the face.

I wince and turn my head, then move my arms and legs. Even my limbs feel tired. I've woken up in the same fetal position I remember I was in when I fell asleep, Joseph pressing himself into my back, his arm around my waist.

Joseph isn't there. I rise from the bed, putting my feet gingerly on the floor. Strangely, my hips and thighs feel sore and I stand with difficulty. I try, but I can't keep track of everything I'm feeling. The fact that I've slept through the night is astonishing and new. It must be the champagne he gave me again last night; I'm more sensitive to its effects than I thought. I don't like it and I'm not doing that again, anytime soon, even if it makes me sleep. This kind of sleep feels wrong, as if I've stolen it from someone, and now I'm probably going to pay.

I move to the gently percolating bath in the corner of the room, sink under the water, and allow the sleep to be washed from my body. The hot, scented water doesn't lighten me in the least. As I bathe, I fade into a strange vision of Joseph tying weights to my ankles and wrists, a belt of worries tied around my waist. He leads me out to the middle of a large, crystal-colored lake, and makes me lie down on the surface of the water. I'm dragged down to the bottom of the lake, while Joseph swims strongly back to shore.

The problem with insomnia is that everything feels like a dream, even being awake. It's dangerous not to know the difference between dream and reality.

I dry myself off, get dressed, walk into the kitchen. Joseph is making an omelet.

"There you are!" he says. "You fell fast asleep. I thought I'd let you rest, so I slept in the other room." He cracks open two cultured eggs, then scans his kitchen display to see what he should add to it—cultured meat, vegetables, or bio-lab cheese; the display will decide based on what Joseph has been eating over the last few days. "I haven't been getting enough vitamins," he says out loud. I know he's talking to himself, not me.

The display beeps and an image of a pig appears. "Ham it is," Joseph says cheerfully. They haven't killed an animal in Green City in fifty years. All beef, eggs, in fact anything natural, is created in a lab with synthetic polymers, proteins, DNA. It's how Joseph was able to have his liver transplant five years ago, and go on living as a healthy man.

"Imagine, Sabine, a hundred years ago, the only way to get a new liver was to take a piece of a healthy one from a close relative and implant it in my diseased one and pray that it took." He laughs at the barbarity of blood and being opened up like an animal on an operating table with knives. Ancient history, he calls it.

"Aren't you glad we live in today's age? Nothing to it. A few hours being injected with the right formula, and in a few weeks, I had a healthy liver again."

"Did you never think about not drinking, not eating so much rich food?" I ask.

Joseph laughs so hard that his belly quivers. I blush, not liking the tone of Joseph's laugh. It says I can never understand the world he lives in, a stranger to the liberties he's granted just because of his status in Green City. Then he sees me glancing in the direction of his paunch and puts his hand over it defensively.

"Darling Sabine," Joseph says. "There is nothing in this city that isn't available to me. Food, drink, drugs. Riches, power, pleasure. I'm in the taxation business. That means I am in the fortunate position of being the guardian as well as a consumer of things that people spend their lives working to attain and obtain. Why on earth would I restrict anything for myself, when science has given us every way of eliminating their consequences?"

Joseph calls me names like *sweetheart* and *darling,* expresses longing for my company, fusses when I have to leave, but I never feel that I've moved him anywhere deeper. I'm supposed to make him feel cared for and wanted, but I think I hold the same importance for him as an expensive suit, or a car. I'm there to scratch an itch that has nothing to do with his skin.

I clutch a cup of coffee in my hands as I watch him bend, move, reach for dishes. An image comes to my mind, unbidden, of him crouching over me the same way he's hunching over the counter. Of him watching me as intently as he watches his eggs cooking in the pan. Of his leg touching my thigh, his knee between mine. It's the first time I've had thoughts like these, and I'm not used to them either. They evoke a sensation in my body that is unsettling and electric. I drop my head, hoping Joseph can't tell what I'm thinking.

Joseph hands me a plate with my breakfast on it, but I push it away and put my coffee cup down. "I'll eat later," I say. "I have to go. The car is going to be here any minute."

For the first time, he doesn't protest. He sits down and starts to eat, as if I've said nothing. He barely glances at me as I go to his bedroom to anoint myself with gold silicon, my fingers trembling. An inexplicable tension ignites in my body. I'm certain I've missed a few spots, but fear and fatigue make me careless and clumsy. Hopefully it's enough to fool the scanners. Not even machines are foolproof; science is only as good as its gatekeepers.

I stumble out of the bedroom, my veil askew. I need to hurry, I feel as though there's a train rushing through me. "I have to go," I say again to Joseph, wanting to avoid the familiar struggle between going and staying.

Immediately, he pushes his chair back, stands up, sees me

to the door, without reluctance, which surprises me. Joseph holds my arm for a moment, lifts the veil back from my head to look deeply into my eyes. I'm reflected in their depths, falling backward. He's infinitely tender as he replaces the veil on my head, straightens it, and then kisses me on the lips.

"Go, Sabine. Go now or I won't be able to control myself." He laughs at his own confession. It terrifies me and I don't want to know why.

I lurch through the lobby of the building and make it onto the street outside. At this time of year, it's hot enough to strip paint from buildings, incinerate small flowers, boil cultured eggs on your car.

I glance around frantically, but the street is empty. There's nobody on either side of the road, which works to my advantage.

But then a wrenching, sharp pain tears through my abdomen: I press my hand to it and gasp at the pain, ten times worse than period cramps. Where did it come from? I was fine just moments ago. There's a strange soreness in my back, too, but nothing in comparison to the tumult inside my belly.

Sweat beads on my forehead. My ears are ringing, my face is turning hot. My sight grows dim. Am I dreaming that the black car drives up just at that moment, stops a few feet from me? If the car idles more than a few minutes, the heat of the engine will register on the scanners; they'll send an Agency car to investigate. The level of threat is too high; the algorithm is triggered to abort the mission.

I float down to the ground like a flower wilting slowly, its head bowing to gravity. I slip a little as I fall, my limbs splayed out around me. I'm beyond knowing this now. I'm gone from this world, and it is the second time I'll sleep so deeply in a space of twenty-four hours, as if I'm trying to catch up with the last twenty-four years of my life.

S he sat in the rose garden with Reuben, at the end of another night. The sky was overlaid with thick clouds, the sun struggling to break through. They were both silent but satisfied, unneedful of words to maintain the connection between them. The high walls around the garden added to the illusion that the world could not intrude on their momentary refuge.

Reuben had his arm around Lin's shoulders. His usual restlessness had ebbed away, leaving the essence of the man behind, what he would be like all the time without the demands of the City and his job.

Lin wondered to herself, *Is this what it feels like?*

Just as she was about to lean her head on Reuben's shoulder before kissing him goodbye, her device let out an urgent beep, followed by a pulsing that grew stronger with every second. This wasn't the usual alert to announce the arrival of the car. This was something different.

Lin took out the device and pressed the key to display the message. As she read, Reuben watched her face change expressions and her skin drain of all color.

"What's wrong?"

Her hand was at her mouth, and for a moment she couldn't speak. Reuben had to shake her before she could tell him.

"It's Sabine. She was out last night with—with Joseph. She was supposed to be picked up right now."

"What's the matter? Is she all right?" Reuben had heard about this man, how he was enamored of Sabine, who was like steel, Lin had said, she wasn't interested in that sort of thing with a Client. And so far, Joseph had kept his hands off her. Reuben believed the young women could adhere to the no-sex contract, but it was no surprise the men grew tired of it. And what girl could withstand that kind of pressure, if a man truly wanted her body?

Lin shook her head. "She wasn't there at the pickup point. The car left without her. She never came back."

Reuben knew he had to act fast, before Lin put herself in danger. As she jumped up and began to stride towards the gate, he caught her and held her back. "Go home. Go to the Panah right now."

"How can I?" Lin was incredulous. "I can't just leave her there. I have to go get her."

"I'll do it," said Reuben. "Just tell me where he lives."

PART 2

REBELLION

FROM *THE OFFICIAL GREEN CITY HANDBOOK FOR FEMALE CITIZENS*

The Gender Emergency is in its last years; we are fully on the way to recovering the population numbers of Green City before the War. You have been crucial in boosting the numbers up to normal levels, but we still need your efforts and your devotion in order to stabilize and secure Green City's future. Your sacrifices will not go unrewarded; your pain will not have been in vain. When you can look upon a city bustling with girls, you will know that you had a direct hand in turning this dream into reality. If you willingly give your bodies to us in trust, we are honor-bound to return your trust a thousandfold. This is our promise to you as full citizens of Green City. Rebelling against our generosity, on the other hand, is synonymous with transgressing against society and will be answered with reeducation as deemed necessary by the authorities. So be mindful you do not even come near the limits of rebellion, in thought or in action.

JULIEN

As he walked into the hospital, Julien Asfour tripped on the same crack in the floor he'd been complaining about since he first started work at Shifana Hospital six months ago.

His toe caught well and truly in the crack, he lost his balance, and he landed on the floor on his hands and knees with a sickening thump. A current of pain shot all the way up his wrists. A violent blush galloped from his ears and chin to his cheeks and forehead. Two nurses standing nearby hid their grins, then hastily looked the other way as he got up with a grunt and dusted off his hands, grimacing. His knees would be beautifully bruised tomorrow.

The youngest doctor appointed to the best hospital in Green City, Julien was mindful of his reputation as a medical prodigy: he had graduated first in his class, winning a gold medal for pioneering a cancer treatment that sent medication through nanopores right into the lung cells. He couldn't afford to show any sign of personal weakness, or vulnerability. He was being watched by his superiors, by his professors, by his former classmates. Maybe the Leaders, quick to reward exceptional performance, might keep an eye out for his progress. If he did well, who knows where he could end up in five or ten years' time?

His name was Asfour, the ancient Arabic word for *finch*, the most ordinary of birds. Finches were not showy, they didn't sing like the nightingale or distinguish themselves with honor as birds of prey. They were Green City's most popular pets, one or two in almost every home, living in cages for most people's amusement. Julien had always identified with the tiny creatures, thinking himself ubiquitous and sturdy, nothing out of the ordinary.

As he dusted himself off, making a note to warn

Maintenance for not yet repairing the broken tile, a nurse came running up to him.

Julien waved the nurse away. "I'm fine, I'm fine." Then he saw the worry twisting the man's face like crumpled paper. "What is it?"

"Dr. Julien. There's an emergency! I can't find any of the senior physicians. Dr. Falak is already in surgery and Dr. Seremian's off today."

A few doctors were away on scheduled leave, but a mystery stomach flu had sickened some of their replacements and the hospital was struggling to keep up with the flow of patients. Julien's shift wasn't due to start until the afternoon, but he thought he might make himself useful in the meantime.

He frowned. "Has Dr. Bouthain been informed?"

"Bouthain's at a conference. I didn't know who else to go to." The nurse was already a few steps ahead of him, urging him onward. But why was he signaling Julien away from the main emergency hall and down a corridor that few people used at this time in the day?

Julien sprinted ahead of the nurse, turned the corner and nearly knocked into the young woman lying face down on a gurney, unconscious and unveiled. Her face, turned to the side, was clammy and pale, her breathing shallow. There were streaks of gold dust on her cheeks and arms.

Julien stopped short, staggered by the sheer impossibility of such a sight. "What the hell. . . who is this?"

"I don't know," stammered the nurse. "Someone left her outside the hospital, just dumped her on the ground and drove off. I've never seen anything like it, I didn't know what to do."

Julien tuned out the nurse's babbling as he bent forward to help the young woman. It was second nature to him, to speak to her and see if she was responsive; to see if her pulse was strong or thready; to find out if her airways were obstructed.

He was forming a list of possible diagnoses—brain bleed, overdose, electrocution—before he touched her skin to lift her chin and observe the rise and fall of her chest. When he pulled her eyelids up, her eyes were rolling back in her head, pupils unfocused and unseeing. All this he observed in an instant, before making a choice that would lead to another and another, a tree of choices that could lead to either life or death.

"Miss? Miss! Miss, can you hear me?" Julien called out. She was unresponsive to his voice, the pulse at her wrist the weak thrum of swallow's wings underneath his fingertips. The only signs of life: a heavy sweat on her forehead and the whisper of her breath on his cheek when he turned his head to watch her chest.

Julien ran the body scanner over her from head to toe, and an alarm immediately rang out. As he read the results, his throat tightened: she was suffering from a ruptured ectopic pregnancy, with possible—no, probable—internal bleeding. Her blood pressure had dropped and she was already in shock.

"What do we do?" said Mañalac, the nurse who had brought him to her. As their fearful eyes met, Julien realized that Mañalac had never dealt with a female patient before. In five years of medical school, Julien had treated only a few women for minor, insignificant problems: a chest infection here, a broken ankle there. Women came to the hospital to give birth, but the students were not allowed to see them or observe their labor until their final year, and that, too, only behind heavy walls of observation glass. Pregnant women were only handled by the most senior doctors. Their heavy stomachs were treated with the reverence assigned to only the most complicated, challenging diseases; the senior doctors fought among themselves for the prestige that came with treating them on a completely different floor of the hospital that was heavily monitored and guarded; regular workers never even laid eyes on those women. Julien had yet to be given the opportunity to start his specialization in women's care.

The robots he had used in all his surgery drills were constructed in exactly the same way as the female lying pale and unmoving on the table in front of him. Only the janitor or a training bot would have been more forbidden to help the girl than Julien and Mañalac. But today the surgical department was operating half-staffed, as Mañalac had said. It would be at least fifteen minutes before the proper surgeons could be notified, and by then the girl could die.

"We have to get her into surgery right now," said Julien authoritatively, to disguise how badly he was quaking inside.

"No, Dr. Julien! We can't." Mañalac shook his head vehemently. An old hand at Shifana, he was trained to obey the doctors without question; however, he was even more well versed in the repercussions of breaking with hospital protocol. Hospital admissions were entered immediately into the city records; the use of all surgery rooms, drugs, and supplies were recorded, down to the smallest bandage. Putting the first cannula into her hand would set off a cascade of electronic tags that would lead right back to them.

Julien heard himself saying, "Do you trust me?" This time his voice was strong and sure, coming from a place as yet unsounded inside him.

Mañalac stiffened, as if insulted by the question. "Of course I do, Dr. Julien."

"Then please, help me. I'll answer for everything." Could Mañalac see how much Julien's hands shook? "I'll handle the system. And don't worry: I'll take complete responsibility for everything." Mañalac had to know he was lying; Julien waited for him to refuse the order. He looked over Mañalac's shoulder once more, to make it clear that he already considered the girl his patient. He gave Mañalac a moment to realize that Julien would risk everything just to be able to see her open her eyes.

Mañalac turned and followed his glance to stare at the unconscious girl, unable to beg for her own life. He sighed softly. Julien knew he'd won when the nurse nodded, tapped his device to look for a free theater, then carefully waited for a response. But instead of triumph, all Julien felt was a sudden wave of gratitude—and hope.

Soon they were wheeling her through back corridors to an outpatient surgery wing in the basement, where all the day's scheduled procedures had been canceled because of the unexpected shortage of staff. Julien hoped the rest of them would be too overwhelmed to notice what he and his team were up to.

Two surgery assistants appeared like ghosts in their gray surgical scrubs, the same color as Mañalac's uniform. The first, Ram, prepped Julien, while the other, George, hooked up Sabine to the monitors and put an oxygen tube into her nose. He quickly removed her clothes and wiped her stomach clean with antiseptic, then raised her legs.

Julien, waiting, glanced around at the intricate machines, the high ceiling, the observation panel—all empty now. How intimidating he'd found it as a medical student during his surgery rotation. Now he was a captain commanding a ship, Mañalac and the two assistants his able seamen, and the ill young woman his passenger. He was determined to bring them all to safe shores. He closed his eyes for a moment and was astonished to find himself asking an unknown force for help, for steady hands, for success. Doctors weren't their own gods, after all.

JULIEN

Mañalac had been keeping an eye on the cardiac monitor as it tracked her heartbeat and blood pressure. Ram and George pushed IVs into her arms, administering saline in one and keeping the other free for anesthesia. Shock could claim a patient faster than any other malady; they had to stabilize her quickly so that her body could cope with the surgery ahead.

"I need her blood count, please." Julien said. "Give me her serum lactate levels, the metabolic panel, type and cross-match, Rh factor, everything. Oh, and be gentle with her. Treat her as if she were your sister," he added. George's eyes narrowed quizzically above the surgical mask over his nose. Even Julien was surprised at himself. Something had truly taken him hostage, making him say and do the unthinkable. Was it her femaleness or the fact that he held her life in his hands?

All Green City citizens had blood taken from their heels at birth, dried and stored on special filter papers. Digital microfluidics could be used to make a quick analysis on the sample, if a citizen was ever in a medical emergency. Julien had been thrilled to learn how all was hidden in that tiny drop of blood, a ruby-red treasure that revealed its secrets only to those who knew how to read its arcane code. And he was one of those few code-breakers to whom drops of blood and strands of DNA and cells and atoms could actually speak.

Ram quickly took a drop of blood from her finger, put it onto a digital blood chip, and waited thirty seconds for a quick reading. The sample wasn't matched to an official Green City ID, but it revealed that she was twenty-one, young and strong, never pregnant before. Julien listened as Mañalac rattled off the woman's blood type, hormone levels, genetic history, previous diseases.

"Drugs?"

"There's something, but I can't tell right now. We'd need to do more tests. Still, yes, I think she ingested some kind of chemical in the last twenty-four hours."

"Any abortifacients?"

"I don't think so."

"Do you think she's had a reaction to it? Is that why she collapsed?"

"Could be, but it's not anaphylactic."

"All right, let's have twenty units of O positive ready. She's going to need them soon."

George removed the bags of serum from the blood safe, while Mañalac quickly performed more scans. She was roughly five weeks pregnant, but the fetus had implanted itself in the fallopian tube, which was ruptured. An ectopic pregnancy, and now blood was just beginning to pool inside her abdominal cavity. Julien was both vindicated and horrified when he realized that if they didn't operate now, she'd die.

Her blood pressure was back up just enough for Julien to start. Mañalac handed Julien the laser scalpel, and they all watched him intently as he readied for the first cut. Their eyes were anxious but trusting. George and Ram held their instruments poised to follow his lead. Mañalac held Sabine's hand and whispered words of reassurance to her, as if she could hear him, in whatever realm she was in, halfway between life and death. "You'll be all right, just hold on. Dr. Julien will take care of you. Don't worry."

Julien had already ruled out a laparoscopy; radical surgery was the only option. All his medical texts and lectures in Kolachi came rushing into his mind. Nothing, however, had prepared him for the reality of this woman on the table in front of him, This was not the way he'd imagined a real woman laid out before him for the first time.

Julien aimed the laser scalpel at the woman's smooth, pale skin. He was aware, at the far edges of his focus, of the roundness of her belly, the light hairs below her navel. With a delicate touch, almost a lover's caress, he traced the beam of light down her abdomen, three inches in length. The blood swirled around the incision; Ram quickly suctioned it away.

Deeper and deeper, past thin layers of tissue, then thicker layers of muscle, until he penetrated the layer that enveloped all the vital organs. A few deft strokes opened up the cavity. While George kept suctioning away the blood, Julien quickly found what he was looking for with the help of the scanner: the internal reproductive organs, uterus, fallopian tubes, and ovaries. "You'll recognize them because they look like the scales of justice," his professor had said in the lecture hall, then quipped, "Although there's no justice as far as a woman is concerned." They'd laughed then, but Julien remembered his words now and winced. They were operating on her without her consent, without informing her next of kin. Would she wake grateful or violated? He'd had no choice when her life was at stake. He put his thoughts aside and concentrated hard, examining the ovaries. "Small and white, of healthy size and color, they look completely normal—no pathology, no injury here," he said out loud. "The uterus, too, is healthy pink—that's very good."

"Hypovolemic shock?" said Mañalac.

"I don't think so, we're lucky, but let's keep an eye on her blood pressure now. If it surges, we might have a bleed, and that'd be a disaster."

Next, he had to find the damage. The scanner grew smarter with each procedure, but it had definitely not been programmed to identify this kind of problem in the female body. Julien put the scanner aside and tried to spot the ruptured tube with his naked eyes. He wondered aloud: "Which one? Left or right?"

Then he spied a small rending apart of tissues, like fine frayed threads, in the lateral wall of the left fallopian tube. He caught his breath: he'd have to widen the space and tease the fetus out, bit by bit. Could he save the tube, rather than removing it completely? He couldn't stand the idea of making this woman anything less than perfect and whole.

He used tweezer-thin robotic forceps and clamps to lift the tube up and away from the surrounding organs. The tube came up easily in his grasp, the small curved funnel a place of transition, too narrow to bear the burden of a growing embryo. Normally the fertilized egg would drop into the uterus, ready to catch the small clump and hide it deep within its protective folds. Nature had made a mistake this time, and he would have to work fast to rectify it. At least now the end was in sight. . ..

He nudged the tear farther apart. A tiny lump no bigger than the end of his finger slipped out from the tube, accompanied by a fresh spurt of blood. It had not yet assumed the curled shape of a fetus, with rudimentary hands and feet, dark spots for eyes, a small hump where the brain was growing larger than the rest of the body. But it still was the earliest stages of a living being, and its miniature size threw them all off balance.

"My god," breathed Ram.

"God has nothing to do with this," said Mañalac testily.

"Oh my god," echoed George, provoking another glare from Mañalac.

"Quiet, please." Julien kept his gaze steady on the tube. As soon as the entire sac was out, he judged that the tube couldn't be saved after all. The rupture was too extensive, damaging too much of the tube, as well as the artery that supplied it with blood. He quickly removed what was the rest of the fallopian tube, incising and cauterizing once again, precisely and efficiently.

"Well done, Dr. Julien," said Ram, when it was finally over.

"What are her vitals now?" he murmured, listening to George rattle them off. But Julien felt little joy at the success of the operation. He'd ignored all the rules of the hospital, as well as the Perpetuation Bureau's directives on the immediate reporting of endangered pregnancies. The adrenaline was fading away, leaving him afraid once more. He had succeeded as a doctor in Green City by obeying the rules so far. In a single morning this woman had made him break every rule in the book.

"Thank you, good work. Clean her up, please. Let's get her. . . Ram, can you check the rooms, please?"

"You're going to put her in a *room?*" said Mañalac.

"I'll have to talk to Dr. Bouthain, figure out how to enter her into the system," Julien hedged. The clarity he'd known during the surgery was fading fast. He should have reported her presence, the emergency, to the Bureau immediately. Why hadn't he done that? Surely they'd understand that he'd acted as a doctor; saving a life first; filing the necessary reports later.

George and Ram were bustling around the table, unhooking the woman from the oxygen and anesthesia lines, settling her limbs and cleaning her up. Soft beeps from the machines punctuated the distant, tinny voices on the announcement system that signaled the end of the early morning shift and the beginning of the next one. Julien would have to return to work soon.

Mañalac bent his head to his device, pressing buttons again and again and shaking his head. The device chirped. Mañalac read the new information and whistled. "Dr. Julien, look at this!"

"What is it?"

"There's a private room showing up, on the thirty-second floor. Instructions say *post-operative. VIP, Do Not Disturb.* And there's no name on the room, nor a Green City ID. It just says, *Patient X, female, 21.*"

Julien's eyes narrowed and his teeth bit hard against the inside of his lip. Someone was making deliberate changes in

real time to the hospital records to accommodate her. Whoever had brought her to Shifana was monitoring exactly what
was happening to her. And sending out a message that she
was under that someone's protection. But whose? Julien's
stomach clenched at the idea that her protector was watching
their every move.

Julien studied her face closely for the first time. Her dark
hair, smooth olive skin, and full lips denoted youth and good
health. She had a slight scar under her lip. Her narrow jaw
and small ears were almost elfin to look at. Her fragility was
deceptive: even though she was still unconscious, now she had
power, because there was a nameless, faceless someone pulling
all their strings like puppets, directing them to save her life.

"What are you going to do?" said Mañalac, with a slight em-
phasis on the word *you*. No matter what his complicity in Dr.
Julien's actions, people like Mañalac survived by never ques-
tioning their role. Dr. Julien would take the blame for whatever
had already happened, and whatever would come next.

Julien wiped the sweat off his forehead, then raked back
his hair with his fingers, tugging on his hair until his scalp
tingled. "Let's get her in that room, quickly. I don't want anyone to see her." He scrubbed his hands clean, peeled off his
surgical suit, and dropped it into the incinerator.

Mañalac's shoulders slumped. Dr. Julien should have
said he would report to Dr. Bouthain first, before deciding to
move the woman into the room. But look at how he'd acted
to save the girl, not even thinking of the rules and regulations. It was what every good doctor should do, but in Green
City, flouting the protocols was classified as rebellion, and everyone sooner or later paid for the crime. There was already
someone watching them, the person changing the records.

Everyone at Shifana knew the young doctor had a golden
future ahead of him; he wouldn't stay a junior for long. Already word of his talent was reaching the ears of the Bureau,

the Agency, the leaders, and higher-ups. They'd pluck him away from the hospital one day and put him in a position where he would make decisions concerning all of their lives. Mañalac hoped that Dr. Julien would remember him for his loyalty and dedication when that time came. Maybe Dr. Julien would even take him with him, as an assistant or right-hand man. In Green City you survived when you learned how to control others, bend them to your will, make them think that your subtle manipulation was for their own good. Mañalac hoped Dr. Julien was his bridge from one class to another, which most men of Mañalac's background could never hope to achieve.

There was only one thing that stood between Julien and his destiny: Julien himself. Dr. Julien mistakenly thought that each person's individuality mattered as much as the collective duties the authority figures had assigned them according to their station. Nor did Dr. Julien sacrifice his own autonomy for the greater good of society. It would not serve him well once *they* took notice.

Mañalac had spent hours observing the young doctor, attending to him during the long work days and nights at Shifana. While Julien was correct in his interactions with the senior doctors and the hospital administration, he lacked the deferential manner that his position demanded and his seniors expected. He ventured his own opinions without fear or embarrassment; he never indulged in the obsequious bowing and scraping that a junior doctor was expected to show. He remained quiet throughout floor meetings, listening calmly, usually not saying a word among other juniors too eager to impress the seniors.

Mañalac knew that Dr. Julien's patients always recovered quicker than the others, that he was requested again and again whenever former patients returned to the hospital. He delivered results that nobody else could match, and there was talk of him winning the Green City Doctor's Award this year, although it usually always went to someone far more senior than he was.

Mañalac admired and feared for Dr. Julien in equal measure. As he watched Julien's eyes move all over the girl's face, a painful sorrow came over him. He could see, with dangerous prescience, where this would lead: they would both be caught, Dr. Julien and the girl, and punished by the Agency for rebellion, if not revolt.

"Ram, you'll stay here and clean up?" said Julien.

"Don't worry, Dr. Julien," Ram said, busy with trays and instruments. "It'll look like nobody's been in here for a week when I'm done with it."

Julien stayed behind George and Mañalac as they maneuvered the young woman onto a stretcher. They wheeled her away from the main areas, again using private corridors and elevator. The elevator sped up to the thirty-second floor in a matter of seconds, blocking their ears up with pressure and making Julien slightly dizzy in the ascent. He kept wondering what was at work here other than the usual authority. Clearly it was someone with the access to the hospital system, someone who was, obviously, incredibly powerful.

When they reached the preassigned room, Julien spoke his name quietly to the electronic lock, "Dr. Julien Asfour."

The door recognized his voice and immediately unlocked itself, revealing a luxurious room usually reserved for only the most important patients: Leaders and their families. The walls sparkled with fresh leaf-green paint, the air maintained at ambient temperatures, and the lighting in the room changed color depending on the time of day. Right now the lights were pulsing a gentle blue, to match the powder-light sky of the early morning just beyond the walls of glass. Julien shook his head, amazed. He'd lost all track of time in these past hours, and was astonished to realize that the world was going on as normal, while he was plunged in this unfolding, complicated situation.

The small entourage paused before entering, even though the hermetic seal was already broken. But once they crossed the threshold, there was no going back. The scent of lemons wafted out from the room as they stood there, hesitating and shuffling.

"Look," said George, pointing at the display on the inside of the door. "There's a name. And an ID number."

Julien stared. *Faro, Female. GCID 9301102-2* read the display. Faro. Faro . . . where had he heard that name before?

Currents of fear buzzed through his body. *Who was this woman?*

As Mañalac and George eased the woman into the bed, Julien strode to the window and looked out at the sea, close enough to surround the hospital on three sides, like a protective moat. He was worried about the medical supplies they'd used in the operating room. Everything from the oxygen and drugs down to the last strip of gauze was automatically recorded on the hospital's internal databases. Everything—the IVs, the monitors, the syringes, even the doors opening and closing—talked to the network to tell it how much was being used and what for. The hospital could be resupplied, expenditures tracked, and performance of the staff monitored, a system that eliminated wastage and stealing from every hospital in Green City. How could he have forgotten the precision of the system? It would betray him, even if nobody else in this room did.

George suddenly laughed "Wow. Unbelievable. The records don't show anything. Look. I've never seen anything like it." Julien looked at George's device, followed his finger pointing to the rows and columns on the sheet: all the supplies for the operating room they'd just vacated were at full levels, at least according to the device. On the record, it looked as though the operating theater hadn't been used since the day before. The benefactor again, resetting the system so that nobody would know they'd been in there.

"What the. . . ?" muttered Julien. The continuing mystery was fraying his nerves, but he didn't want them to know that. "All right, let's get Mrs. Faro comfortable."

She was not Patient X anymore, but Mrs. Faro. Julien couldn't place the name, familiar as it sounded. Perhaps one of his schoolteachers was called Faro, or he'd known a boy with that name. It was a long time since he'd felt like a boy, or thought of his days in school. In the space of these short hours he felt like an old, old man.

He leaned his head against the cold window and let his eyes grow unfocused, soothed by the white-capped waves fighting each other on the water's uneasy surface. He put his hand on the window to steady himself: it was cold outside, too, the sun barely making a dent in the gray clouds. He thought idly of his sweater, wondered whether it would be warm enough for him on the way home. He wondered why the woman in the bed wore no wedding rings.

"Dr. Julien?"

"She's doing well," said Mañalac, nodding his approval. "Strong girl." Julien started at the sound of Mañalac's voice. George and Mañalac stood back from the bed, the girl lying in it, her head and shoulders propped up by pillows. Her eyes were closed and her mouth lay slightly open, revealing the white tips of her teeth.

She looked anything but strong to Julien. Patients were at their most vulnerable post-op, no matter how many antibiotics and bio-healers were pumped into them to speed up their recovery. Yet as much as infection threatened her, the possibility of discovery and denunciation added an extra sheen to the pale translucence of her unmoving body.

"What should we do now?" George said. "Do you want one of us to stay with her?"

Julien studied the girl, trying to pinpoint when he'd acquiesced to the plan laid out before him by this mysterious force, or person, whatever it was, who was responsible for her. And how could this benefactor have known that he would break all the rules to save her life? That he would instinctively agree to shelter her until that benefactor came to claim her? But how would he monitor her while shielding her from the prying eyes of everyone else at the hospital, much less any Agency spies that might be wandering the corridors?

"No, I'll stay here with her for now. Start over with your new shift, tell them if they ask that you were with me. Inform Ram, too. None of you have to worry about this anymore. It would probably be best if you just forget all about it."

"My tracking record?" said George. "It's been almost three hours now. If anyone checks, they'll know where I've been."

"I'll fix it," said Julien. He didn't have access to the hospital records the way the woman's benefactor did, but he would try to make it look as if all three nurses were carrying on their normal hospital routines.

George nodded, then left. Mañalac hung back, shuffling from foot to foot.

"My shift's over. Ended an hour ago. I can come back whenever you need me, Dr. Julien."

Julien clasped Mañalac by the shoulder. "Thank you," he said quietly. "I won't forget this." His fingers tightened on Mañalac's sleeve for a moment, then let go. Mañalac nodded, embarrassed. Then he, too, disappeared.

When Julien was alone with the woman, he sat down in the soft chair opposite her bed and watched her sleep. Color was seeping back into her face, her cheeks turning from ivory into a sunrise. Her chest rose and fell smoothly, a bow slowly moving back and forth across the strings of a violin, sounding out long, clear notes of rest and healing.

Julien was still too young, too low in status to be assigned a Wife through the Perpetuation Bureau. His only chance of romance would be to strike up a relationship with one of the female robots in the hospital that smiled and moved their heads, extended their arms and legs, breathed in and out in a maddening verisimilitude that allowed men to pretend, for just a while, that they were human. Compared to the real women he'd known—his mother, an aunt on his father's side, a grandmother who'd died when he was young, the robots were perhaps a little lacking in spontaneity or vitality, but they'd been engineered to be warm and pliable enough.

The first weekend after his eighteenth birthday, Julien went with two friends to the decrepit downtown area of the city known as Red Town, searching for a brothel that would accept the "comfort money" given to them by the Perpetration Bureau. Sleeping with a prosbot was something that everyone did at least once, if only to prove they were real men. It wasn't something you bragged about, but single men had needs, and this was the only legitimate way to satisfy them. Thinking that it would help men control their impulses toward real women, the Bureau subsidized the first visit to a prosbot when men came of legal age, so it cost next to nothing. After that, it was true, some men became addicted to the physical release; others, to the deception that these were real women who cared about them, who truly liked them, who enjoyed their company, not just their money. Visiting prosbots could become an addiction as much as any of the rest of the pharmacological cornucopia that Green City had to offer.

A visitor spent an hour in a private room with one of the prosbots. Any act was allowed, as they had been constructed more sturdily than the anatomical ones in the medical school; they only were not allowed to willfully damage or dismember them.

Julien found no real pleasure in the female's limbs around his neck, her synthetic lips on his, or her recorded voice;

his body responded, but it felt like cheating on an exam or stealing money. Immediately afterward, the emptiness in his head and the pit of his stomach made him want to weep. He decided that he would not return. He would wait for something better, more human. And yet it was depressing to think that any woman he'd end up with would have two other husbands, at least.

At the same time, Julien decided to sacrifice all hopes of companionship in return for professional success. So far he'd been on target, working days and nights, taking on extra hours and emergency calls that had gotten him noticed by the hospital administrators. There was even talk that he might be promoted in the next year if he kept the pace up. He'd be the youngest doctor in history among the ranks of the elite surgeons; he might be deemed worthy enough by the Bureau to have a Wife sooner rather than later.

Julien was completely exhausted and suddenly felt a desire to lie down next to the woman in the wide hospital bed, to curve himself around her body and put his arms around her, bury his face in her hair, and simply close his eyes and drift away. It would be such a clean forgetting, a knife cutting time into *before* and *after*. It wasn't his habit to seek comfort from another person in that physical way. Yet feeling the warmth that came off her like waves and inhaling the scent of her skin and hair, he longed for relief by her side.

Julien settled himself into the chair next to the bed and closed his eyes. He thought about how he'd taken out pieces of her flesh and blood and removed the life growing inside her. Her body had been violated enough by his hands. He would not impose himself on her even more in what remained of this day. Besides, she was married to J. Faro, whoever that was. He fell into sleep as quickly as a child in its mother's arms.

SABINE

When I was eleven, I began to ask my mother questions. "Why do you only have one Husband?" She sat at her dressing table, carefully blotting her face with powder. She had a drawer full of makeup that she used only on special occasions. Women weren't encouraged to paint their faces too much, to avoid drawing attention to themselves when they went out.

She dabbed powder under her eyes, first the left, then the right. Her mouth was pulled down into a funny shape, one that I imitated when she was gone, looking in the mirror and pretending I was applying makeup to my face, too.

"Our family is different," she said. "One mother and one father and one child."

"But my friends—Irene has three fathers, Jana has two. There's one girl in the class above me who has four!"

"Do you want to have more fathers?" She turned to me and watched my face carefully.

I felt bad saying *yes*. "I don't know."

My mother's hands fell into her lap. She bowed her head for a second, deep in thought. When she lifted it again, her eyes were clear, guileless as they looked into mine. "It's my fault, Sabine. I can't have more children, so they don't want me."

For years afterward, I believed her. When I was old enough, I imagined the pain my mother endured, the humiliation of monthly examinations, the prodding and poking of her body. For years in my mind she lived a martyr to infertility, a poor invalid who had to make monthly declarations that her body had failed her and Green City.

What I didn't know is that instead of submitting to the rules of the Perpetuation Bureau, my mother defied them. She had been bribing a doctor who faked the results of her hormone tests, so she got classified as temporarily infertile. This momentous lie exempted her from having to marry two, three, or four men. The lie bought our family years of normality.

When I turned twelve years old, the doctor was exposed and betrayed by one of his patients. Panicked, my mother confessed everything to my father, who urged her to pledge herself as a loyal rule-abiding citizen of the Green City. When questioned by the Agency, she said she was ignorant of the doctor's actions.

The doctor was swiftly arrested, underwent a public trial, and was eliminated. All the women he'd helped were ordered to take more husbands immediately. They wouldn't be punished; the doctor corrupted them, led them astray from their paths. They could earn forgiveness in return for their complete obedience from then on.

My mother waited in dread for the notification, knowing that it would come soon. Probably on a Monday morning, when the most important missives arrived through the Network to the families of Green City. There was no question of my mother rejecting the assignment, of even choosing the Husband.

But before the notification ever came, my mother died, suddenly. When the Officials visited and the crews came to take my mother's body away, they labeled it a suicide. They painted a compelling portrait of my mother's mental state before her death. The psychological counsellors sent by the Agency wrote in their reports that the guilt and anxiety my mother underwent was too much for her; it drove her to an impulsive, impetuous decision to remove herself from our lives, so that we would be spared more repercussions of her rebellion.

My father accepted the official version of events. I was sure it wasn't true. She would never leave me like that. They probably knew she'd refuse to take another husband and quietly eliminated her, stole her life from us as if she were their property. She had no more moves left, so they checkmated her, and left us to live with it forever.

I often relive the moment when I found my mother in the bed, face down, clad in one of her afternoon robes, a flowing blue kaftan slit high up the legs to afford her freedom of movement. I wait to see her head move, her legs shift, the usual signs of her waking up.

I wait and wait and wait.

Then I touch her hand, shocked at how cold it is, and I begin to scream.

An alarmed neighbor calls the emergency line. When the ambulance arrives, the paramedics cannot pry me away from her body. I'm clinging to her, begging her to wake up. "I'm sorry, Mamma, I'm sorry! I didn't mean it! Please wake up now."

I lay in bed for countless nights after she died, half terrified, half hoping that I would see her in my dreams; she might be laughing and happy in them. Sometimes I was afraid to fall asleep and sometimes I couldn't fall asleep because I believed that she'd killed herself because of me.

Hissing, a soft beeping, a low hum from deep somewhere— inside me or outside?

Is it morning already? I should get up, they'll be waiting for me.

Hearing muffled sounds, like being underwater. Rising, rising, the surface not far above my head. . . Sharper now. That's a door opening. Closing again. Opening. But why?. . . doors in the Panah never make any noise.

My mouth is dry. My throat hurts—

I'm cold, so cold. Shivering—

A tube snaking out of my nose, smelling strangely anti-septic, delivering the purest air I've ever breathed, a cool breeze whistling into my lungs.

I move my hands instinctively to pull out the intruding

tube, the prongs scratching at my nostrils. At the same time, darkness starts to lift, brightening to red, then orange, and pink. A sunrise behind my eyelids.

But where—

My eyes snap open. Nausea claws its way out of my stomach. I retch and try to sit up but the muscles of my abdomen won't tighten, as if everything is disconnected from my very core. Then I notice the throbbing, aching weight all across my belly.

I flop over weakly to the right and retch over the side of the bed. Nothing comes out. I'm clutching at my belly with my hands. There are starbursts of white heat when I twist. I press my forehead into the cold railing at the side of the bed and groan with each stab of pain.

"Wait, wait, wait!"

In an instant an unknown man is at my side, holding a metal pan to my mouth. "Easy, easy. We don't want you to burst your stitches. Well, they're not really stitches, we just call them that out of habit, but we still don't want anything rupturing after we've done such a good job of fixing you up."

I barely hear him. My abdomen still throbs, the sensation that someone's rummaged inside me. I whimper softly, and he pats my back, his hand calming against my spine.

"I'm sorry, I know it hurts. I can give you more medication for the pain. And the nausea. It's a common effect of the anesthesia. Luckily the gels we use to knit your skin together after. . ."

I raise my neck to try and look down at my stomach, but the smallest movement draws a gasp from somewhere shallow in my chest. At once his hand is behind my head, cradling it until I sink back down on the pillow.

His hands on my head and back are gentle and firm, holding me where I need support the most.

"Where am I?" I whisper.

He falls silent, moving away so I can get a good look at

him. I stare at him, trying to recognize this tall, thin man with blond hair and blue eyes. I've never seen him before, but he seems more familiar with my body than I am right now.

I glance around uncomprehendingly at the darkened room, with only a glowing light on in the corner. The large displays that run all along the wall to my left are switched off. Only a small machine beeps softly from an alcove. I look up at the ceiling and see small twinkling lights, arranged in tiny constellations.

For a moment, I think I might already be dead.

"You're in hospital, Mrs. Faro," he says and looks perturbed when I give him another blank stare. "That is your name, isn't it? Mrs. Faro—that's what it says on your records."

My records? I don't have any records. I don't exist, officially speaking. "Am I still in Green City?"

His sudden smile breaks the tired shell of his face, giving way to a young boy's friendly gaze. "Yes, you are. You're in Shifana Hospital, the best in Green City. And I'm Dr. Asfour. . ." He pauses. I realize: he's in complete control of me. For all I know, he could be the reason why I'm lying in this hospital bed, wires running from my fingers like snakes, this flower of pain growing from my stomach.

A small chirp emits from the monitor. I flick my eyes to the display and see that the numbers on it are rising, matching the drumbeat of my pulse beating faster in my ears.

The man glances over at the machine, then at me. "I'm Julien," he whispers. "I'm a doctor here. You don't have to worry. I'm not going to hurt you."

I nod at him, as if there could be nothing more logical than for me to wake up in a hospital, my insides aching. I open my mouth to tell him that my name isn't Mrs. Faro, it's Sabine, but the pain momentarily leaves me mute.

"Why am I here?" My voice scratches against my throat. "What happened to me?"

"Do you mind if I sit down?" Julien pulls up the chair next

to the bed and perches on its edge. He puts his head to one side, like a bird, his blue eyes growing brighter and his gaze more pointed as he allows me to watch him.

My eyes are clearer now; I can see the faint blond stubble on his jaw, the slight bags under his eyes. He's tall, almost spindly, with elongated wrists and a pronounced Adam's apple at his throat. His long legs stick out from beneath his doctor's coat. Life hasn't yet etched its scars on his face; his forehead is smooth and unwrinkled.

"You're. . . too young to. . . be a doctor," I say, as scornfully as I can. But my words come out a pathetic mewl. The tube in my nose makes it hard to speak clearly.

He laughs, a short, explosive sound, as if he's been sucker-punched. At the same time, his skin turns a shade of scarlet I've never seen before. "That's a great way of saying thank you."

Thank you for what? "It's true. You look younger than. . . than me."

"I'm twenty-six." His color stays high and bright.

I frown. "It's still. . . not right." The words aren't coming easily to me. If only I can just lay my head down on the pillow and go back to sleep. Just drift away, back to the dark water from which I've emerged, where there's no pain, no nausea, no strange man talking to me as if he's my friend.

His expression remains pleasant, relaxed. The blue eyes keep searching me for clues. I avert my eyes. "Tell me why I'm here, before I get sick again."

He leans back and sighs. The beeps begin to issue faster again from the monitor, and he frowns momentarily, before beginning:

"Someone dropped you at the doors of the hospital early this morning. You were unconscious and in shock. We had to take you to surgery immediately."

"I had an. . . operation?" That explains all the pain, and his earlier talk of anesthesia and nausea.

"We found that you had suffered an ectopic pregnancy, which had ruptured in your left fallopian tube. Do you know how long you were pregnant?"

Pregnant? The word ricochets in my head, bringing out beads of sweat on my forehead and under my arms. The small machine begins to beep faster still.

My hands go instinctively to my stomach, but my fingers only find gauze, not the reassuring feel of my own flesh. "That's impossible! I don't understand. What are you telling me?"

"I'm sorry, Mrs. Faro. . ." He reaches out and holds my wrists away from my body. "Don't, Mrs. . . .. Please. You'll hurt yourself. I don't want you to feel worse than you already do."

I struggle, resisting his hands for a moment, then go limp in his grip.

"Didn't you know?" he says, gently. His eyes widen with dismay when he sees my face crumple.

Mortified, I begin to weep. He releases my wrists and sits forward on his seat, watching me cry. He doesn't move or make a sound.

The racking sobs hurt my stomach too much, so I push them under the surface again. No words, no thoughts, just silent despair. How could I possibly be pregnant?

The small lights shine overhead, some switching on, others off, changing the constellation above our heads. The hospital around us continues to hum, although we seemed to be shielded from the sounds of activity outside the door of this room.

He waits. He's patient. Perhaps ten minutes pass until I let out a deep sigh. He interprets it correctly: I've prevailed over my private misery, for the moment.

"I can see what a shock all of this is for you. I'm sorry."

I'm beginning to notice some of the things that they — *he* — has done to me. I don't understand what's really happened, but the feeling of a wound in my lower stomach, the pulse monitor attached to my finger, and the soreness in my throat mean he can't be lying.

"So, Mrs. Faro. Let me explain what happened to you. If you don't understand something, please just ask me."

Someone else has baptized me with a fake name, Faro. I haven't chosen to come to this hospital, to have things cut out of me. Was I really pregnant? It might all be a lie, designed to get me to confess who I really am, and where I've come from. There's a name tag around his neck that confirms Dr. Julien Asfour is a member of staff at Shifana.

I know I'm not thinking straight, but in a moment of sullen irritation, I mutter, "Call me Julia."

He looks down; he knows I'm not telling him my real name.

"All right, Julia. So. An ectopic pregnancy is when a fertilized egg gets stuck somewhere it shouldn't be. Usually it travels down to the uterus, where it implants itself in the uterine wall."

I have a vague idea of all the things he's telling me, from my classes in school. Still, everyone uses devices when talking about medical procedures, giving directions, holding a lecture. This Julien Asfour has no device anywhere on his person. *How odd*, I think. Am I really in a hospital after all? Or am I dreaming and I'll wake up in my bed at the Panah now? Maybe I'm dead and have yet to realize it.

Lin's face flashes across my mind. How will I get in touch with her? How will I tell her what's happened when I don't even understand it myself?

The room starts to spin around me. Julien is still talking, oblivious to my state of mind.

"But in your case, the egg implanted in your fallopian tube, and from there, it began to grow bigger. And we think it was there for about five weeks, before it got too big. Then the tube burst. You began to lose blood and you went into shock. I had to operate on you right away. We couldn't wait to obtain the consent of your Husbands. . ."

He glances at me, but I stay mute.

"So we had to perform an emergency procedure to remove the embryo and your ruptured fallopian tube. And we gave you blood transfusions. You're out of danger now.

"The good news is, it was just the left side. Your right tube is unharmed. You can have children in the future. . . What is it, Mrs.—Julia?" He leans closer to me with new concern. "Are you in pain?"

I shake my head, but my face tells the truth. Julien leans across the few inches between us, and puts his hand on my shoulder. The palm of his hand feels warm to my skin, as if he's transmitting safety and security, or perhaps friendship, in the only way he knows how. The physical contact, made without demand, merely meant to comfort me, draws fresh tears to my eyes. I turn my head aside and give in to them.

"You're very tired. You should get some more rest. We can talk more when you're feeling up to it."

He's looking at the monitor now, tapping on the display. I hear a beep, then a fresh wave of drugs enters my system, killing the pain and pushing me backward again.

I'm asleep before he finishes speaking. I close my eyes just as I see the blush spread across his face when he withdraws his hand from my shoulder, and his fingers are wet with my tears.

REUBEN

The coordinates of Sabine's location were buzzing in Reuben's device, his cup of tea still cooling on the bench in his garden as he drove his car fast into the City. Far safer for him to go than to send someone; in matters of discretion, he trusted only himself. And nobody would question where he went, or why.

It would take him twenty minutes to get to the side of Green City where Joseph lived. Reuben wasn't worried that his car would show up on the Agency registers at the electronic checkpoints. Reuben could stop traffic anywhere in Green City, shut down any of its elevated roads or underground intersections. He'd never be questioned by an impertinent young man in a uniform, brandishing a weapon that Reuben was most likely responsible for issuing him. The Agency watched everyone, but its higher-ups insisted on complete privacy, autonomy, and impunity for themselves. Their unlimited freedom kept everyone else in line: they needed absolute power to guarantee absolute civic order.

He hoped Lin had obeyed him and gone back to the Panah. She was not one for obedience; yet it was he who obeyed her plea and was making this mad dash to save Sabine from whatever danger she was in.

Oh, Lin. What could he say about Lin that he hadn't told himself a thousand times before? He couldn't refuse her. He never could. Since they'd begun their affair, she'd ruled him, and he'd enjoyed it. She conquered his body with a skill or a magic that had taken him prisoner from their very first night together.

Green City survived on hierarchies: the rich over the poor, the strong over the weak. And high above them all, the Leaders, watchful hawks circling over a society in crisis. Reuben wasn't religious, but sometimes he wondered what force had overseen his meteoric rise to power. Which god ensured that he stay at the top, eluding his enemies, gaining more strength year after year?

Maybe it was the god of war he had to thank. Reuben had always been fascinated by the idea of war. He paid close attention in school to the lessons of how the first leaders of the new Green City took power swiftly, stepping into the vacuum brought about by the chaos of the Final War.

The phrase "Final War" was a misnomer; it referred not to just one conflict but to a series of wars across Asia, from the former Levant all the way to the former subcontinent. From Sham and Iraq to the old Religious territories along the sea to the monarchists in the new Religious territories along the northern coast of Africa: the history texts chronicled the desperate days of mass migration, the dissolution of old boundaries, the bloody unseating of old kings and dictators.

In university, Reuben studied the War carefully, making special note of how the seemingly unshakable structures of power crumbled under multiple heavy forces, both from within and without. These forces came under what the historians called the three waves, knocking the foundations of society down not all at once but over decades of slow collapse.

In Green City, the first wave came from the east. The middle of the twenty-first century saw devastating climate change in South Asia, bringing floods and unprecedented torrential rain for months on end. Mudslides and avalanches in the northern territories damaged so much infrastructure that the locations of certain nuclear facilities became compromised. Militants took hold of the weapons and launched them at each other, destroying much of the subcontinent.

The shock waves juddered both eastward and west, claiming not just lives, but also millions of acres of arable land and drinkable water. The second wave destabilized the economies of all the countries in the region, shutting down major trade routes that stretched from China to Europe, as if a part of the world was simply amputated from existence.

Every student knew what the third wave was, hearing about it straight from the mouths of their parents and grand-parents, when the women of Green City began to die, and Green City started to sink into anarchy. Groups of young men roamed the city's streets in packs, committing violent crimes—robbery, destruction of private property, assault, and rape. Murder rates climbed. Common custom in the City was to leave one's front gates wide open, denoting a welcome to anyone who needed shelter. Reuben's father told him he knew Green City had changed forever when he drove down its streets and beheld one locked gate after another.

Reuben's father was never invited to join the Agency, or the Perpetuation Bureau, or any of the Leaders, when they declared the Emergency over Green City. The security directives came to him like everyone else; he had to obey the 7 p.m. curfew designed to keep the men off the streets, even though he was never one of the criminals.

Throughout his childhood, watching his father obey notifications and fear the Agency, Reuben grew hyperaware of who was powerful, who was weak, and who was so insignificant that they never mattered to anyone. His father belonged in the second category; Reuben swore to never join any but the first. Not for him the humiliation that his father endured. Reuben decided to never marry, but to concentrate on his upward trajectory into the elite. He had a vision of what his life would look like when he was rich and powerful; he obsessed over its contours and details with a focus that other boys around him gave to their toys and games. When they were playing, he was reading the works of the Leaders and memorizing their famous speeches. When they beat him on the playing field or in exams, he doubled down on his practice or his studies and eventually showed them up. He had the discipline and stamina of an adult, a man's control over his emotions when he was a boy, and his friends were only children squabbling in the playground.

Nobody had ever seen Reuben Faro cry.

Over the years, Reuben excelled in his studies and cultivated friendships with classmates who had powerful fathers. Reuben addressed those fathers as "uncle," speaking to them respectfully but with confidence. They didn't mind the familiarity; on the contrary, they seemed to relish it, found it surprising. Their own sons never exhibited any sort of interest in their work. Yet here was this new boy, tall and handsome, a star on the sports field, fascinated by every aspect of their professions. Over time they began to regard him as the son they wished they'd had instead of their own short, thin, socially awkward goslings. They described their jobs, hinting at official secrets they were privy to, which tantalized Reuben.

Reuben studied his uncles keenly, looking for blueprints of the man he wanted to be, not the father he had in his own life—quiet, subservient, the spirit and drive drained from him like an exsanguinated corpse. He openly admired those uncles' lives as important and thrilling, their power such a contrast to his own father's weakness.

Reuben's uncles kept track of him when he went to university. They sent gifts and messages of congratulations when he completed his degrees. One of them, tipped to become a Leader of Green City, arranged an internship at the Agency under his direct tutelage—the one whose son dropped out of school and joined the Army the same year Reuben graduated with honors. That young man was killed in a small skirmish with a group of militants from the north, who still fought for control of the Levant decades after the wars had begun.

The uncle grieved for his son for an appropriate amount of time, then dedicated his life to lavishing on Reuben Faro whatever hopes and ambitions he had nurtured for his offspring. Through his uncle's patronage Reuben joined the Agency the day after he graduated from university.

He racked up triumph after triumph. In his first few years he'd smashed a huge smuggling ring, stopped the trafficking of brides out of the territories, cracked a scam involving gold-backed digital tokens in which the principals didn't have any gold to speak of. Within five years he was promoted, then made a division chief.

His success had become the Agency's legend.

He used his new cachet to assemble a loyal circle: bureau-crats and junior Officers in the Agency or the Bureau. He gathered them in weekly councils and they came faithfully, week after week, hoping that his proximity would inflate them like balloons and they, too, would float up through the hierarchy. One day one of these small men might succeed him. Who would it be? Sulayman, with his habit of siphon-ing off crumbs from the Treasury? Behrani, whose military service and the loss of one eye in combat made him think he'd gained in intelligence what he'd lost in vision? Zimmer, whose Levantine connections bought him his place in the Agency? It was too far off in the future—probably after Reu-ben's own death—for him to care much who among them would rise when his sun finally set.

Discovering the Panah had not been part of Reuben's plan. Five years ago, his daily intelligence reports uncovered a woman who was using outlawed cryptocurrency to buy food from stockpiles meant for hospitals. Reuben investigated the companies that supplied food to Green City's institutions and found that one of their delivery services was making random trips outside the City, miles away from any of its hospitals, universities, or prisons.

The owner of the delivery service was brought in for ques-tioning. Simply mentioning the Agency was usually enough to frighten most Green City citizens into obedience; the man broke almost as soon as Reuben entered the interrogation room. He confessed that he was being paid a large amount of illegal currency to deliver pulses, rice, and dried vegetables twice a month at a warehouse in the desert north of Green City.

"Who are you dealing with? Who's the buyer?" asked Reuben. He sat in a chair, gazing pleasantly at the merchant who stood before him in a sweat-stained vest and trousers. They hadn't even begun to beat him—the oldest methods worked the best, surprisingly—yet the man was already squeezing out a jumbled-up stream of tears and words, pleading for forgiveness between hiccups of fear.

"I don't know her name. I just drop the goods where she tells me to leave them. I've never met her."

"A woman?" This made Reuben sit up straight.

The man swallowed his tears and lifted his head. "I think she runs a brothel or something. What else would a woman be doing, buying so much food? Please, can I go now?"

Reuben examined him from head to toe. Anyone could fake a slumped posture and a tremulous voice in order to portray abject submission. But the man's bare feet twisting nervously into the floor, the fleeting, imploring glances that met Reuben's eyes and then quickly flicked away betrayed his honesty. Still, the merchant had to be embellishing his confession so he'd be released sooner.

"After you've given me the coordinates of the location. And your communication codes."

The man complied, but Reuben threw him in jail for five years anyway, and forgot about him.

The location trace turned up one thing. Decades ago a pair of scientists had applied for a research permit to find out how much radiation the land just outside Green City had absorbed from the nuclear explosions of the Final War, twenty years after it had ended. The application bore two names: F. Dastani and I. Serfati. Ilona Serfati had worked for the Per-

petuation Bureau; she was the original author of the Handbook for Female Citizens. And both of them had disappeared
not long after the date mentioned on the permit.

Reuben made a note of the name *Serfati* and ran it through
the Perpetuation Bureau records. It brought up an unsolved
case of a girl who had been kidnapped from a quiet street in a
well-to-do neighborhood, in the wake of her mother's death.
This couldn't be Ilona: the years didn't match. But the girl,
Lin Serfati, would be around forty years old now.

Serfati... Reuben made a note of the name and wrote down
next to it, *disappearing women and disappearing girls. . . .*

He found a picture of the child and aged it digitally; within
seconds the infant turned into a child, then a teenager, and
then a woman. Was she the secret buyer, this woman on his
display? There were no brothels of real women in Green City,
but for whom was she buying so much food? Was she alone,
or did she have accomplices? Was she working with the rebels
active along the southern border of Green City?

As he studied her photograph, his eyes narrowed. This Lin
Serfati was a woman with a composed face, and confident,
cool eyes. Yet there was a warm femininity in her curved lips
and cheeks. It occurred to him that she would be his first
female capture. But first, he had to find her.

He used the merchant's communication code to send out
a signal to the mystery woman across the uncontrollable,
unsurveilable Deep Web. Any citizen in Green City caught
using it would be severely punished, but it came in handy for
the Agency's covert activities. Disguised as the incarcerated
merchant, Reuben told her he wanted to change some of the
terms and conditions of their agreement. Could they meet in
person? He was careful to use the same language and phrases
that the merchant employed in their communications so she
wouldn't grow suspicious.

"That isn't possible," she responded, a full twenty-four

hours after his query. "Neither the changes nor the meeting. Our contract was binding for a full year. We'll renegotiate when it's time."

Reuben couldn't help scoffing aloud at her tone. An illegal acting like a queen. Queen of what, a band of insurgents? He had no proof of anything, he knew that. She was probably just a petty criminal, a black-marketeer. Or even more brazen than that. What if she and a group of others were providing unsanctioned sexual services to the men of Green City? Why hadn't he known about this? If the woman was really a whore, he wanted to see what she had on offer.

He tried again a few weeks later, writing to her as the merchant that he'd imported some contraband hashish—the real thing, not the fake stuff that went into those useless e-spliffs— from the North African territories. Would she like to try some? He couldn't trust it with the usual couriers. When could he see her?

After that, Reuben was certain he'd offended her, or scared her off. Waiting for her response, he became as impatient as an addict craving the next hit. A full day passed, and Reuben wondered whether his plan had backfired. He'd have to arrange a security detail to find her quickly, before she could run. He was just about to give the orders when her message came through, agreeing to a meeting. No more circling around each other, just a businesslike note fixing the time of their meeting: 11 p.m. the next night, at a neutral place: "I only work at night."

So she liked drugs; one more thing to trap her with when it came time to take her in. He wrote back to suggest a greenhouse in the eastern quadrant of the City Park, a popular spot for Green City marriages. At night nobody ever came there, and he could make sure the usual Security patrols left them undisturbed (he didn't tell her that). They could meet there in anonymity, talk safely in the silence and the darkness.

She agreed, then cut the communication channel permanently.

He knew she would come, like a hawk returning to its master's arm. Plotting out her arrest in his mind, he waited for the hours to roll around with feral, almost sexual anticipation. Would she fight him, try to get away, or acquiesce meekly to his authority? He felt the keen thrill of success in his grasp, the jolt of the moment between the first cut of a knife and the blood welling to the surface of the skin.

Reuben drove to the greenhouse at ten in the evening. He'd had the area cleared on the pretext that he was conducting a sweep for a visiting dignitary from Kolachi the next week. He would personally inspect the eastern part of the park, where a reception for the dignitary would take place at the end of the week. No, he didn't want to take anyone with him. And he wanted to be alone while he was there. His subordinates obeyed; they were frightened of displeasing him.

When Reuben arrived at the park, there was nobody else there, not even the Security patrols or the maintenance workers. The far-off lights of the city glimmered in the distance, but darkness and a sad silence misted the park's myriad wonders: the rainforest simulation, the massive food gardens, the xeriscaped terraces. They all thronged with crowds during the day but lay empty and barren now. Reuben strode past them all, toward the edge of a burbling stream. He waited anxiously for the bridge to unroll and flatten so he could cross over to the cooled conservatory on the island in the water.

He let himself in through the main door—all government-owned buildings and public spaces allowed him immediate access—and keyed in a code to keep the door unlocked. It took him a moment or two to orient himself to the greenhouse's blanket of cool, humid air. Small phosphorescent bulbs illuminated curving pathways, and fireflies, glowworms, and bioluminescent millipedes moved and shimmered all around him in points of flickering light.

Reuben edged his way along a pool where oversized lily pads covered the water like lush dark teacups. He sat down by the side, breathing in the slightly mossy, moldy scent; he trailed his hand in the water and drew it back quickly, smiling, when a fish nibbled at the tips of his fingers, breaking through the furious concentration with which he was watching the doors, waiting for her to arrive. He couldn't remember the last time anything had made him smile, especially before an arrest, when the teeth-chattering adrenaline coursed through him like this. But he found himself savoring this interlude punctuated by trickling water and the clicking of geckos hidden in the plants. All the pieces of his plan were in place, and he only had to wait for the queen to step into the square he'd marked out to checkmate her.

The woman appeared at the door of the greenhouse, spectral and shapeless in her full black veil. Reuben watched her from his hidden vantage point as she glanced around, then opened the door and stepped into the entranceway. She looked not quite real as yet, with the glass ceiling arching high above her head and the breezy mist from the humidifiers pushing the veil around her body in gentle undulations.

Reuben forced himself to get up and move calmly, approaching her as if she were standing on a ledge and might topple over if he came close too fast. When he stood face to face with her, he held his breath and waited to see if she'd stay, or flee. He would be behind her in two seconds if she tried to escape. But as she pushed her veil back from her face, it was he who felt his legs tremble, the immense kick of attraction at the pit of his stomach. Close to her, he could see now that it was Lin Serfati, but that his digitized photograph had lied. Her face radiated a type of beauty that no camera could capture: a perfect symmetry of features, translucent skin that held a shifting landscape of emotions—boldness, fear, certainty, doubt. Sharp hazel eyes that looked as though they knew melancholy well peered at him defiantly, fixing him in his place.

"Lin Serfati?" He tried to sound authoritative, but inside he felt as lost as a motherless boy. His heart beat fast, throbbing in his own ears. She must be wondering how he knew her identity, and who *he* was. She'd have to have been living underground for years to not know Reuben Faro, by name and deed.

She nodded. "How do you know who I am?" Her voice was low, with an accent he couldn't place. Where had she grown up? "And *you're* no merchant. Why have you called me here?"

"My name is Reuben Faro."

"I know who you are." She tilted her head, angling the lower part of her face up to peer down at him from the lower corners of her eyes, as if she were measuring him up. "Who doesn't know Reuben Faro in this town?" Then, unexpectedly, she leaned close and whispered, her lips nearly touching his ear, "Are you here to arrest me?"

"That depends on your crime." His whole body tingled at the sensation of her breath on his skin. She was so close to him, close enough that he could smell her scent. He leaned away, doing the exact opposite of what every cell in his body was urging him to do.

She smiled in the darkness; he couldn't see it, but he knew that he was being mocked from the lightness in her voice. "And *this* is where you conduct your interrogations?"

How dare she sound so amused? Surely it was his place to toy with her, not the other way around. Every muscle in Reuben's body strained with the effort to stand completely still. She should talk more, to truly incriminate herself. He'd always found it more satisfying when they trapped themselves in their own attempts to escape the reckoning, but he knew he was lying to himself. He only wanted to hear more of her voice.

"You have to admit, this is an unusual place to meet. There are eyes everywhere. But then, I suppose most of them belong to you."

"I had to resort to unusual measures to bring you out from your hiding place. You weren't exactly easy to find." A moth flitted by, brushing its wings against Reuben's cheek. He waved it away, irritated, snapping back into the reality of why they were both here: so he could arrest her. But the woman wasn't reacting the way he'd expected her to, with tears or fright. He guessed she'd start to bargain now, or offer a clumsy attempt at seduction in order to sway him from his path.

"And yet you found me after all," she said. "How clever you were." She averted her body to move past him, cutting a path through the foliage as if she knew exactly where she was going. Reuben followed quickly, wanting to reach out and catch her by the arm, yank her back, and haul her to the Agency. She wouldn't be so reckless in an interrogation room, stripped of all her pretensions. *Clever?* Nobody had ever used that word for him before. *Brilliant. Genius. Power-ful.* But *clever?* That was praise for a monkey who performed tired tricks in front of a bored audience.

He allowed her to keep walking. At last she stopped abruptly in a clearing, a small grotto of bottle palms that grew only slightly taller than their heads. A few spotlights picked out the clearing, a circle of light in the surrounding gloom. The trailing fronds of the palm trees tapped like gentle fingers on Reuben's chest.

She spoke again, an edge in her voice that hadn't been there before. "Don't you already know my crimes? Reluc-tance, rebellion, revolt. I've committed them all." She held up her slim fingers and counted them off, her hand in the air like a curse in front of his face. Here was the defiance that

he'd been expecting, the show of anger. He suddenly imagined her palm on his cheek in a stinging slap. He could feel
himself craving the blow.

"You'd better tell me everything," Reuben said. "The out-
come will be more favorable for you if you do."

"Oh, I will tell you everything. Did you know, there's one
thing you left off your holy list of gender crimes. Can you
guess what it is?"

"We left out nothing. It's a perfect system." He spoke with
the certainty of someone who had worked his whole life to
uphold it. Why she wasn't begging him to let her go? He'd
seen men drop to their knees, pleading for leniency, for their
lives. She was hissing at him as if he were the criminal. Did
this woman truly not know what was at stake for her?

"Perfect for *you*. Perfect for Green City. Reform, repopulate, redress the imbalance that we were left with after the
War. But it all fell on *us*. We're the ones you relied on to make
the system work. You didn't even ask us if we consented to
your grand plan. And if we'd said no, would you have even
listened? *Understanding is better than blind compliance.* You
want us to choose our prisons willingly. Oh, I can see you
already know that phrase. I know every word of that wretched
Handbook. I ought to."

Could she truly be this preternaturally calm, or was she
terrified inside, he wondered. No man could have acted this
well. "Because of Ilona Serfati?"

"My aunt."

"Is she the one who took you?" The pieces were all coming together now. But why was his breath coming and going
so heavily? His intellect was still working, despite the antago-
nistic, animalistic response of his body to her presence. "She
worked for us, you know." He watched her face carefully for
her reaction, but found himself staring at her lips as she spoke.

"She saved me. She taught me everything. The procreation schedules. The fertility testing. You pump us full of hormones and expect us to produce children as if we're cows. *With each new baby, a new hope for Green City and South West Asia is born.*"

"It's not like that. We preserve your dignity and your respect. Without this, you'd be bought and sold on the open market, like slaves."

"Don't you see? We already are." She frowned, as if he had given her a gift she didn't like. "But as I said, there's one crime you didn't write about in your Handbook. You weren't so clever after all."

He wished she would stop saying *you*, as if he was the one who had come up with everything. "What crime is that?"

"Refusal."

"What?"

She lifted her chin. "I refuse to be part of your system. Arrest me for that, if you have to."

Just then a lock of auburn hair escaped the veil and fell down to her shoulder. An urge seized him to wind it around his hand and pull her head back to expose the lines of her throat, then trace the vein in her neck with his fingers. He didn't know what force compelled him forward, but he pressed his mouth against hers long and hard. She strained against him, but he could not stop himself. After a moment, it seemed that neither could she. He kissed her angrily, greedily, as she shivered in his arms.

The kiss hurt as much as it helped, bruising their lips and knocking their teeth together. He thrust his hands under her veil without refinement or control, feeling the contours of her body from shoulders to hips as she pressed her legs all the way down the lengths of his own.

* * *

Reuben drove up to Joseph's apartment building and immediately spotted Sabine lying on the ground. A curse escaped
his lips. She was on her stomach, her black cloak obscuring
the upper part of her body, her arms and legs bent, a broken
doll, not a girl. What on earth did Lin think he'd be able
to do for her? Sleeping with Lin was one thing, but helping
a woman of the Panah once above ground was collaboration, something for which he would not avoid censure. The
Agency would never spare him for the crime of interfering
with their self-designed order. Such a transgression, even for
him, would be fatal. For an Agency official, or a Leader, collaboration was worse than reluctance, rebellion, and revolt
put together. Collaboration equaled treason, and there was
no coming back from that.

But there was something about the girl's body that made
him feel uneasy, as if he'd unwittingly had a hand in bringing
her to this point. If he left her there, she'd be discovered by
someone else, and they'd follow the trail all the way back to
Lin. He had to take her right now; he'd figure out the next
step once she was somewhere safe.

He angled the car so that she was shielded by it as he
pulled the emergency brakes and threw open the door. A
glance up and down the street revealed nobody else, though
any moment the robot cleaners would come trundling down
the street with their chemical blasts and hygiene fumigators.
Joseph resided in a high-security, low-crime neighborhood;
early-morning Agency patrols occurred less frequently than
in the more populous areas of Green City. Although it was
never publicly stated, to better maintain the illusion that all
Green City residents were safer because they were always
watched. Not a soul lurked in the doorway of Joseph's building, but someone might still be spying on him behind one of
the reflective blue windows of the high-rise tower.

Reuben hurled himself out of his seat, ran a few paces,

and crouched over Sabine. He pulled the veil off her, revealing her face. At first glance he could tell that she was lovely,
but her pallor was alarming. He lifted her and carried her
quickly to the car, trying to be gentle. If he had a daughter,
he'd want the world to be gentle with her, too.

In a moment she was inside on the back seat. The car
engine hummed a strange lullaby for the girl. Reuben was
alarmed by her lifeless face, her closed eyes, her head loll-
ing back. He raised her arms and tried to tuck her head in
between them, then he straightened her tunic, uncomfortable with her naked back showing. He had at least to give her
some dignity.

Reuben climbed into the driver's seat. He set course for
Shifana Hospital, then erased the route. He'd drive without
navigation; he knew the way well enough, and it wasn't far
from here. And there was someone there who he thought
might come in useful in helping him make sure Sabine was
all right, before he took her back to the Panah, if he could.
He glanced in the rearview mirror to check on the girl. Her
chest seemed to rise and fall, although whether due to her
breath or the vibrations of the car, he couldn't be sure.

He gunned the engine, driving the accelerator almost
down to the floor. Only after he pulled away from the curb,
leaving the streets of Joseph's colony far behind, did he remember her black veil still lying like a shroud on the pavement where she fell.

PART 3

REVOLT

FROM *THE OFFICIAL GREEN CITY HANDBOOK FOR FEMALE CITIZENS*

The use of contraceptives is strictly prohibited in Green City. Anyone caught trying to buy or sell, deal in, or trade any substances used to prevent or end pregnancy will be dealt with severely by the Perpetuation Bureau. All citizens are charged with the duty of aiding any and all pregnancies to go to full term; every new baby is a new hope for Green City. By the same token, abortions are forbidden in all South West Asian territories. Under no circumstances will any pregnancy be terminated at any stage. Anyone caught trying to procure an abortion, for herself or others, will feel the full wrath of Green City's authority. Order brought us out of the near-collapse of our nation, but chaos is a danger to the future of Green City. The authorities consider anything that harms an unborn child no less than treason against the state. Beware of those who urge you to revolt against Green City; they cannot be trusted, and you, no matter how young, will receive the same punishment as your cohorts.

SABINE

Standing is uncomfortable; walking requires more effort. I plan each step carefully to minimize the jolt it sends up my spine. Julien tells me I'm lucky: I haven't lost as much blood as he'd feared, which will make my recovery faster.

"We've pumped you full of bio-healers and chemical endorphins. It's a cocktail of drugs and natural hormones that stimulates the body into repairing itself," explains Julien, like a professor. I nod gravely at him as if I've understood him, when in reality I'm still dazed by everything that's happened to me so far.

At first, even getting up out of bed is agony, but I push myself and make it to my feet. Then I attempt a few steps from the bed, only to collapse back into it. After a few tries, I reach the bathroom and back. Again, again, again, five times an hour, as much as I can bear the weight on my legs. Julien says the drugs work better if I keep my circulation going: my heart will pump all the drugs to all the right receptors in my brain. Right now my heart is trying to dig its way out of my ribcage.

Finally, I make it all the way to the window, a distance of about six feet, and stand there, trembling with weakness. For the first time I realize the room is at a great height; at least thirty stories above ground. I've never been so high before—Green City's skyscrapers are built for the rich and powerful, and we crawl close to the earth. I didn't know people could live this high and perform all their functions without the ground underneath to steady them.

Dizziness strikes when I peer down at the rows of houses. Maybe we're closer to forty stories. The windows are polarized; they keep changing color with the ambient light and the sun's journey across the sky. Right now they're turning everything outside to notes of blue and green and soft gray, taking the glare away so I can look at everything without squinting. The solar panels are catching the brilliant early morning light even though the sky hasn't yet taken on the punishing white heat of the daytime. The buildings form grids intersected by neat roads ribboning away towards the sea, the cars traveling on them small bullets moving in all directions. I'm calmed by looking out at the sea, a flat sheet of deep blue in the distance, and I feel as though I'm in an airplane, moving quickly over the rippling greenish-blue waves massaging the shore.

I sleep for most of the first day. The next day, just as the room lights are beginning to turn midday bright, Julien comes to my room. My thoughts are surprisingly focused; the dull fuzz of the anesthetic has worn away and the nausea's died with it. I can recognize my surroundings immediately, as well as the thin tall man who stands there before me, holding a tray of food that he's sneaked out from the hospital kitchens.

"It's my lunch. I hope you like fish."

The aroma of grilled fish provokes in me a strong, gnawing hunger, as well as a distant memory of being at the seaside with my parents when I was five or six, eating spiced fish out of wrapped banana leaves. My hand goes instinctively to my belly, pressing down: someone has replaced the gauze with a small, lightweight bandage while I've been sleeping. I feel raw, scraped out, but the incision is already halfway healed; all that really remains is tiredness and a heaviness over my stomach, and this new sensitivity, as if I've been stripped of my outermost layer of skin.

"It's all right for you to eat now, Julia," Julien says, as I hesitate. "It won't hurt you."

I don't like it, his ability to discern my innermost thoughts as easily as he takes my temperature. "What about you? I don't want to deprive you of your meal."

"There's enough for both of us. They always try to fatten me up. They think I'm starving to death."

"We'll share, then. I'm not that hungry." I am, actually,

but in my state of confusion and discomfort, I find myself craving companionship and kindness.

I pull myself out of the bed, rearrange my hospital gown with as much dignity as I can, and shuffle like an old woman to the sofa under the window, where we sit side by side, not quite touching, but he's close enough that the warmth of his skin radiates against my bare arm.

We eat in silence. The food is unmemorable, the fish slightly cold and rubbery, the vegetables an indescribable color halfway between orange and brown, the rice overcooked. It's my first solid meal in seventy-two hours. Nevertheless, it is delicious.

Before this day, I've never set foot in a hospital. Whatever small illnesses we suffer in the Panah, we treat ourselves. We're young and strong; none of us has to deal with grave problems. When it comes time for me to die, Lin's brisk efficiency will see me placed in the small crematorium at the end of the garden and incinerated within an hour of my death. Where I go after that doesn't matter much to me.

I watch Julien's fingers as he holds his fork, scooping up his half of the fish and the congealed vegetables expertly. I can tell that he's used to wolfing down these institutional meals. It strikes me that his hands have been inside my body, a fact about which he seems completely unembarrassed. I remind myself that I am just another body in the lineup of bodies that he deals with every day. But does he sit side by side with those other bodies, eating calmly and turning his head to look out the window, his face softening as he looks out on the city and the sea?

I've never really spent any time with a man of my age before. I could have had a brother like him. Or a Husband. Or even a lover, although I bat away the thought as quickly as it comes to me. When Julien meets my eyes, he blushes, and I realized that for all his talents as a doctor, he has no idea what to do with me, now that he's saved my life. I want to reach out and touch his face, to warm my fingertips against his flaming skin.

Julien looks around at the room, observing its corners and features, his eyes bright with interest. "It's a VIP room," he says eventually. "This part of the hospital isn't operational yet. That's why there's so much furniture in here. If you were a regular patient you'd be on a ward, with others. If you were a man, that is," he adds carefully.

I exhale slowly. We are beginning, at last. "How did I get here?"

"I was waiting for you tell me that, Julia."

I look down at the single red dot where he put a needle into the vein on the back of my left hand only a few hours ago. "I don't know anything. I can't remember." It's true. I can't remember what happened after I went to Joseph's apartment.

He tilts his head away from me, examining me with a sidelong gaze, perhaps as sharp as one of his surgeon's tools. "Well then, let me explain. Someone drove up in a car and dumped you outside the hospital like a corpse. You would have died if we'd gotten to you just ten minutes later. My question is: Who would do such a thing to you? Where were your Husbands?" His voice cracks on the word *Husbands*.

Again, that dreaded assumption that I'm a normal Wife of Green City. I want to escape as fast as possible. How can I run, though, from this wretched room, this wretched hospital, when my body now feels as though it's made of different parts and pieces sewn together by him, guarded by the machines, and owned by this hospital itself?

"I couldn't have been pregnant. . ." My voice sounds small to my own ears.

Julien says, "I didn't keep any of the ultrasound images; I had to delete them. The recordings of the procedure I performed on you, too. Or else I would show you that you were definitely pregnant."

"Why?" I say. I need proof if I'm to believe his crazy story. "Why did you have to delete them?"

"I had to make sure there was no evidence. Otherwise I'd have had to report the whole thing. How you got here. What kind of shape you were in. What we did for you." He runs his hand through his hair, not for the first time. I'm beginning to recognize it as a sign of his nervousness.

"And then they'd come find me," I say.

He shakes his head. "Not just you. They'd take me away, and all the nurses that helped me. There were three of them. I can't believe they all agreed to keep quiet about this, but they have. For now."

"So if it's so dangerous, why did you help me? You wouldn't have had to take any risks. You wouldn't have to answer any questions afterward, or get rid of the evidence. You'd be safe. Why do you care so much what happens to me?"

He answers with spirit, "I wasn't trained to let anyone die on the side of the road like a stray dog." He pulls on his hair so hard I'm amazed clumps of it don't come away in his hands. He's fidgeting, breathing heavily through his nose. But his eyes are intense, fixed on mine, and in that moment I believe him utterly.

Still, dare I trust him? I've never heard of anyone in Green City acting unselfishly, putting someone else's safety ahead of his own. "But that's against the rules."

"I know. Well, we'll see what happens. For better or worse, we're in this together now."

I stand up abruptly in a show of strength to conceal the turmoil inside. "I have to use the toilet." A cramp ripples across my belly and I grit my teeth, my vision blurred with tears of pain and confusion.

"Do you need my help?"

I use his offered arm to push myself away from him. "I can do it myself. Don't look at me," I add, and am pleased to see him flinch.

He averts his eyes as I wobble to the small door of the bathroom cabin. Once inside, I lock the door behind me, lower myself down to the toilet. Relief is slow to come, stopping and starting, causing pain deep in my pelvis.

I think back desperately to every assignation, every Client. I've been obsessing over it all the time—those men the only explanation I have for Julien's wild assertions. But no matter how many times I go through the lists, the names, visualize their faces, nothing clicks. The answer's not going to come to me like this. Maybe I'm just imagining it so this impossible scenario makes sense somehow.

Grinding my teeth, I rip a piece of toilet paper off the roll on the wall and shred it to pieces, throwing them on the floor. The toilet flushes itself, and my heart skitters along uneven beats. I have to touch my face to reassure myself that I'm still here, alive, if not whole.

A voice calls out through the door. "Are you all right, Julia?"

"Yes." I unlock the door and go back to the room. Julien is standing at the window gazing at the sea, his back turned to me, as I'd requested. I walk slowly over to him and we stand side by side, looking in the same direction at the tall wind turbines, sentinels guarding the coastline against an enemy that might never come. We're just like them, but we know the enemy is going to come, sooner or later.

I lower myself down to the sofa. "So I was pregnant." How hard it is to say the taboo word; in the Panah, we never talk about it, as if mention of the word is enough to bring about conception. I can't look Julien in the eyes.

"About five weeks, maybe six, yes."

"And it went wrong. So you had to take it out."

"I had to remove the fallopian tube, where the pregnancy had implanted itself. It's not supposed to do that." His tone is kind, but still professorial, a little condescending, as if he's explaining things to a child.

I'm struggling to not cry. "Why didn't you ask me?"

"I would have obtained your permission if you were conscious. But I didn't have a choice. You would have died."

"How can you be so sure?"

"It's a medical fact. It's one of those unfortunate risks of pregnancy. I know it's a tough burden for women to bear." He shrugs, then he sits down next to me again on the couch. "Did your Husbands know?"

"I didn't even know," I say, needing to make it very clear to him that all of this is a lot more complicated than he thinks.

He nods. "Sexual reproduction is far from perfect. But considering our circumstances, these days, it's all we have, really."

"I didn't consent."

The skin near his eyelids flickers. "To the operation? I know, I explained. . ."

"Not that."

"What are you saying?" He stops short.

"If it happened," I swallow hard, "it happened while I was asleep. Or unconscious. I don't remember anything."

Furrows appear in his forehead as if time and worry have troweled them in so deeply that they spring to life at the slightest provocation. And I know that this is a big one. "Your Husbands?" he says, gently. So he's heard the stories, about Wives and what really goes on in Green City marriages. But that's not my problem right now.

"I don't have any Husband. I'm nobody's Wife. I'm not even supposed to be here in Green City. I'm illegal."

Julien's eyes slowly change from warm blue to cold and

unforgiving gray. His pupils narrow and he shifts away so our arms and knees are no longer close enough to touch. My bare feet are naked and vulnerable next to his white shoes. There's a spot of blood on the right one. Is it mine? Does he understand, at last, who and what I am?

After a long pause he speaks again. "I'll go back and look again at your tests." His voice is calm, his expression neutral. But now he realizes fully what he's done. Only now does he know that when he opened me up like a gutted fish, he reshaped my world, but also his, and linked his fate inextricably to mine.

I'm overcome by weariness, sudden and bewildering. I want him to go away. "I think I need to sleep some more."

"No," says Julien. "Don't sleep. Walk as much as you can. I'm sure you want to get out of here as quickly as possible. It will speed things along if you walk."

He's already got one hand on the door as he gives me these instructions. He's the one who wants to get out of this room as fast as he can; I'm the one who can't escape. I glance toward the window—if only I could open it and fly out, straight back to the Panah. But I will be here at Julien's pleasure, for as long as he wants to keep me here.

I doze for a fitful hour or two in the evening. I'm startled out of sleep when my hand hits the steel railing at the side of the bed. I jerk awake, breathing unevenly, the darkness disorienting me, making strange monsters out of all the shapes in the room, and I can't tell where the door is. Then it all comes back to me.

If only I'd had access to hospital-grade anesthesia all those nights in the Panah, when thoughts marched across my brain like ants, when the mornings were a sick fog and my body felt like it was bursting at the seams with exhaustion. I would have done anything for this kind of rest. And then I remember: that last night at Joseph's, I had fallen asleep in his bed. Was it because I was finally, utterly exhausted, or was my body, burdened by this deformed pregnancy, already starting to betray me?

I push away the recollection and try to think of Lin instead. Is she looking for me now? But my mind careens to the moment after I stepped out from the building and looked for the car. I remember the road, the way it tilted and seemed to come up and meet me as I tumbled down. Then this strange room with Julien's unfamiliar face hovering above me. And all the pain, the disorienting drugs, pointing the way to somewhere in the past, an action against my body that I can't remember. . .

Again I'm straining to pull out the memory: which one of my Clients would do such a thing to me? None of them touched me as far as I know. I don't recall being injected with anything, being told to smell anything. I'd been pregnant for at least five weeks, according to Julien, so it didn't happen when I fainted just before coming here. Can I even believe what he said? Maybe I wasn't pregnant, and this is all a trick, a way for the Agency to capture me?

Why can't I remember anything? I press my fingers hard into my eyes. If I press hard enough, will they make me see the truth? Was I awake when it happened, or unconscious, on my back or on my stomach?

All the faces of my Clients appear in my mind, yet none of them strikes any notes of recognition, any instant of pure and absolute knowing that *he* was the one. My sense of the hours I spent with those men is expanding and contracting. I can't pinpoint the moment five or six weeks ago where I may have fallen asleep long enough for one of them to steal his act of sex from my body. That makes him a thief, not just a rapist. But he gave me something in return, something that I lost before I even knew I had it.

I have to get away from here. I have to run.

Swinging my legs over the side of the bed before I even realize what I'm doing, I put on my shoes, and begin to walk, cringing in pain. My feet hit something lying on the floor between the bed and the door. I stifle my scream. It's a person huddled in a blanket; I've just narrowly avoided kicking him in the head.

He turns so that the moonlight shining in through the window illuminates his face, his wide-awake eyes. It's Julien.

"What are you doing here?"

His eyes focus on me. "Where are you going?"

"I'm getting out of here."

"You can't just. . ." He sits up and pushes the blanket aside. He wears a light sleeping shirt, and in the light, his bare, thin arms gleam.

"I can't stay here. I have to go back. . ."

"Julia," he says, "it's not safe. Please don't do this. I don't know where you want to go or what you're going to do. Stay here!"

"You can't keep me here."

"You're not well enough, can't you see that?"

"Don't tell me anything more. I have to go home." I have no plan, but all I need to do is find a display—there has to be one somewhere in this hospital. I'll send a message to Lin across the Deep Web, to tell her where I am. I still remember how to do it. She'll find a way to help me, to get me home again.

"But where is your home?" says Julien, as he rubs the sleep out of his eyes. He blinks at me owlishly in the half-light. "You said you don't come from Green City. Where do you live?"

"You didn't tell me why you're in my room."

When he speaks again, after a minute or so, it's too dark to see but I can hear the blush in his voice. "Keeping an eye on you."

"Am I a prisoner?"

"I'm watching out for you," he mumbles. "You're my patient."

"You do this for all your patients? Sleep on their floors?"

"No. . ."

"So open the door."

Any moment now Julien will reach out to catch me by the leg; I'm ready to kick out with all the strength in my weakened body. He slowly rises to his feet, hands raised to show me he won't touch me. He puts his hand against the door handle, which beeps softly as it unlocks. Then he pulls the door open for me. "Go," he says, under his breath. I watch him, wary and confused. I'm unaccustomed to an enemy that gives in so easily. "Leave, but do it fast. There's an emergency exit on the fourth floor; it leads to a corridor which heads north, towards the Old Quarter. But there are alarms everywhere. You won't even be able to see them."

I haven't even thought about alarms. "I—I just need a device or a display. That's all. I need to send a—message to someone. Do you have one?"

He shakes his head. "I can't let you do that. They track me. I'm a doctor, but that makes me a government official. A minor one. Whatever I do on my device, they can see it."

I slump down, feeling trapped.

"But there's an office downstairs that staff are allowed to use. There's something there, I think. A public display or two. I've never been, but we all have access. But you'll have to go on your own. I can't go there for you. I could be tracked."

Not quite understanding, I say, "How will I know the right room?"

"There's a symbol on the door. Looks like a monkey's tail. They have it on all the places where there's display access."

"Just in this hospital?"

"All over Green City. I think. But I've never needed to use one."

He takes my hand, writes something on my palm with a pen he takes from his pocket. A short series of numbers is glowing on my skin.

As I brush past him, he leans over and presses his lips to my cheek, just once, a tenderness that makes no sense in that moment. His lips against my skin are soft and tentative.

"What are you doing?" I don't want his touch, I don't want any man's touch on me ever again.

He stiffens, then backs away. "I'm sorry. I'm sorry."

"Don't do it again!"

This time when he blushes, the moonlight is bright enough that I can see it.

The corridor floor has rows of phosphorescent lights that mark a trail to the service elevators in the dark corridor. Specific security codes haven't been set in this unused part of the hospital, hence the general code that Julien's written on my hand with his dermapen. I place my palm on the wall next to the elevator shaft. In a few seconds, the door slides open and I step inside, shivering. The elevator plunges down, down, down, and my stomach cramps while my ears fill with the pressure.

I'm in shadows as I step gingerly down the hallway, my eyes darting left and right. I'm looking for a small alcove where a few displays are recessed into the tables, just before the main hall of the hospital.

I quickly assemble a plan as I move: I'll try to access the Deep Web to send Lin an SOS. I go over it in my mind as I follow the trail of blue lights, praying that there will be no guards along the way, that the communication channels are still open on the Deep Web since the last time I used them.

A luminous thermometer on one of the walls glows as I pass by. Somehow the cold muffles all sounds, as in an underground cave. I shiver, as much from fear as from the chill in the air.

To distract myself, I search for that strange symbol Julien mentioned—the monkey's tail. Above ground there are so many things I know nothing about: gestures, ways of speaking, jokes, signs. I'd have to learn a whole new language if I ever reemerged into normal life.

I edge around a corner toward a warm light emanating from the end of the hallway. I slow down, my eyes sliding along the walls. Is this it? No, it's a toilet. How about here? No, an office.

The locks on each door pulse soft green, inviting a handprint, but the wrong touch will alert Security in an instant. I round another corner and suddenly the main hall appears, an empty cavern. Where are the patients and doctors and nurses coming together and moving apart? Where is the dance of life in the hospital? This is more like an abandoned airplane hangar, desks empty, chairs pushed back and left. The main lights are switched off; the amber lights of the night cycle pulse overhead in a pattern that resembles blood rushing through the four chambers of the human heart.

But this means I've gone too far. Or that I've gone down the maze of corridors in the wrong direction.

I retrace my steps back to the beginning of the corridor. I still can't find the strange little symbol or anything even close to it. Maybe it's so small that it remains hidden in the gloom. I drop my line of sight, looking lower, and that's when I see the sign embedded in the door handle. It looks nothing like a monkey's tail, I think, in annoyance. *Stupid doctors.*

I reach out to grasp the handle, matching the dermacode to its imprint. It glows green, and smoothly the door unlocks and opens.

Just then, another door right next to the display room begins to open. I've only got a split second to react: terrified, I push myself into the alcove, where I cower, legs shaking, as the alcove door stays open for an eternity, like a yawn that won't come out.

Someone's emerged from the room into the hallway. I don't recognize the shadowed face—he's not tall enough to be Julien. My own door isn't closing quickly enough. Whoever it is will peer inside the room, if he's curious. He'll see me, if I make any noise.

He stands in the hallway, a blue ghost. Then he goes back inside and the alcove door slowly shuts. I release my breath sharply, pressing my arms into my stomach.

The lights flick on as soon as the door closes. I'm in a simple storeroom, nearly empty except for a few bedding supplies. But wait: in the corner, a desk, with a single display on top. I don't know if this is the place Julien meant.

I inch toward the desk, reach up to the display, and wait for the dermapen code to be accepted. I blink once or twice and see the message flashing across it:

Code invalid. Access Denied. Contact IT for more information.

"No!" I moan out loud.

There's no time to think, to fantasize about my life underground, to wonder whether Lin's upset, or Diyah's lighting candles for me in the shrine in the Charbagh. I retrace my steps all the way down the corridors, back to the elevators. The corridors, empty as starving bellies, are haunted by guards and Agents only in my imagination.

Soon I'm back in front of my room door, shaking and sweating. I lean against it, too tired to lift my hand to the handle. The door swings open for me, sending me stumbling, off-balance, into the room.

"Julia?"

Julien's been here all this time, waiting for me, good as his word. He sits on the edge of my bed, his hair pushed back from his smooth forehead. The darkness marks out the hollows beneath his eyes. What makes a young man look so old?

"I couldn't do it. I. . . the code didn't work," I say.

My knees buckle. Julien reaches out soundlessly for me, and I fall towards him. He enfolds me in his thin, strong arms and helps me to the bed.

The moon observes us through the window; we're both spirits in its brilliant wake. I won't sleep for fear of what will happen to me tomorrow. At least for now, in these few bright hours, nothing can touch us while we shelter each other.

JULIEN

When had they lain down together? After Sabine had come back from her failed mission, and Julien put his arm around her to comfort her. He couldn't remember how it happened, but suddenly he and Sabine were pressed together in the narrow hospital bed, two people holding on to a raft for fear of drowning. He shifted his body away an inch or two to put some distance between them, but they always seemed to come back to one another on invisible currents.

She'd finally told him that her name wasn't really Julia, but Sabine; she had been in a place called "the Panah" since the age of seventeen, when she had run away from home. She'd contacted the Panah over illegal channels. She disappeared into an underground life: he couldn't even imagine her daring, her foolishness. Her job: to spend nights with the rich and powerful men of Green City, nights that were not marked by sex, but rather to share sleep, a type of contact and comfort that had become impossible decades ago. She'd been in the Panah so long, she said, that she didn't desire any other life.

"Where are your parents now?" Julien had asked her.

"My mother died when I was twelve. My father. . . I don't know if he's dead or alive."

"What happened? The Virus?"

Her fingers, resting lightly on top of his, had stiffened. He could feel her tense up; he loosened his arms around her until she settled down again, like a hawk rousing its feathers. "She killed herself."

"Oh, god," he said. "I'm so sorry."

"Oh, god? I haven't heard anyone say that in a while."

"My grandparents used to say it a lot. I guess I picked it up from them. They were Religious. Old-fashioned." He was glad the darkness hid his blush.

His mind always moved in a practical, scientific way. To

put a man and a woman alone into a room together, and expect nothing to happen. . . What an impossible paradox. This
was a game of the most dangerous kind. And how vulnerable
those women were to those powerful men. No wonder Sabine had ended up here. He didn't know what to be more
amazed by: the women's courage or Sabine's naïveté.

He believed she was telling the truth. He had gained some
understanding of human nature, listening to patients all day
long. Their history, how much they exercised, how much they
ate, smoked, drank—he could discern who was honest and
who was being evasive; he had developed an ear for the unsaid,
the unexplained, the unarticulated. Sabine, he could tell, told
the truth as if her life depended on it. He shook his head, bewildered at the scenario he'd gotten himself into. Holding this
woman in his arms was like pulling a time bomb close.

"What?" she whispered.

"Aren't you afraid?"

Her quiet laugh had so many colors that he couldn't tell
if he was being mocked or reassured. "You would never hurt
me. Would you?"

Julien grew instantly alarmed. He meant her life in the
Panah, but suddenly he felt like an assailant. "But. . . after
what happened to you, and then I operated on you without
your consent. How could you not hate me?"

"I can't hate what I don't remember."

Julien had treated victims of male-on-male sexual attacks,
reported immediately to the Agency, punishable by immediate execution. It was an inevitable part of life in Green City;
the absence of women caused more harm than the authorities let on. Julien had been trained to handle them clinically
and procedurally. He knew which reports to file and which
Officers to alert. He followed the DNA protocols precisely,
referred the men to the right department in the hospital for
deprogramming to treat their trauma.

There was a parallel track at the hospital: a more compassionate philosophy, pioneered in part by Julien's senior and informal mentor, Dr. Rami Bouthain. White-haired, wrinkled, and grand, Bouthain was still strong on his feet even at the age of sixty-eight. He worked six hours a day as Shifana's senior consultant in the department of internal medicine.

As a young medic in the army, Bouthain treated many wounded men in the border skirmishes, where unspeakable things happened between men. Rape, torture, mutilation were all commonplace, haunting the men for years after their military service. Only talking of their experiences relieved their mental burdens. As a result, Bouthain developed a keen interest in psychiatry and psychology. Most psychiatric aid was now relegated to psychotropics that targeted gut bacteria and body inflammation rather than the brain. Talk therapy had gone out of vogue decades earlier. But when Bouthain came to Shifana Hospital after the fighting, he created a trauma program where military veterans underwent counseling and rehabilitation. Most important, they could talk about what had happened to them, a curious route to healing, but one which Julien found himself agreeing with as he witnessed its results with the patients.

Now Julien asked himself: what else could he have done? The procedure he'd performed on Sabine was a complete success, medically speaking. But as he listened to Sabine talk in the dark, he recalled Bouthain's work and wondered what he could do about the trauma of her experiences. Her mother's suicide, her father's indifference, her life in the Panah, the assault at the hands of an unknown monster. All stacked one on top of the other; if one were touched, all would fall and shatter the woman who contained them.

During the night Sabine shifted and turned in the bed, away from him, toward him, pressing against him until he was squeezed to the edge, pulling away from him so that he felt cold when their bodies separated even by an inch. Julien told her a little bit about his childhood and family, his days in school. He couldn't explain his intense loneliness, his furious drive to succeed. He couldn't tell her that he was unable to trust the boys he'd grown up with. How there was always a wall between him and other people.

She said very little, but she put her arms around him and squeezed, and he lay there, breathless and stunned. The points of pleasure electrified by her proximity weren't located in his body, but in his mind, and by morning, he'd come to believe, in his heart.

Alternating between waves of contentment and anxiety, Julien riffled through plans like a pack of cards, shuffling and turning up the same dog-eared ones in the same order and combination. He was risking his life, and others' lives, in helping Sabine. Yet he couldn't just abandon her the way the man who'd dumped her at the hospital had done. So now what: Hide her here for another few days until she was strong enough to walk out on her own? Send a message for her to the Panah for them to come and collect her? Or wait for the Agency to find out about them and arrest all of them for their crimes? By saving her, had he sentenced himself and his colleagues to certain death?

Julien pressed his thumbs between his eyebrows to release the knot of tension in his forehead. Then he leaned back into her warmth again and tried to shut out all thought from his mind until the predawn light began to filter into the room. But his mind drifted back to earlier in the day, when Mañalac had caught him in the corridor as Julien was on his way to his rounds. "Wait, Doctor Julien, wait. That test you asked me for, I have the results."

"From toxicology? And?"

"It came back positive. An experimental drug. Ebriatas. We don't have it in the database. I had to check it with the

Science Bureau. That's why it took me so long to get the results."

"What does it do?"

"Works like Midazolam used to, before they discontinued it," whispered Mañalac. "Treats insomnia without as much disorientation or nausea. Anterograde amnesia is common. But one more thing: it causes all sorts of problems with pregnancies—miscarriages—especially in combination with all the fertility drugs the women are taking. That's why they haven't released it on the market as yet."

After Mañalac delivered this information, Julien had tried to understand how Sabine had gotten her hands on an experimental drug that even he, a doctor, hadn't heard of. Could it have have caused the ectopic pregnancy? It certainly explained her amnesia. He'd have to bring it up delicately with her; she would be reluctant to confess to using illegal drugs. She must have been truly desperate, going to such lengths to find the sleep that eluded her.

He'd tried giving Sabine a synthetic morphine to knock her out in the night, but it had no effect. That was when she told him how she'd lie quietly in her bed for hours, trying to fall asleep, her mind racing and becoming more and more anxious about the coming daylight. Only the anesthesia she'd had during the procedure had kept her under, and he couldn't exactly dose her with it just to help her sleep. Julien wondered if Sabine might be suffering from a form of hypervigilance—a symptom Bouthain had said he'd seen in traumatized patients, especially the ones who had returned from war. Sabine hadn't seen any heavy combat on the battlefield, but that didn't mean she hadn't fought her wars.

Julien decided to try a simple relaxation exercise on her: he told her to count her breaths. "It's a natural tranquilizer. It relaxes the whole nervous system. In for four, hold for seven, out for eight."

At five in the morning, Sabine was finally lying silently beside him, breathing evenly. Julien's device began to glow orange, rousing him in time for early morning rounds in the main ward. He raised his head from the bed, then levered his body into a sitting position, his long legs easily reaching the floor. He sat there for a few moments, blinking in the morning light. He was light-headed, but it didn't matter. Having spent the night beside this woman, he felt rejuvenated, ready to face whatever the day would bring him.

He turned to look at her over his shoulder. "Sabine?" There was a frisson when he said her name, a feeling of expansion in his chest.

She stirred and opened her eyes, red and strained with dryness and lack of sleep. He wanted to give her drops to soothe the dryness; he wanted to stroke each eyelid with his fingertips to relieve her pain. "I have to go now. I'll send someone with something to eat in an hour. His name is Ram: he's a surgical assistant. He helped me during your procedure."

It would be better to protect everyone's identities, so that later, when questioned—and that time would come, Julien knew Shifana and Green City too well to pretend it wouldn't—they wouldn't be able to incriminate themselves, or each other, to the Agency. Yet Sabine needed to know there was a family of a sort, a temporary one, that she could trust in, here in the hospital. Ram, and Mañalac and George, in those heated hours in the operating theater, had become her surrogate kin.

"When will you be back?" Sabine's voice was low and papery. The morning light was having the opposite effect on her that it did on Julien: she shrank into the bed, smaller and more gaunt than she had looked the day before.

"On my break," replied Julien. "Around eleven." He was already worried how many times he could steal away from his duties and come to see her on this unfinished floor, worried that sooner or later someone was going to notice his absence.

She raised herself up on one elbow, propping her head in her hand. "You should go. I'll be fine." The tired corners of her mouth lifted in a small smile that brought an unexpected calm into his heart. His nerves, tight as wires, suddenly relaxed. "Come back as soon as you can."

Walking down the corridor, Julien considered his next move. Sabine should be safe for at least today, but Green City Security made routine sweeps of the hospital every week. There were unannounced inspections during times of heightened conflict with the border insurgents, but the administrators refused to let Security just barge into sensitive areas and treatment rooms whenever they wanted. Because of this, tension always simmered between Security and the hospital administration. But Security might demand to inspect the unfinished floors, claiming that since there were no patients there, prior warning was unnecessary.

"Hello, Julien."

Julien froze in the middle of the corridor. His heart kicked like a mule in his chest and a wave of cold sweat broke out across his back.

The stranger's voice was unknown, yet familiar. There were shadows on the man's face, but Julien could still make out his size, his height, the well-developed muscles underneath his jacket. The faint smell of cigars and leather surrounded him like a mist.

"I've been waiting for you."

"Who are you?" said Julien.

"My name is Reuben Faro. I don't think you remember me."

It came back to him in an instant: the large fleshy man who bent down to put the medal around his neck. That man had been fatherly, jovial, offering a smile for the cameras that bathed everyone in protection and warmth. This was a different person looming in the shadows. Gone was the avuncular pride; menace emanated from every pore of his body.

Then another piece of the puzzle suddenly dropped into place. "Reuben Faro?" Julien gasped. "You're married to Julia—I mean, Sabine?"

Reuben Faro let out a short sharp laugh. "Not quite."

"I don't understand. Your name was on her records."

"A placeholder of a sort. Nobody's ever going to see those records once this is over."

"What do you mean, 'over'?"

"Oh, Julien. Dr. Asfour? No, I think Julien suits our relationship better. We aren't doctor and patient, so I don't have to go by hospital conventions. I'm sorry for keeping you in the dark. But this is a complicated situation." Faro swept his arm around in a wide circle.

Julien wondered if there were more of them coming: Agents, Officers, Security waiting with weapons, restraints, and chemicals. "I'm the one who decides what's complicated here, Mr. Faro."

Faro's hand landed on Julien's arm in a tight grip just above the elbow. "You make the decisions between life and death for one person at a time, Julien. I'm in charge of who lives and dies on a much bigger scale. I don't think you'd want my job."

Faro marched Julien to the elevator, then pushed him inside. He waved his hand against the display and brought up a colored administrative panel that Julien had never seen before. Faro tapped in a short code. The elevator moved up halfway between two floors, and stopped with a judder.

Faro smiled at Julien. "Isn't this better? We can talk privately now. Man-to-man."

Julien kept his voice calm and low. "Open these doors immediately and let me go."

Faro leaned back and folded his arms across his chest.

"I've actually been following you, Julien, since I came to your graduation all those years ago. When the time was right, maybe a year from now, maybe in five years, I would have come to you and asked if you'd wanted to join us. We're always looking out for leaders, for people with potential. But it seems your chance has come sooner than expected. If you help me, I can make big things happen very quickly for you."

Faro's presence was so imposing that Julien almost felt a lack of oxygen in the elevator; he didn't want to look at the man but Faro's eyes followed him everywhere, like an optical illusion. The wrinkles were cut deep into the older man's forehead and cheeks.

"Now listen to me carefully, Julien. I want you to answer my questions. It'll go better for you, I promise. How is Sabine? Can she stand? Can she walk? Is she well enough to leave here?"

"I'm not required to tell you anything about her."

Faro spun Julien around until he was pressed against the back wall of the elevator. Faro's left arm, sturdy as a ship's mast, pressed down between Julien's shoulders and neck, his fist bunched against Julien's lower spine, applying a subtle pressure that could turn into disabling pain with one short, sharp punch. Julien was younger and taller than Faro, but he possessed none of the oaken strength of Faro's body, nor his edge of violence.

"Look, you have Sabine. Nobody else is going to find out; I'll make sure of that. But I want her ready to be moved in the next four hours, and then I'm taking her."

"Taking her where?" Julien gasped, twisting his head around to look at Faro out of the corner of his eyes. The pressure in his head made him feel his eyes might burst. Faro could easily snap his neck and leave him dead there in the elevator.

"That's none of your business."

"You've made it my business! When you dumped her here and left her in my care, you made her my business!"

Faro suddenly released Julien from the bind and took a step back. "You're right. My apologies. But I still can't tell you anything more than what you already know."

Julien turned around slowly, coughing. "Are you going to take her back to the Panah?" he managed, between wheezes. Faro did a double take, and it pleased Julien, beneath the pain, to wrong-foot the man.

"She told you about the Panah, did she? Did she tell you about Lin Serfati?"

Julien watched him warily, wondering why the man was bringing up Lin's name. "I know about the Panah," he said cautiously, not wanting to reveal anything to Faro. "It's where she wants to go. Back home."

"She'll be dealt with appropriately. You've done your job. Let me do mine."

"You're willing to eliminate a *woman*?" Julien leapt to what seemed like the most logical conclusion.

"I wouldn't be, but the authorities would, if they found out about her. Now you know how serious this really is. I'm the only one who can protect her from them."

Julien knew that Sabine was of equal value to both of them, though for vastly different reasons. For both of them to fight over her went against every rule in Green City: women were to be valued, respected, shared, never the source of conflict between men. Men were, after all, the protectors and guardians of Green City's most precious resource. They had been noble enough to make the sacrifice of sharing wives: they must not belittle themselves by letting their jealousy or competition come to the surface.

Julien straightened himself with difficulty, tried to inject as much strength into his voice as he could. "You *are* the authorities."

Faro's voice was low-pitched and urgent now. "You really don't understand, do you? She's not a bag of groceries that I can just lift and haul from one place to another."

The colorful panel started to flash a silent alarm. In a few minutes the main system would summon Security to investigate. Julien pointed silently at the panel. Faro turned around and glanced at it, puzzled.

"Oh," Faro said, "I forgot about that. You see? I can't make everything go according to my wishes. Not all the time, anyway."

"Then you're not as powerful as you'd like to think," said Julien.

"Power's an illusion," said Faro sadly, before he waved his hand in front of the panel. As the doors slid open, he turned back to Julien, his confidence and authority back in place, as if the mask had never cracked. "Four hours. Then I'm coming for her. A word of advice: don't risk your career for her sake. She's not worth it. Nobody is." Faro brought his lips very close to Julien's ear. "But if you try to stop me, you'll share her fate. You'll leave me no choice, Julien. As much as I like you, I'll have to eliminate you as well."

LIN

"Was there news of a missing Wife on the Info Bulletin? Has any other Client mentioned Sabine? Has anyone acted strangely in any other way?"

Lin's eyes raked one woman's face, then the next, looking for answers. They were all silent and frightened. Only Rupa had color in her cheeks, her bright eyes and the high pitch of her voice betraying her excitement at being the one to deliver the bad news.

"Nothing at all? Fine." Lin turned on her heel with the precision of a soldier and walked to her room in measured steps, calling out behind her, "I don't want to be disturbed." She was in no mood to stay and reassure them. She would not participate in a public show of fear, even if she was more terrified than the rest of them.

She locked the door, then sat down at her desk and typed out a desperate message to Reuben: "Any news of bird?" They'd always made their messages as short and cryptic as possible, working out a mutual code that relied on innocuous symbols and images. She steeled herself, then sent the message.

How could this catastrophe have happened? Lin paid exorbitant sums of money to certain Officers and Agents. She kept scrupulous tabs on Clients, tracking the details of their homes and offices, finding out about their finances, their vacations, their families. She'd vetted them all until her suspicions were allayed, because any link in the chain was an opportunity for betrayal. Whatever had happened to Sabine had to be because of an outside force, something entirely beyond her control. Every moment that passed by without word from Reuben felt like a noose tightening slowly around her neck. Her mind churned furiously, trying to imagine exactly what had happened to Sabine. Had she been captured? Kidnapped? Fallen ill? Gotten lost?

Then, the horrifying thought: had she betrayed them all by turning herself in? If Sabine had surrendered to the Agency, she would receive a lesser punishment if she surrendered information about the Panah.

Lin thought back to the Info Bulletin they'd seen weeks ago, the Wife—Nurya Salem—found in a pool of her own blood. How had that slipped by the censors? The Bureau trotted out women regularly on the Networks: young, beautiful faces unlined with care or worry. Those winsome puppets testified to the happiness and success of their blended families, how well looked after they were, how they were treated like queens by their Husbands: breathless, saccharine testimonials to the perfection of life in Green City.

Whoever had allowed the news of Nurya Salem's suicide to go on air was sending a warning to every woman in Green City. The Agency must have instructed the censors to leave the news item uncut, so that everyone could see that there was no redress for anyone who resisted. Had Sabine been undone by their cunning?

For hours Lin sat bathed in the eerie red-orange glow of the Moroccan lamp, the cutout designs on its four sides casting shadows like large flowers on the walls of her room, on the table and bed, moving and changing as the lamp turned above her head. The lamp etched tattoos of light on her skin and she looked down at them, wondering how it had all come to this.

When Ilona died twenty years ago and Lin had taken over the Panah, she'd wanted to help the young women who were running away from horrible futures. They were brave; Lin met their courage with strength of her own. For twenty years she had performed her duties with a devotion bordering on obsession.

She'd thought they were escaping the system, but when it came down to it, she'd still had to ask Reuben for help. Truth be told, she was as dependent on a man as if she'd been married to one. For the first time, Lin broke down and wept freely. She wondered if she should turn herself in to the Agency before she slipped under the waterline of sanity.

At last, many hours later, the return message from Reuben finally arrived, the notification sending a jolt straight to her heart: "Located bird. All well. More later."

Her fingers hovered over the device, but the words wouldn't come to her head. She slammed her hand down on the desk, then screamed out in frustration and pain. Damn him! Why couldn't he tell her any more than that? Didn't he know she needed every detail from beginning to end? This was his way of keeping her under control, in breathless anticipation of his next message.

As she searched frantically for the right response, she heard a noise coming from the other side of the door. Damn them, she'd told them not to disturb her. She pushed her chair back from the desk, ignoring the ugly squeal as its legs scraped across the floor. When she reached her full height her head struck the Moroccan lamp overhead, sending it into a wild orbit that threw a kaleidoscope of stars jittering back and forth across the walls.

She threw open the door: nothing there. But she hadn't imagined the noise. She was about to close the door and turn back into the room when she heard the noise again, coupled with a shadow crossing the wall across the door. She slipped out of her room to track it, followed it all the way down the hall, past the kitchen, and then toward Sabine's door. Lin flattened herself against the wall, listening to the muffled sound of a hand trying out the handle cautiously against the electronic lock Lin had activated an hour ago.

Lin stood and waited until the woman turned around. She slowly met Rupa's beautiful brown eyes, full of shock and fear.

"What are you doing?" asked Lin.

"Nothing."

"Why were you trying to go into Sabine's room? *Answer me.*"

"I wasn't doing anything, I was just worried about Sabine, I came here to see if I could help, do anything. . ."

Something slipped just then from Rupa's grasp, landed with a metallic *thunk* on the floor, and rolled towards Lin's feet.

Lin bent down to pick it up. She held it up to the dim light of the corridor. It was Sabine's flask, the one that Lin filled with tea and sent to her in the car every time she came home from a night with a Client. She turned it around in her hands, feeling its weight and circumference. It was still full; the mixture sloshing inside took on a new significance, now that Sabine was missing.

"Why do you have this, Rupa? It belongs to Sabine."

Faces, stretched and pale, appeared in the gloom of the corridor: Diyah, Su-Yin, a few of the other girls. Lin searched for Sabine's face among them, then remembered again that she was gone. "What are you doing with this?"

Rupa whispered, "It was in the car. I was washing it."

"Why? It's not your job to wash it." She waved the flask threateningly in Rupa's face; Rupa flinched and reflexively lifted her arms to protect herself.

"Please don't. . . please, Lin. I came here to tell you something. It's about Sabine."

Lin moved only her eyes, but her sidelong glance made Diyah and the other women step back hastily. They'd all known fear and anger in their lives, but none of them had ever seen Lin like this, her features twisted with a fury they could not relate to the poised, dignified woman they knew.

"Go away," Lin said to the other women, without looking at them. They skittered away like birds startled by a gunshot. She didn't care where they went, what they would talk about among themselves. She needed to concentrate on Rupa right now.

Rupa sat on her haunches, her hands resting in her lap, the position of the penitent. Lin realized that she had never understood this girl, haunted by ghosts that she could not exorcise. Rupa had chosen to carry her secrets inside her skin, where they ate into her and poisoned her from the inside out. She mumbled over and over again something that Lin couldn't make out.

"What did you say?"

"It's my fault."

"What?"

"It's my fault Sabine's gone. This happened because of me."

"What are you talking about?"

"Joseph. He's in love with Sabine. . ."

"I know that. What does that have to do with you?"

Rupa raised her head to look at Lin, her rich, beautiful eyes red with embers of fear. "He's crazy about Sabine, but she hates him, and he knows it. He asked me what to do, and I wanted to help."

"I don't understand. How were you supposed to help?"

"He wanted me to tell him how to make him like her. I told him to give her a drink and see if it helped her relax around him."

"What do you mean, a drink?"

"You know, something with alcohol. Her assignations with Joseph would go better if she was more. . ."

"But she doesn't drink!"

"I know. I told him not to get her drunk. I didn't think it would do any harm."

And then suddenly, Lin remembered. *The drug.* Sleep, the one Reuben had given her, that she'd been administering to Sabine. His warning that it wasn't supposed to be mixed with alcohol.

Lin forced herself to think hard. Sabine only drank from the flask of tea when she was in the car, returning from a Client. But if the drug had been in her system over the weeks Lin had been putting it in the tea—oh God, what if she'd

been giving Sabine too much? If Joseph had given her alcohol, could it have made Sabine sick? Could it have killed
her, or was it more likely just to render her unconscious? Lin
shuddered thinking about what Joseph might have done to
Sabine, vulnerable and insensate.

Lin put her hand out to the wall to steady herself. "When
did this happen?" she asked Rupa. "When did you tell him
to do this?"

Rupa said, "My last visit to Joseph. A couple of months ago.
I wasn't trying to hurt her. I only wanted to help, I promise."

Lin stared at Rupa. The girl's words were an echo of her
own thoughts. She'd been so worried seeing Sabine night
after sleepless night, her cheeks drawn and dry with lack of
sleep. Lin made so many decisions over the course of the day
to safeguard the women of the Panah, over so many years.
Sabine's stubborn refusal to accept anyone's help for her insomnia had irked Lin more than she liked to admit. She was
no better than any Bureau worker, exercising her dominion
over Sabine's body. But now she knew she'd miscalculated.
She should never have experimented like that with a drug
without Sabine's knowing.

Rupa was still talking, unaware of Lin's inner tumult: "I
thought she'd enjoy Joseph's company more if she was less
stressed about being with him. It's not easy to do what we do,
you know. It helps if a Client is—well, if you like the Client.
And Sabine doesn't like her Clients. She isn't like me: she's
not as friendly as I am. . . or as open-minded."

Lin heard the words through the fog in her head, and
something in them made her realize that Rupa, too, had lived
among them while not truly wanting to be there. Her heart
had never been with them in the first place.

Whenever young women climbed down into the elevator shaft and knocked on the door of the Panah, they were
always high on adrenaline, euphoric with triumph at having

escaped. Their eyes shone and their skin glowed. It took a few days, maybe a week, for the high to wear off. Then the realization crept into their minds that their lives had been bisected by their escape into *before* and *after*. There would always be a date in each woman's mind to mark the death of everything they'd known before entering the Panah. What came, usually after a few weeks, was a deep depression as the women came to terms with where they were now, as well as the constraints of life underground, the rules and the regulations of Panah life. Those, like Diyah, who did well accepted where they were and tried to make the best of it, choosing to turn the date of arrival into a second birthday, a second chance. Once a woman was at the Panah, she was granted sanctuary for the rest of her life—if she wanted it.

But clearly Rupa had never really wanted this. She had come to the Panah by force. No wonder she'd held so little regard for its structure and rules. In her mind, she was only waiting for the day that she could leave the Panah and never come back.

"Come with me, Rupa."

Lin took Rupa's hand and pulled her down the corridor and into her own room. She prodded Rupa into the middle of the room and made her stand there while she checked her device again for news from Reuben. She already knew there would be nothing, but she couldn't stop herself from pressing the device over and over, hoping that if she tried enough, a response would miraculously appear.

Her eye caught the tiny memory slip, resting in a small receptacle at the edge of her desk. Rupa's diary! She'd put it there, meaning to confront Rupa after having worked out a rational response to its contents, but things had happened too quickly after Sabine's disappearance.

Rupa's words came tumbling into her mind again: "He was so good to me. So kind and gentle. And when it was over, he kept touching my nose pin and telling me how beautiful it made me look. Like a Gedrosian princess." In light of everything that had happened, the words had new weight; they felt like murder instead of betrayal. Lin was certain now that Rupa had slept with Joseph and had sent Sabine to him for the same purpose. Either he was paying her, or she was getting some obscene feeling of power out of pimping herself and then Sabine to the same man. The very thought made Lin recoil in disgust. But Lin's own guilt was clamoring at her now, whispering that she was the one truly responsible for Sabine's disappearance. Not Rupa. Not Joseph.

She turned around to face Rupa, who was sitting on the floor, one knee up, her face hidden in the crook of her elbow. "You had sex with Joseph." It was not a statement, but an accusation, savage and furious.

Rupa lifted her head, her eyes wide. "No!"

"I read it. In your diary."

"What diary?"

Lin held up the memory slip to the light in front of Rupa's face. "You should be more careful with what's precious to you."

It took Rupa a moment to focus on the tiny slip, but then her face darkened. "That was mine. You had no right. . ."

"You slept with him. And then you thought you'd give Sabine to him. I don't know what kind of sick game the two of you thought up, but. . ."

"No, you're wrong. I swear, I didn't sleep with Joseph."

"The truth? What is the truth to a Gedrosian princess?"

Lin expected Rupa to flinch, but to her surprise, a small, rueful smile crossed Rupa's face. "That was someone else, not Joseph," she said.

"Who, then?" Lin crossed the room and sat down next to Rupa. "*Tell me.* Sabine could be dead because of you." *Because of me*, she thought.

The girl winced when Lin reached out to her, expecting

a blow, but Lin held Rupa's chin in her fingers and turned the girl's face gently towards her. The nose ring sat delicately in the fold of her skin, the diamond mocking Lin and all her illusions about her role in these women's lives.

"It was Le Birman."

"Le Birman?" For a moment the name made no sense to Lin. Then she remembered: he was the head of a pharmaceutical company, a widower, innocuous. She'd even asked Reuben to check him out before she'd added him to her list of Clients. "The *businessman?*"

Rupa nodded. "He was kind to me. I wanted to know what it was like, and he was willing to show me. But he told me he was still in love with his wife, who died a long time ago, so I shouldn't get any ideas. Lin? What does this have to do with Sabine? Do you think Joseph hurt her? I didn't mean for any of this to happen."

Lin tapped her device to quickly check her records. The Client called Le Birman had asked for Rupa on three different nights in the last eight months or so. He was reluctant to talk, or to leave many messages, but he'd always paid for each assignation promptly and generously. Lin had studied him thoroughly, had even asked Reuben to run a security check on him. Reuben had said he was no threat: a businessman whose wife had died of the Virus, like so many women. Rupa would be safe in his hands.

Lin needed to think coolly and calmly, to get her mind around all the new information. She still wasn't sure if Rupa was being honest. She let out a long, slow breath and touched Rupa's nose ring with her forefinger. "This is so beautiful. Strange how I never saw that before. I've made a lot of mistakes, Rupa. And I'm sorry for all of them. But please, if we're going to help Sabine, you have to tell me the truth about Joseph and Le Birman, about everything. I promise I won't be angry anymore."

JULIEN

Julien sprinted to Bouthain's office, the muscles in his calves and thighs burning as he ran in long, desperate strides. He'd hated leaving Sabine lying there alone, but if he didn't get to Bouthain, someone would alert Security and have them all arrested as soon as she was discovered. Julien would plead for a misdemeanor charge, arguing that he was a doctor, in the business of helping first, asking questions later. But god knows what the Agency would do to Sabine if they found her. Bouthain's sympathy, if not his permission—he would certainly not give his blessing, Julien wasn't naïve enough to imagine that, but he could promise to look the other way—might buy them a little more time.

Bouthain's office was at the top of the building in a skyway that connected two wings of the building. He perched up there like a bird, keeping an eye on everything that happened down below. The room was simple and sparse, brightly lit. On one side of his wide desk was a bank of displays showing him different scenes of the hospital: he surveyed the operating theaters, the busy wards, the consulting clinics, and even the men trooping in and out of the staff rooms throughout the day. From his vantage point Bouthain could see if a doctor was sleeping too much, and make a note to have the doctor evaluated for depression. He could tell if a patient was being cared for properly or mistreated by the night staff, and he reprimanded or commended the supervisor accordingly.

He was standing at the window, looking up into the sky, when Julien burst into his office without knocking.

"What on earth—Dr. Asfour?"

"I'm. . . sorry. . ." Julien pushed the words out with effort, then bent over and clutched his knees, gasping for air. "Didn't want to. . . disturb you. . ." He'd neglected his body during his medical training and his work at the hospital; there was never time to exercise, once meetings, rounds, clinic, and more meetings had eaten up most of his day.

"Is it an emergency? Tell me quickly."

Bouthain had an unwritten rule: any doctor could interrupt Bouthain's office time if a medical emergency presented itself and Bouthain's assistance was needed. The medical emergency for Sabine was over, but Reuben's threat had catapulted both of them into danger again. But how to tell Bouthain about Sabine? Where to begin?

"Dr. Bouthain, I. . . I've done something terribly wrong. Promise me you'll hear me out until the end, and then you can discipline me, or kick me out if you want to. But please, I need your help." His voice had risen as he shrank in both age and stature. He was no longer a junior doctor consulting with his superior; he was a desperate boy begging his father to step in and fix his mistakes before it was too late. Taking in Sabine, helping her, reporting none of it: he didn't even know if there was any way to fix everything he'd done wrong.

Bouthain regarded Julien for a moment with an inscrutable expression. Then he went over to the display bank and waved his hand across it. All the displays instantly turned black. When he spoke, his voice was low and hoarse. "Is this about the woman in Room 3214? The unfinished floor?"

Julien blanched. "How do you know?"

"I saw her," Bouthain said, simply.

"I tried to be careful," said Julien. "I erased everything. Did I forget something? Did you get an alert?"

"No. I was working late two nights ago, and I went down to the reception to look for someone on the night shift I needed to speak to. I couldn't find him. I was passing by the storeroom on my way back to the elevator. That's when I saw her in there. I hid myself around a corner until she came out, and then I followed her up to the thirty-second floor.

You were there, too." Bouthain paused. "Playing doctor after hours, were you?"

Julien blushed. Bouthain was long rumored by the doctors to be superhuman: he could discern many hidden things about patients just by sizing them up with those pale gray eyes of his, half hidden by heavy, white-fringed eyelids that hid and revealed them like the blinking of an owl. "Why didn't you say anything? Why didn't you report me?"

Bouthain shrugged. "Not until I spoke to you. I was just waiting for you to come and tell me. It wouldn't have been fair. So who is she?"

The nights of disturbed sleep, the tension-filled days, and the fear and worry all gathered into a mass that hit at Julien's knees, and he staggered. Before he knew what was happening, Bouthain was leading him to a chair and pressing a glass of water into his hands.

Julien felt thankful for the shelter of Bouthain's momentary tolerance. Usually, when something was wrong, everyone rushed immediately to the authorities. People feared anything that would implicate them; they needed to announce their innocence as loudly as they proclaimed another's guilt. Bouthain's kindness made Julien want to clasp the man's hands in his own and kiss them in gratitude. Instead, he put his arms around Bouthain and hugged him hard. Bouthain seemed nonplussed, but he held Julien for a few moments, then pushed him away.

When Julien calmed down, he confessed to Bouthain. The whole story: Sabine, the operation, the recovery in the hidden room. The mysterious drug, Ebriatas, in her body. The Panah, and Reuben Faro: it all came tumbling out.

"A place for women? Where they've been hiding from the Agency all this time?" said Bouthain.

As Julien explained, Bouthain whistled, a small appreciative wisp of sound through his thin lips. "Insane. Brave, but insane.

So she isn't just illegal, she's a Rebel. No wonder she's so dangerous to Faro."

"He mentioned another one that he seemed to know already: a woman called Lin Serfati. She's their leader."

The older man narrowed his eyes. "I've never heard of her. But the name is familiar. I don't know why. How does Faro know her, though?"

"He's probably been trying to capture her, but I didn't ask. I just wanted to get away from him, and make sure Sabine was safe."

"And who helped you during surgery? Ram? Mañalac?"

"And George," said Julien, reluctant to name any of them, but there was no point keeping anything from Bouthain now. The blush bled from his face down to his neck and chest as he thought about the night he and Sabine had shared the room, and then the bed. "Do you have a display on in her room? Did you alter the records?"

Bouthain shook his head. "There wasn't one there to begin with, and how would I have one installed without alerting maintenance? Besides, I prefer to do my spying the old-fashioned way. You were in the room with her. She wasn't in any shape for you two to get up to any trouble." He grinned, his face breaking into a dozen wrinkled segments. Then he became serious once more. "However, we've got a real problem with Reuben Faro. He's the one that changed the records, not I. He's got the power to do it."

"I know," said Julien. "He wants Sabine."

"And he'll get her," said Bouthain. "If I know Reuben Faro."

"What? Do you?" Julien was taken aback. How many surprises did Bouthain have up his sleeve?

"He was at school with me. Don't look so surprised. Green City's a small place. Or you didn't realize I was that old? You're shaking your head no, but I know you mean yes,"

Bouthain chuckled. "He was younger than me. Nobody liked Faro. He was the one who'd do anything to get into teachers' good books, ingratiate himself with anyone who had power or privilege. He was always ambitious, even back then. But he's a ruthless man. I don't know who's more unfortunate to know him: his friends or his enemies."

"I can't let him take her."

Bouthain tapped his fingers together. "How will you stop him?"

It was like being back in medical school, sitting his exams. If Julien could only pass the test, then both he and Sabine would be safe. "I'll get her back to the Panah somehow."

"But Faro must know where this Panah is, no? I doubt he's going to take her there himself, though. Probably wants to get her into a cell and save his own neck."

Julien bit back a curse. "Why has he let them go on?"

"If I'm guessing right, he thinks of the women as toys, or puppets. It amuses him to let them exist in their own limited way, doing what they do. In a way, he thinks of those women as his creations."

"He's a hypocrite."

"Well, he can afford to be, because it's rebellion on such a small scale. But he's not invincible. Those women are supposed to quietly do their job behind the scenes, and then conveniently disappear. Not pop up in a hospital for all of Green City to see. Faro will be blamed."

"So why did he bring her here? Why didn't he just let her die?"

Bouthain rubbed his hands together, then shook them out to relieve a cramp. Julien noted the knottiness of arthritis in Bouthain's fingers. It was strange to think Bouthain was as human as the rest of them. "I don't know why he helped her. Maybe he was afraid to leave her there in case someone else found her. Or maybe he felt sorry for her, and couldn't just leave a young woman to die. It's a sign that there's still a human being left in there somewhere. But he's unpredictable, dangerous, and therefore an even bigger threat to you. I guarantee it."

Julien nodded. "I think he's going to make a show of 'capturing' her, bringing her to justice. As a way of distracting from his own crimes."

"Yes," said Bouthain. "It's about keeping up pretenses. Saving face. She's going to be sacrificed as a 'clean-up' so that the larger rot can remain. That way Faro gets to maintain his position, his status. And even the Panah is permitted to continue. But he'll also have to deal with you."

"What can I do?"

Bouthain turned his chair around to face the window once again. The view from his office, on the fifty-sixth floor, was spectacular. On overcast days, the clouds made a thick white carpet through which the upper halves of skyscrapers pushed like trees made of steel and glass. It was hard to imagine how the business of Green City went on underneath: the three-dimensional kaleidoscopic movement of cars and buses, high-speed trains, and Metro cutting through the air at different elevations, pedestrians flowing in and out of buildings, rising up and down in glass-walled elevators. It was as if this room existed on a different plane, purer and more elemental than the one closer to the ground.

With every passing moment that Bouthain spent in contemplation, rocking slightly in his chair, Julien grew more and more convinced that he would have to give Sabine up to Reuben. Maybe Bouthain would tell him to let Sabine go, and save himself. If so, he might as well sign her death certificate then and there. He lowered his face into his palms.

Bouthain tiptoed over to Julien, put his hands on Julien's shoulders, and bent close. "There is a way to get Sabine out of Green City."

Julien looked up at him, scarcely breathing. "How?"

"Reuben may be Leader, but he doesn't know the human body as we do. We can fool him into thinking Sabine is already dead. He'll report it back to the others, or maybe he'll cover it up. He can't make an example out of a dead woman. It won't matter."

"I don't understand. . ."

"I'm going to inject Sabine with a substance. It's something I've been working on for a while. Induces a coma with a heart rate so slow that even you'd be fooled."

"What is it?" said Julien.

"Ebriatas."

He stared in horror at Bouthain. "But. . . you can't be serious, Dr. Bouthain. It's not safe. It nearly killed her! You can't possibly use it on her again. I won't allow it."

The white-haired man shook his head. "I understand your concerns, Dr. Asfour. So let me explain: A few years ago, I was working on Ebriatas at the Science Ministry with the company that was producing it. They sent it to me for trials, after its early versions looked promising. It wasn't meant to be mixed with alcohol, but that was a minor issue; that only intensified the sedative effect. But we couldn't run as many tests as we wanted to because there weren't that many women for the clinical trials. The few women whom we could test it on handled it well at first, but after the trials were over, when they got pregnant, they underwent spontaneous abortions. Miscarriages. I advised that it not be used because its safety was in question."

"Exactly my point! I can't imagine how it ended up in Sabine's system."

"They shelved it as far as I knew. They said they didn't want to bother with more tests. But I continued to experiment with it on my own. I thought it still had some promise. Then by sheer chance I isolated an active molecule in Ebriatas that deepens the REM cycle of sleep. At least, that's my theory.

It produces a syndrome not dissimilar to sleep paralysis, but the patient is also unaware of her surroundings, as if she were asleep."

"But how safe can it possibly be?" said Julien, struggling to make sense of Bouthain's revelations.

"I combined it with a few other compounds to refine it, and I tried it out on myself before I gave it to anyone else. It seems safe enough for our purposes."

Julien pulled his hand through his hair, trying to ease the ache at the top of his skull. "Safe enough. But have you given it to anyone else?"

"Let's just say that your Juliet wouldn't be the first woman I've helped in this manner."

"Julia, not Juliet," Julien corrected Bouthain automatically. The Agency had so many ways to spy on citizens: electronic tracking, digital surveillance, following any display transmissions or emissions of energy from a vehicle, for example. Yet Bouthain, whispering into Julien's ear, seemed more concerned about the old-fashioned ways, the bugs in the room that could watch or listen to people's conversations, planted under a desk or chair, or in a corner of a room.

"Never mind. You young people don't read enough. Shame. Medical education turns out good doctors but vastly uneducated human beings, sometimes. Not you, of course."

Was Bouthain crazy? In the midst of this most dangerous crisis, Bouthain was going on about Julien's lack of education. "What about the effects on fertility? The miscarriages? She's just been through surgery. . ."

"Dr. Asfour, it will work. It'll slow her heartbeat down to almost nothing, and to the whole world she'll appear to have died. We'll say that she died of the Virus. And then we'll get her out of here to the crematorium for Virus victims, the one that's just outside the border. From there, she can move on to safer territory."

Julien tried to compose himself. "So we manage to get her out of the hospital and take her all the way across Green City. Say she gets across the border. Then what happens to her?"

"That's up to you, isn't it?" Bouthain said. "You'll have to go with her, too. The same way."

"*Me?*"

Bouthain gazed at Julien with fatherly concern. "Do you really think Faro's going to let you live out your life here, work peacefully for the rest of your days at Shifana after this?"

"But. . ."

"You'll sleep for a good six or eight hours, then you'll wake up."

"You're sure?"

"I added an extended-release ampakine in there; it'll get you going, don't you worry. It's a bit of a brain-booster, actually. Good for memory, so you won't have any amnesia. Too bad they didn't have it when we were in medical school. You'll wake up smarter than you were before."

"When do we do it?"

"The sooner the better. We'll need some help. Whom do you trust the most of the men who helped you?"

"Mañalac," said Julien automatically. "I'd trust him with my life. I already have."

Bouthain moved to a locked cabinet at the far corner of his office and opened it with a verbal command. Withdrawing two unlabeled vials, he took them over to a countertop, where he used a pipette to mix the contents of both in a third bottle. His hands moved surely, his eyes steady on the drops falling from the pipette like liquid diamonds.

The Virus was a disease that only women could catch, but men could give it to them—a fact that nobody liked to discuss in Green City. Yet their hand in the decimation of the women made the Perpetuation Bureau defensive, the Leaders tight-lipped, ordinary men fearful enough to respect the boundaries of marriage. The Leaders made a border agreement with the adjoining territory of Semitia to allow the crematorium in a no-go zone between the two countries' borders. If any woman died of the Virus, to safeguard the rest of the population her body had to be sent there to be burned and forgotten. Only a few hospitals were authorized to handle Virus victims: Shifana was one. The Virus, Bouthain found, became the perfect pretext through which to smuggle a woman here and there out of the City.

While Bouthain worked, Julien looked down at the city through the panoramic window. He'd lived in Green City all his life, never contemplated leaving. Was it really as Bouthain had said: would Reuben Faro come for him when he found Sabine had gone? The red-purple bruise was already developing on Julien's arm, where Faro had gripped him just above his elbow.

He thought of his gentle parents, Johannes and Celine, tending to their balcony plants, setting out dishes of water for parched birds in the summer. Would Faro go after them if he couldn't find Julien? He wouldn't be able to say goodbye. He knew he would lose them to disease and death one day, but he'd taken comfort from the thought that he'd care for them in their last days.

They lived in a small apartment in the poor eastern neighborhood of Keliki. They were not young anymore, his parents: Johannes grizzled and slightly stooped, Celine afflicted with osteoporosis over the last few years. She'd never passed the medical tests that all participants in the Perpetuation scheme had to take before being declared fit for remarriage; she'd suffered malnutrition as a child, and it affected her well into adulthood. That and pernicious anemia earned her a merciful exemption from the Bureau's rules.

The last time he'd gone home, Celine had greeted him at the door, leaning heavily on a cane. Julien quickly saw that she struggled to keep her balance; he was shocked at the sudden deterioration in her mobility. Instead of embracing her immediately, he hesitated, worried he would hurt her. Celine drew back, her pale blue eyes watching him with nervousness and reserve.

"What's this?" said Julien in a half joking tone, to cover up his disbelief. "Are you going to beat me with that if I don't do the washing-up?"

"I use this so I don't fall. Who will look after your father if something happens to me?" Celine replied. "Come in, I've got dinner waiting for you."

Julien convinced Celine to go for a long-overdue body scan the next morning, which showed she'd been losing bone density for several years now. He squeezed her hand as she lay on the body scan table, wiped her tears when she got the poor results. In five years she'd be in a wheelchair; no science could reconstruct her weakened bones.

If he left Green City for good, who would look after both of them? The Leaders claimed nobody ever suffered from neglect, hunger, or violence in Green City, but the fate of the elderly was less clear-cut. They were expected to fade away from sight when they were no longer able to care for themselves; they would go into a Green City institution from which they would not return.

He wanted desperately to tell them what he was doing: fighting for a woman he had only just met but already loved. He wanted to ask them if in their thirty-year marriage they'd ever felt anything like this wave of certainty, the renewed sense of resolve, the determination to survive so strong for both of them that they'd go to the border of death to escape Green City's wrath. If he and Sabine didn't make it, his parents had to know how hard he'd tried. But how to tell them without alerting the Agency to his movements? It was an impossible situation. He had no idea what to do.

Frustrated, he shifted his mind elsewhere: he wanted to

know what exactly Bouthain would do after he'd put the drug into Julien's veins, and Sabine's. "What if Faro follows us all the way to the cremo? And makes sure they dispose of us while we're still alive?"

"He won't be allowed in," said Bouthain confidently. "Quarantine regulations. In fact, he shouldn't even be allowed near your bodies. Of course, he'll break the rules, but he'll be too squeamish to get too close. Sex with a carrier is what infects the women, but there's so much ignorance about it all. If you've even been in the same room as someone with the Virus, you have to go into quarantine. Faro won't want to risk being quarantined himself. Once you're at the border, Semitian rules apply; he won't be able to circumvent those."

"Why do they call it the crematorium? I've never understood that," said Julien, to distract himself from his fear. The method of getting rid of the bodies had nothing to do with fire: corpses were dipped in liquid nitrogen, then shaken to dissolve them into powder. The process took all of five minutes, prevented postdeath Virus transmission, saved space, was eminently respectful of ecology and the environment. And yet the idea of being irreversibly turned into powder made Julien shudder, even though it hardly mattered what happened to people's corpses.

"It's historical," Bouthain said. "War camps where thousands of bodies were burned en masse. Everyone in Green City is so obsessed with wiping out the old traditions and names, replacing them with those that have no ties to anything that happened before the Final War, and the new regime. Maybe in Semitia they're more sentimental about the old days and the old ways."

Seeing the vials in Bouthain's hands, Julien was struck by a concern: "She was just under anesthesia three days ago. Will that affect her in any way?"

"This drug affects different receptors in the brain than

anesthesia. She's young enough, and healthy otherwise. She's recovered well so far, hasn't she? Her bloods are all back up to normal range."

"You checked her records?"

"Of course I did. Look, I can't say how this is going to work out for either of you, Dr. Asfour. This drug of mine will probably affect you two in different ways."

"If we both appear to be dead, won't it make Faro suspicious?"

"Of what? That she died of complications and that you committed suicide because you didn't want to be caught? Sounds reasonable to me. Look, here it is." Bouthain crossed the room and held out his hand, showing Julien the final vial. The colorless liquid moved slowly inside the container, shiny as oil. "Beautiful, isn't it?"

"What about my parents? Will he go after them?" Julien said desperately. "You know what they do to the families of criminals. How do I warn them?"

"It's not safe for you to leave now. But I'll tell them, once you're out of here. Reuben won't bother them. They're helpless. Harmless."

Julien considered this. Bouthain was right. There was nothing to be gained from hauling in a lonely old couple, torturing them to extract information they didn't have. They'd live out their lives, lonelier and sadder than they'd anticipated, outwardly mourning the death of their only son. If they knew he'd disappeared, at least they'd have that secret to comfort them. It would be a life devoid of joy, but perhaps they would learn, in time, to accept it. He'd trust Bouthain to make it right somehow.

Julien's eye was caught by a tornado of several hundred black kites swirling around in a funnel cloud that went right up to the sky. Behind the birds, a backdrop of towering orange clouds moved in swiftly from the east. A storm was predicted for tomorrow evening; was it coming already? In answer, the wind began to whip up, sending dusty gusts barreling through the spaces between the high-rises. A canopy of sickly yellow wavered overhead, instead of the bright blue sky that always hung over Green City like an unremembered dream.

"Sandstorm," said Bouthain.

"What!" said Julien. Summer sandstorms could be deadly, the northern winds sending debris and detritus flying through the air, blinding motorists, causing the giant digital billboards downtown to fall down and crush or decapitate passersby. The storms appeared several times a year without warning; nobody in the Environment Agency had discovered how to control or prevent them, and the death toll from the worst ones could be high. With no announcement yet, at least fifteen or twenty minutes still remained before Shifana Hospital would go into high alert in order to deal with the casualties.

Bouthain murmured, "Let us proceed, Dr. Asfour."

Julien stared at Bouthain. "*Now?*"

"Everyone will be too busy to notice," said Bouthain mildly. "Do you want to wait until Faro arrives here to escort you to the Agency himself?"

The growing sandstorm, the orange cloud approaching from the coast, was casting a baleful shadow on the cityscape. Bouthain was right: it had to be now. Reuben would be stuck in the Agency, the roads would be closed to all traffic but emergency vehicles and ambulances. Bouthain was already out the door.

Julien chased after him down the emergency staircase. He cursed himself for having become flabby and unfit, for eating terribly, for not taking care of himself, but doctors weren't supposed to be athletes. How the hell did Bouthain manage to move so quickly? Was he dosing himself with youth-preserving drugs that he'd designed for himself in his laboratory?

Bouthain muttered terse instructions through clenched teeth as they rushed down the stairs. "Call your man. Tell him to get an ambulance ready. Tell him to have two stretchers ready at the service elevator in fifteen minutes. He's going to have to drive a long way, so tell him to make sure he's got his pass. It's a Virus death, so quarantine rules apply: I want two sets of full gowns, masks."

"*Two* sets?"

"What, did you think I'd let you do this on your own? Really, Dr. Asfour, after everything I've taught you. You do surprise me."

SABINE

I lift my gown to look at my stomach, fascinated by the neat red incision that bisects the length of my stomach from navel to groin. The line is less angry than yesterday, and where I run my fingers up and down it, more firm, too, a zipper-like texture where my skin's already joining together. The pain of the surgery is already receding.

Hidden away in my hospital room high above Green City, the hum of traffic and the glare of the sun are both blocked out by the thick, tinted glass windows. I'm meant to feel nothing but restful calm. The climatized air ruffles my hair as if I'm at a lakeside somewhere in a cooler country, far away from Green City. But I'm not calm: over and over in an endless loop runs the thought that Julien has left me and he isn't coming back.

As the sun begins its climb across the early morning sky, my heart hurts so much that I imagine my ribcage bursting open and hundreds of black birds flying out of me, darkening the air and blinding me with their flapping wings, their desperate bodies beating against whatever light remains in my head.

When I rise to go to the toilet, I feel steadier on my feet. Julien said I should try to move my bowels, the most important sign of a good recovery. By all accounts, I'm recovering well.

I lie back down and close my eyes. How I miss my bed, my room, the chatter of the other girls, the stale food we cook, and the perfume of the Charbagh's flowers. I long for it all so powerfully that I have to raise myself from the bed to rock back and forth like an abandoned child. I miss Lin's smile that always starts from the corners of her mouth, and then spreads across her face. Her eyes light up last, like morning stars in a dawn sky. How I wish she could take me by the hand to lead me back where I belong.

Other thoughts intrude: the memory of Julien's body

against mine, his hand twisted back on itself, pressed under his body as he slept. I straightened it carefully, trying not to wake him. And then I couldn't resist slipping my fingers between his, entwining our hands. His hand was firm, his fingers long and finely shaped, the hair on the back of his hand soft, instead of the wiry threads I'd imagined. His nails were neatly trimmed, the nail beds slightly blue. I caressed each finger one by one and ran my thumb over his palm, feeling his lines with my fingertips.

I told him things I've never shared with anyone, not even Lin. Even though I'd already told him my mother killed herself, I confessed that I actually feared the authorities had killed her for revolt. That's a secret thought I've always guarded from everyone, even Lin. But with Julien, it slid out of me as easily as blood from my veins. He pulled me to him in a long, silent hug. I didn't push him away. I simply collapsed there, limp, empty at last.

Neither of us were the same people we'd been at the beginning of the night. Julien's eyes changed; there was a tenderness to them when he glanced at me that I realize actually reflected the softness he saw in me.

In the dark of that sleeping-not-sleeping, for the first time in my life I took comfort from a man's presence, instead of being the one to provide it to him. Our presence together wasn't a transaction to fill the Panah's coffers or fulfill a Client's ego. Nor was I tossing and turning in my bed alone at the Panah. To have someone keep vigil with me in those long hours, to spend the night in Julien's embrace, defined the physical boundaries of my body and the edges of my soul. At last I had weight and heft. I was real and I mattered to someone other than myself. The comfort of his body, his closed eyes and sleeping breath, lulled me into a state of calm that was as close to real, natural sleep as I'd ever experienced.

Through the window I see a demarcation between the clearer parts of the atmosphere, miles away out to sea, and a thicker, more pallid set of clouds racing in over the shoreline. The sky's grown blurry and orange, as if the entire City is reeling from some kind of sickness that's corroded it down to its bones. Birds are flying in confused circles just ahead of the storm, because that's what it is, I suddenly realize—a huge sandstorm that's traveled over the sea and come to bear down on Green City. They are terrifying enough to live through when we're all safe in the Panah, with the wind howling and things banging and crashing above our heads. I'm ill prepared for its naked fury above ground.

A huge gust of wind spatters what seems like barrels of sand at the window. I gasp and draw back, terrified the wind is strong enough to shatter the window and bring the storm straight into the room. The tightly fitted panes don't rattle, but they can't fully block out the high-pitched and angry howl of the wind as it rounds the corners of the hospital, seeking out any weakness in the walls. Below, the cars on the street have put on their high-vis beams and are moving slowly; the few people still outside scurry for cover in the buildings that line the street; they appear to sway like trees. I wonder if I should run to the door: maybe I can find cover deeper within the hospital building, in a windowless stairwell.

The door to my room unlocks with a soft hiss, and three men enter: Julien first, followed by a white-haired man I've never seen before, and then a small, lithe nurse, wearing a gown over his hospital uniform, gloves, and a surgical mask on his face that reveals only dark, almond-shaped eyes. The third man wheels in two hospital gurneys, one after the other. I back up against the wall, my fingernails scraping against the electrical board where the displays and other machines are plugged in.

"We have to leave, Sabine," says Julien, looking panicked. I haven't seen him like this before.

"What's going on?" I say.

"Reuben Faro is coming after us." He sees my blank look, and starts to explain. "He's in the Agency. He knows about you, somehow. And the Panah. I think he's coming to arrest you. And me. He was here, he threatened me in the elevator."

I begin to tremble and my breath becomes locked in my body.

"Hurry, hurry," says the older man, throwing a glance at me that sizes me up in an instant. I shrink from his gaze, unsure whether he's there to prepare me for another operation or to arrest me and take me away.

"Oh, sorry, Sabine, I'm sorry," says Julien, stretching out a reassuring hand to me. "Sabine, this is Dr. Bouthain, my supervisor. He knows everything. And this is Mañalac. Don't worry, they're both on our side. They're going to help us." I look down at his hand, which trembles slightly. Waves of nervous energy radiate from him; his lips are clamped together in concentration, his face drawn.

"Help us with what?"

Julien doesn't answer me. He turns to Bouthain and says, "You're sure it won't augment the effects of the first dose? We don't even know how much it was."

"It's out of her system by now. It should be all right," says Bouthain, in a tone that brooks no argument.

"What are you talking about?"

Bouthain and Julien glance at each other. "She doesn't know?" says Bouthain.

"I haven't had the chance to tell her yet." Julien looks into my eyes and speaks in a low voice. "We think you were given a sedative. One that made you forget what happened to you while you were asleep." His voice cracks on the last word.

I unpeel myself from the wall and step forward, forcing my voice to remain steady, not to shake or rise in pitch. He can't bring himself to say it; I know I have to. "Someone gave me that drug on purpose. Without telling me." My cheeks burn with indignity, but I stare defiantly at them, from one to the other. "So that I wouldn't remember being raped."

Only Bouthain meets my eyes directly, displaying no discomfiture at my confession. "I believe you, my dear," he says, in that rasping voice of his. "Did you ever notice yourself feeling ill, groggy, off balance?"

"All the time. And my thinking was slowed down a lot of the time. As if my head was filled with mud. I thought it was because I couldn't sleep," I tell Bouthain.

Julien and Mañalac are fidgeting by the door, the sandstorm battering the windows outside, but Bouthain pulls me aside to the bed and makes me sit down on it. His body shields me from the other two men in the room.

"My dear, did you notice any signs of trauma on your body? Soreness? Bleeding? Bruises?"

"I thought I noticed some pain. . . sometimes. But I'm not always regular, and I thought. . ." I'm too embarrassed to continue.

"I understand," says Bouthain, his gaze never wavering. "Don't be embarrassed. There's nothing I haven't seen. And I'm older than him," he gestures to Julien, who's turned his back to us to give us more privacy. "Doctors these days, they don't know the first thing about women." He smiles conspiratorially; a little answering grin comes to my own lips.

His demeanor grows serious again. "Chances are, my dear, we may never know who did this to you, but I believe that it happened as you say. And tell me, how have you felt since your surgery? Any problems, any pain? The incision's healing well?"

I nod. "But why can't I remember it? Have I gone crazy?"

Bouthain meets my fearful glance with calm reassurance.

"This is common in people who have suffered trauma. You may not ever remember, or it may not happen until you feel safe enough to remember. And it may take years. But you are not crazy, my dear. Don't even think that for a second."

This gentle man makes me feel as though I could tell him anything without shame or remorse. I wish I could talk to him more; we've only been conversing a few minutes, but Julien can't contain himself any longer. He stands in front of us like a skittish horse, hopping from one foot to the other. "Sorry, but we have to move. I don't think there's any more time left."

Bouthain says, "You're right. But first, we have to explain to her what we intend to do." He speaks more quickly now. "Our objective is to get you out of the hospital. Without detection. And Julien will have to leave with you. You're both in great danger."

"But how?" I ask. "In the middle of this storm? Won't there be a curfew?" The sandstorm isn't even hitting the hospital with full force yet, but the windows are shuddering in the gusts of wind that announce its tangled, swirling path.

"Yes. For everyone. Except for medical emergencies. And we are going to disguise both of you as an emergency."

My hands and feet grow cold as Bouthain describes the plan to me: he'll inject me and Julien with something to make us look as if we're dead, and this man and Mañalac will drive us to the crematorium, where we'll eventually wake up and escape to some place across the border that I've never heard of.

"This is mad," I breathe, saying the words to Bouthain but meaning them for Julien.

"That's what I thought, too, at first," says Julien. "But what choice do we have?"

I instinctively look at Bouthain, who confirms this statement with a grave nod of assent.

Julien goes on: "So that's why you—and I—must take the drug. Mañalac will put us in the ambulance disguised as victims of the Virus. And then he'll drive us to the border."

"And you're really doing this, too?"

Julien nods. "I have to. Faro will certainly come after me. If I don't disappear with you, I think he'll kill me, too. We have to do this. We have to go now."

"Go? Go where?" I say, clutching at the sheets on my bed. "I don't want to go. I want to go back to the Panah."

With a clatter, Mañalac pushes down the rails of one of the gurneys. That's when I notice the body bags laid flat on both stretchers. The monitor at my wrist starts to sing, and Julien holds my arm so he can peel it off. He whispers to me while he's bent over my wrist. "Listen, Sabine. Faro knows everything. About you, about the Panah. He's the one who found you on the street and brought you here. He won't let you go back there. He's scared the Agency will make an example out of him, if he doesn't take you straight to them."

"But why? He can just pretend it never happened, look the other way. . ."

"It doesn't work that way," Julien says. "Once you've stepped across the lines they've drawn, the only thing they can do is punish you. Or kill you." Julien holds on to my wrist as he talks. "You never spent any time with him, did you? He was never your Client?" He sends a quick, deep look into my eyes, before his own dart away again. I would have called it jealousy, in another time.

"No. I never did."

"But at least you knew of his existence. He mentioned Lin. Did she ever tell you about him?"

"Not by name. I knew there was someone important who helped us get food and medicines, but she didn't tell us anything about him."

"She was protecting you by not telling you. And after

meeting him, I can see why. He's dangerous and power-hungry. Lin was risking all your lives getting involved with him."

"How do you know he wasn't the one that drugged me?" I say. "Maybe I just don't remember it. Maybe that's why he wants to eliminate me."

Julien says, "That doesn't make any sense. He brought you here, remember? He wouldn't have done that if he'd hurt you." He pauses, thinks hard. "I think there's something going on between him and Lin. Maybe they both decided you should be turned in, now that you're out of the Panah, to protect the rest of them."

I yank my arm away from his grasp, shaking my head *no, no, no.* "Lin would never do that. And I'm not doing this. Any of it. Let me go."

Julien grasps me firmly by the shoulders. He pulls me up from the bed and walks me over to the window, where he presses his face close to mine. "This might be the only way you can save your life. Please listen to me. You can't go back to the Panah now."

Bouthain is waiting patiently. Behind him, Mañalac stands beside the gurneys. The body bags, black and with a dull sheen, are unzipped and spread out on the flat beds, ready to be occupied. I stop struggling. A strange sort of stillness comes over me, the way they say human life is sometimes blessed with calm and resolution before it abruptly ends. Squaring my shoulders and raising my wrists, I turn to Bouthain. "All right."

Bouthain motions to Julien. "You, too. On the gurney, Julien."

I lift myself up onto the gurney and lower myself inside as Mañalac holds open the sides of the bag like a gaping wound. My stomach twists with the effort, and I break into a sweat from the pain.

Inches away, Julien is doing the same. I'm aware of every

whisper of the body bag as he moves into it, shrugging and squirming as if trying to get comfortable in a too-short bed. His legs are so long that I'm worried he won't fit. How will we breathe once the bags are closed? They're a bioplastic of some sort, thin and nearly translucent. My mother was buried in one of these, inside her funeral pod—they're both biodegradable, the bag and the pod. Then I notice there's a white cotton sheet inside the bag as well. Mañalac is now pulling it out around me, preparing to wrap me in it, like a mummy.

"If you were really a Virus victim," he tells me as he works, "we'd use the Category 3 bags. But we don't want you to suffocate. So I use Category 1 only, but I code you as Category 3. The bags look identical. Hopefully we will fool everyone." His eyes crinkle above the surgical mask.

When I'm wrapped in the sheet with only my face and neck uncovered, Bouthain comes over to me, while Mañalac performs the same procedure on Julien. Bouthain holds a pressure syringe in his hand.

"Now, Sabine, when this starts to work, you'll fall asleep very quickly, and to the rest of the world, you'll appear dead. The concentration I've made will last four to six hours, and you'll wake up within that amount of time. It'll clear your system very quickly—it has a short half-life—so you shouldn't suffer any residual effects. Not like that awful poison—the Ebrietas. Really, whoever made that should be jailed for life. Now count backward from ten to one, my dear."

Bouthain's hand comes down quickly over my neck, and the syringe emits a high-pitched beep just once—

Ten, nine, eight. . .

And then it's as if the sandstorm finally breaks through the glass with a ferocity that only I can see. The winds tear through everything in the room, the whirlwind descends over my body, and the last thing I remember—

seven, six, five. . .

is Julien's face, still and handsome in the moonlight, and—

four, three, two, one.

I think: *He'll make such a beautiful corpse*—

Zero.

THE DREAM

S he is supposed to be asleep.

She is supposed to be dead.

Panic hammers the inside of her chest; she tries to rise from the gurney like a body jerking up in the middle of its own funeral pyre. But she can't move. The drug has paralyzed her, yet she's still groggily aware of her surroundings. Bouthain didn't tell her that it was going to be like this.

Everything is muffled, as if she's underwater. She sees dim lights in the corridor as the little procession—the two men wheeling the two gurneys, hers and Julien's, both of them hidden in the body bags—makes its silent way to the service elevator in the south face of the building. Bouthain whispers instructions to Mañalac, the words sewn together like velvet, not separating into individual sounds she can identify and comprehend.

There's a great coldness in her body; she's become a glacier, her heartbeat so slow it barely registers in her veins, one faint beat every ten seconds or so. Is Julien awake, like her? She tries to move her mouth, but nothing happens. The words bubble up in her head but die on her tongue.

They're entering the elevator now, a wide one with space for both the gurneys and the two men. She is slotted in, side by side with Julien. But she can't look in his direction, because like the rest of her, her eyes won't move.

Bouthain reaches down to pull slightly at one end of the material that covers her face, opening small slits cut into the side to let in air and let condensation out. From far away a series of strange bangs and shudders register on her consciousness.

Bouthain says to Mañalac, "It's strong."

Words make sense to her, just barely. The sandstorm still rages outside.

"How will I drive in it?"

"Slowly," says Bouthain.

Any moment now the doors will open and a Security array will be standing there with weapons, waiting for them. Or Reuben Faro himself. Just the syllables of his name terrify her, even in her stupor. Beside her, she can sense Bouthain and Mañalac tensing, readying for the fight ahead.

Like a snake's slitted pupils widening to take in its victim, the elevator doors slide apart. The shiftless world is waiting for them beyond the light.

Lin lifted her head from the desk reluctantly, unwilling to face the world pushing its way into her consciousness. The device on her desk said that it was three in the morning. Had she fallen asleep for a time, or had her senses simply left her after that ugly moment of epiphany?

Rupa lay sleeping on the floor, her head bent at a painful angle, one arm underneath it. They'd talked late into the night, Lin asking Rupa over and over again to reveal every detail, every moment of her meetings with Le Birman and Joseph.

Rupa claimed she'd never slept with Joseph, that he could only think about Sabine. He was obsessed with her. "He didn't give a damn about me. Le Birman was completely the opposite. Always giving me little gifts and presents. Always talking to me about his work. He didn't just see me as a comfort; he thought of me as a companion, and he made me feel comfortable, too. That's why I decided to let him. . . have me."

"And what about Joseph?"

Rupa gave Lin a shamefaced look and didn't answer right away. "I told you, Joseph loves Sabine. She doesn't love him."

Lin wondered: Could it be the world really was that simple? Where desire justified everything, no matter how dangerous? She couldn't believe the naïveté of Rupa's reasoning, but she had to press on. "What exactly did Le Birman tell you about his work?" she asked cautiously.

"His company makes drugs."

"What kind of drugs?"

"Cancer drugs. Drugs to make the skin younger. A drug for insomnia."

Lin sat up straight. "Insomnia?"

"Yes, that's what he said."

Lin began to breathe faster, her skin feeling hot. "Did it have a name, this drug?"

"Yes. I remember the name. Sleep," said Rupa. "He called it 'Sleep.'"

"Did he ever give any to you? Did he ever ask you to try it?"

"No, never. He said they were still testing it. Because in certain doses, it started to make some people sick. . . and some women miscarry, if they were pregnant. He said it couldn't be mixed with alcohol."

Alcohol. Reuben had said that about the drug he gave her. But how could he have gotten his hands on a drug that wasn't yet on the market, a drug that only could be considered as contraband? This wasn't like procuring cigarettes, which could harm only him. This was taking a risk. And to think he'd actually given it to her! Could it be that he just didn't know how dangerous this drug was? The drug and Joseph's drink clearly had done something terrible to Sabine.

After Rupa had lain down and fallen asleep, exhausted and tearful, Lin went to her desk and stared at her device, too horrified to even cry. She knew at last what Reuben had done. How could he have put them all in danger like that? Or had he decided that the side effects didn't matter because they weren't women of Green City, and pregnancy was not their duty? And after all, he'd given the drug to her; he'd had no idea she would use it on Sabine.

She pressed her thumbs into the pressure points at the corners of her eyes. Then she glanced over at Rupa, asleep, her thick hair in disarray, breath going in and out of her chest in waves. In sleep Rupa was without sin, returned to her primal state of innocence. Lin couldn't bear to think about how Le Birman had unwrapped this girl, revealing her smooth, lovely youth skin, one inch at a time. That was her fault, too: insisting on rules that drove Rupa to hide her loneliness and vulnerability, to keep her search for tenderness a secret that had taken on such ugly consequences.

Lin bent over her device to write a message in code to Reuben:

I know what you've done. Bring Sabine back to me.

She didn't allow herself to hesitate or reconsider. She sent the message as soon as she'd written the last word, stabbing the device with enough force to bend her fingernail backwards. The pain felt clean and right, a clear light through all the murkiness. There was no more time left to wait, to play games with Reuben. She had to force Reuben's hand into returning Sabine to the Panah.

She got up from her desk, stumbled around Rupa, fell into her bed, and sank into limbo.

"Lin?" Rupa was finally awake, raising herself up in one graceful movement from lying to sitting to standing. She rubbed her eyes and stretched. "I'll make tea."

Lin watched her go out of the room. She knew the others would be keeping vigil, waiting for any news of Sabine. Let Rupa deal with them, she thought wearily to herself.

A light chime sounded from her device. She was instantly alert; she scrambled out of bed, adrenaline pushing the leftover dreams out of her head. Another chime, this one louder, more insistent, was accompanied by a message flashing across the display: Reuben was attempting to initiate a visual conversation with her. He'd never done this before; it was too risky for both of them. The chime kept ringing and ringing as her finger hovered over the device. She couldn't bear the sight of his face now; she wanted only to know that Sabine was on her way back to the Panah. But he might not contact her again.

On the tenth chime, she accepted the chat.

Reuben appeared instantly, but it was not the same man she'd known for so long. His face had always been eye-pleasingly rugged, but this was a haunted man, purple shadows descending from underneath his eyes to the tops of his cheekbones. His jowls sagged, his mouth was drawn downward as if gravity and time had wrought ten years' damage in a matter of days. The rueful lift of his eyebrows told her that he was only too aware of his transformation.

"Hello, Lin." His voice, at least, was the same, colored warm with cigarettes and affection.

"Where is Sabine?" she said, immediately. But he appeared to not have heard her.

"Lin? Say something." There was a glimpse of the familiar tender concern that he always carried for her, but it was an illusion, a trick of the light. Or had he not read her message? She could only stare at the man she had once trusted. Of course he would act as naturally as possible; he didn't know he had anything to defend or explain. He couldn't know that his deeds were written on his face.

She'd play it cool until he came out with it himself. "I'm here." Her throat constricted and she cleared it several times before the words came out properly. "I'm here. How are you?"

"I was going to ask you the same question. I got your message, but I didn't understand it. Are you all right?"

"I feel as bad as you look."

Reuben smiled then, even though his eyes remained clouded. He let out that familiar deep chuckle that had always disarmed her. "Oh, Lin. I love you for your honesty."

"You value honesty?"

"Very much. Especially for a man like me, surrounded by people who only tell me what they think I want to hear. You tell me what I need to hear. Thank you for that."

He raised a glass to his mouth and took a long swallow from it. The display cut in and out for a second, with the glass

at his mouth and then out of frame. Lin could tell that he had
been drinking for a good long while already. His nose was
slightly reddened, his mouth a little more slack than normal.
Several times he opened his mouth and then closed it again.
The small movements of his face, the tic in his left eyelid,
made the fear blossom in her anew. "Reuben, tell me. *Where
is Sabine?*"

Reuben brought his hand to his mouth and ran his fingers
across his beard and lips, as if he wanted to keep the words
trapped within. She heard the truth in the long pause before
he could bring himself to speak.

"She's dead, Lin."

Lin strained to see his face properly, but his head was bent,
shadows obscuring the long upper half of his face. "You're
lying."

"Lin, I wish I were."

"What do you mean, dead? Did you see her? Did you *see*
her?"

"I saw her. I'm telling you the truth."

"I don't believe you. You were supposed to keep her safe
until she could come home. What did you do to her?"

"I saw her lying on the ground outside Joseph's apartment.
I knew she was unwell, so I took her to the hospital. They
took her in after I dropped her there. Later I went back. I met
her doctor and told him to look after her. Just for a few hours.
I was going to bring her back to you. I swear it." Reuben took
another swallow from his glass. Lin wished it were poison.

"She was all right, or so he said. Young man, called Julien
Asfour. He was willing to do as I told him."

Another sip. He was rambling now, talking in circles to
himself. A coldness was invading Lin, cell by cell, vein and
artery.

"There was a sandstorm. Did you hear it?"

"No."

"All the roads were closed. It took me hours to get to the hospital. When I got there, Sabine was gone. So was the doctor. And a senior doctor with them, Rami Bouthain. I knew him from school."

"So?"

"So I went after them." Reuben's eyes flicked back to Lin. Reuben the Official was speaking now, the one who spent his days going after traitors and transgressors against the state. Not the man who loved her. "They stole an ambulance, declared a quarantine, and went out into the desert. In a sandstorm. Either they were crazy, or they were trying to escape with her." The ice clinked in his glass as he lifted it to his mouth and drained the last of the liquid in it. Lin could hear the opening of a bottle and the gurgle of another glass being poured.

"Did you catch them?" She could only speak in short sentences: she tried to add other words, but they evaporated on her tongue.

"Eventually, yes. But it took a very long time. We stopped them a few miles short of the border. They were heading for the crematorium. I had the ambulance unsealed. Inside were two funeral pods."

Lin breathed in sharply.

Reuben nodded. "I know," he said. "It was horrible for me to see her."

"Keep going. . . just tell me everything."

He pressed his hand over his face, grotesque on the display. He had the largest hands of anyone she'd ever known, big-boned, broad-palmed. She shuddered to think of them touching her. She felt tainted, as if she'd been with a snake instead of a man.

"I ignored the quarantine, though Bouthain told me it was too dangerous. I had the pods opened."

"And?"

"Sabine was in one and Julien Asfour in the other."

"Who?"

"The doctor. Julien Asfour. The one I'd told to look after Sabine."

"Are you sure she was dead?"

"Yes, Lin. I'm sure. I touched her body. She was cold and stiff to the touch."

Her body. Lin couldn't form the image of Sabine lying there, devoid of life or breath. The barrage of information was too much; she found herself unable to grasp the fact of Sabine having become just a body, no longer a woman living under her protection. She focused on Reuben's face, flickering on the display, with great effort. "Why were they in quarantine?"

His voice dropped lower, as if he were about to speak words too profane to be said out loud. "Bouthain said she caught the Virus. That's why she died."

"The Virus? That doctor, too?"

"No. He killed himself. Because he'd broken a lot of rules to try to save her and he knew he was going to lose everything because of it. Asfour was responsible for Sabine's death, I'm sure of it. I don't know who else was involved but I'll get to the bottom of this, I promise you."

Lin glanced around at her room, her beloved sanctuary within the Panah. She stopped listening to Reuben as he droned on; she was overwhelmed with grief. But then, through the anguish a thought occurred to her: that Reuben wasn't telling her everything; there was more to the story, and that probably he had some hand in the way things turned out for Sabine. "I can't believe you, Reuben. You've lied to me already."

"What have I done? How have I lied to you?"

"Why can I not believe you when you say she's dead?"

Reuben swallowed hard. "All right, then maybe you'll believe this." His face disappeared, and in its place an image flickered onto the display. Lin stared hard without blinking, trying to absorb what she was seeing: a darkened space that looked like the inside of an ambulance; the prone figure, encased within a funeral pod; the familiar, beloved face, pale and so incredibly and unnaturally still. Lin wanted to hold Sabine, to warm her cold face and hands, to see her open her eyes and laugh at the idea that she was dead. It was ludicrous, it was obscene, to witness Sabine as a corpse.

The image vanished after a minute, and Reuben's face reappeared. Lin's eyes snapped to his, red-rimmed and blurry. For the first time she thought it all might be true. That Sabine was really dead. And she realized he hadn't lied to her. He'd just made a mistake. Just as she had, in giving Sabine the drug to help her sleep.

"Well, then *they* lied to *you*. It wasn't the Virus that killed her." She pulled the vial out of a drawer and placed it in front of her as she spoke. She lifted it up so he could see the pills glistening within. "Reuben, why did you never tell me that this was so dangerous?"

"What?"

"This drug. The one you gave me. You knew what it does to women, and you still gave it to me. Why?"

Alarm flashed across his face in the twitch of his eyes, and he swallowed quickly. He took a moment to gather himself, and when he spoke, his voice was low and hoarse. "I didn't know about the other side effects. Just the ones I told you about. That you can't take this drug with alcohol."

"Well, I gave it to her and I know that she drank with it. I'm guessing that's probably what killed her. And I am responsible for that part. Imagine if she'd been pregnant."

"Lin, I was only trying to help."

Lin fell into silence. Reuben leaned back in his chair and looked away, at the ceiling, the floor, anywhere but Lin's eyes. "You don't know what it's like, do you? All my life I've worked for this city. Its security has been my entire focus, all my life. And in return, I was given a measure of power and responsibility. It was a fair exchange. Until I met you.

"Before I met you, I only ever had one mistress. When I first met you, I thought I could be with you, but still stay loyal to Green City. I thought I could keep it all separate. Green City in the day, you in the night. And I thought that even that was part of my job: keeping an eye on you and the Panah, in case it ever got out of hand. I had it all worked out in my mind, how to help if it all went wrong. I'd bring you all in, discreetly, cleanly, and neatly. A few months of reeducation and no harm done: you'd all be put in the system and things would go back to normal."

His so-called reprieve was nothing more than a prison. She knew she'd rather die than be put, no matter how gently, back into the system. "You have your world and I have mine. I wish you hadn't interfered. With your substances. With your 'help.'"

Reuben lowered his head. "I fell in love with you. I know I shouldn't have." The confession, coupled with the sight of his thinning hair, brought a flood of regret that washed over her tense body. He'd had such thick hair when they'd begun, she could put her hands in it and not be able to see her own fingers. "I made a mistake," he admitted, after some thought. "I should have been more careful and not given you that drug. But I never, ever meant to hurt anyone. Not Sabine and never you."

For a few moments Lin couldn't speak. Sabine's death, she knew, was entirely her responsibility to bear. His love couldn't save Lin from that. She leaned in close to the display, taking a deep breath and gazing at his face for a very long time before speaking. It was strange to cherish a last moment of intimacy between them, at a distance. "Listen to me, Reuben, listen carefully."

Again the visual cut out for a second. When it returned,

his expression was smooth and blank, as if he'd washed his face with innocence. "What is it? Tell me," he said.

"Reuben. I need a favor. The biggest favor I've ever asked of you."

"Anything."

"You tried to help Sabine. It wasn't your fault that she. . . that she didn't make it." Lin had to stop for a moment and compose herself before continuing. "But now I need you to help the others."

His expression grew quizzical, then suspicious. "What do you mean, Lin?"

"I'm shutting it down, Reuben," she said, in a soft voice.

"Shutting what down?"

"The Panah."

"Well, at last you've seen reason. You can shut it down and then we can be together, properly. As man and Wife."

She winced at his visible relief, but she had to focus on the next step. "No, Reuben. It's not going to be. You have to help them but we can never meet again."

Reuben scowled. "Lin. I know you're in shock, it's terrible news, but we can still save the Panah, the rest of the girls. One of them died; it's a tragedy, but you and I can go on as we were before. You'll see."

Lin felt a surge of energy now her decision was made. She could see the path in front of her, clear and unhindered. "The others can't stay here any longer. The Panah is finished. And you can't put them back in the system. You have to help them leave Green City."

"And if I refuse?"

"I'll make sure that all of Green City knows you've supplied drugs to Green City women that will kill their unborn children."

"But you aren't Green City women," said Reuben, bewildered.

Finally he was telling the truth: he saw them differently, their lives more expendable than the ones above ground. She replied, "We're women just the same. And I have the proof of what you've done. I have the drugs in my possession. And I would never have gotten access to them except through you. That means you've helped perpetuate something that is against the rules. Not mine, but Green City's rules. You'll be accused of the treachery of killing precious unborn children. They might even think the Panah was your idea in the first place: a harem for the rich and powerful like yourself. Your reputation will never recover."

Reuben jumped up and backed away from his display. She could see him a few feet away, pacing up and down like a caged animal. Then he came back and leaned over his desk, his face so close that she could see the red veins in his eyes, the dark holes of his nostrils. "Don't threaten me! I don't want to hear this nonsense! Do you understand? If you don't stop talking like this, I'm going to—don't make me come over there, Lin, don't."

"Reuben," Lin smiled. "That's what I want you to do. If you loved me ever, you'll help me get these women out of here. Bring transport in an hour. They'll be waiting for you. Goodbye, Reuben."

Abruptly, she terminated the session. Reuben's face instantly snapped to blackness, leaving only her own image staring back at her, twenty years older than she was.

There was a hesitant knock at the door. Lin unlocked it and opened it to find Rupa standing there, two steaming mugs of tea in her hands. "I heard you talking, so I waited outside until you were done." She caught sight of Lin's face, and her eyes widened. "Are you all right? Wait, Lin, Lin, where are you going?"

Lin lunged past Rupa, leaving the girl standing there, holding the mugs of tea. She ran, stumbling through the corridors until she came to a stop in the Charbagh, gasping and panting for breath. The day sky was shifting into twilight, lavender and rose, to simulate the setting sun. The water of the four streams splashed at her feet. Stars twinkled in the eastern corner of the garden, where the night was gathering strength.

As she clutched her knees and rubbed the stitch in her side, the women, who had followed her into the Charbagh, murmured and whispered among themselves. She straightened up to regard each of them with a long, hard stare. Some of them met her eyes, others averted their gaze.

"Listen to me, all of you. Listen hard, now. The Panah is in danger and I have to shut it down. That means that all of you will have to leave."

"*What?*"

Mariya whispered, "But where will we go?"

"Don't worry. I've made arrangements. You'll be safe."

"We want to stay here!" said Su-Yin.

"And wait until Sabine comes back," added Diyah. The rest nodded in agreement.

"You can't," said Lin. "I told you. Things have gone terribly wrong. None of us can stay here anymore."

"But where. . ."

"Don't ask any more questions. Do you trust me?"

They all nodded: Diyah, Su-Yin, Mariya, Rupa, all of them except for the one whose absence was a void in the midst of their tight circle. Lin wished she had warned them when they'd first arrived at the Panah that this could never be more than a temporary resting place, a pause in their lives. The Panah could never have gone on forever as Ilona and Fairuza had hoped. Lin hadn't even known it herself until now. The Panah was the only life she'd ever lived.

Finally Diyah spoke up. "Tell us what you want us to do."

Lin willed herself to stay strong, not to cry in front of them. "You've got an hour to get ready, get your things together.

Pack the essentials. Leave everything else behind." She knew Reuben would come: he would not be able to resist interfering this one last time, to try and dissuade her in person from the path she had decided to take.

"Should we bring food?" said Diyah. Lin heard a new tone in her voice, authoritarian, decisive; she felt unexpectedly grateful. First Rupa's help, now Diyah's cooperation: maybe this could work after all.

"You'll be provided for, where you're going. Now go. Hurry. Meet at the entrance in an hour. *Hurry!*"

They ran helter-skelter toward their rooms. Lin waited until they had dispersed before returning to her own quarters. She was taking a huge gamble, all hinging on the threat she'd made to Reuben. It had to work. He could keep one fallen woman hidden from the Agency; a half-dozen of them emerging from the Panah in broad daylight was completely different. It would be all over the Bulletins; the whole of Green City would know about it by nightfall. And when the women were taken by the Agency and questioned, they would tell all, on Lin's coaching, about Reuben's involvement with the Panah, his collusion with Le Birman, the drug that wrecked women's bodies and killed their children. The Agency would turn on Reuben. Lin knew he had no option but to help the rest of the women escape.

She gathered the half-dozen small devices in which she stored all her records and set them on the floor of her room. On top of that she piled up other objects: cushions, clothes, small decorative trinkets, anything that wasn't too large for her to lift. She took down the silk wall hangings and placed them on top of the heap. It took ten minutes for her to accumulate everything, and when she stopped, her back and shoulders were sweaty and trembling with the strain.

She went to the kitchen, the place where she'd always been most strict about cleanliness and orderliness. Despite her instructions, the women had searched for any food that they could take with them on their journey to parts unknown. Drawers and cabinets gaped open, packages of food were spilled over the counters and the floor. Lin ignored it all and bent down in front of a floor cabinet. She lugged out a gallon bottle of cooking oil, lifting it to her chest with a pained gasp. She could hear the women calling out to each other in panic as she struggled with the canister all the way back to her room.

It only took a few seconds to open the canister and pour the oil all over the pile of belongings: a sorry, sodden mess when she finished. She shook the last drops from the empty bottle on the pile and stood back to survey her work, flicking an unlit match between the fingers of her left hand.

The women would all be waiting for her in the entrance to the Panah. But she would not emerge above ground with them, blinking at sunlight that they never saw. She would not be there when Reuben showed up to take them to their new lives. She was already disconnecting from the world and their faces, all anchors to an existence she no longer wanted to live.

More knocking on the door, this time loud and insistent; the hammering startled Lin out of her reverie. Swiftly she crossed the floor and unlocked it, hiding the match behind her back. Rupa stood there, her hair and clothes disheveled, a bag thrown over one shoulder. "Aren't you coming, Lin?"

Only then did Rupa notice the jumble of devices, clothing, knick-knacks soaked in oil in the middle of the room. Her whole body shook like water, and she nearly lost her balance and sagged against the door.

Lin beckoned Rupa into the room and opened her fist, scratching into it with a derma-pen. Rupa snatched her hand back and stared at the combination of numbers and letters Lin had written on her skin.

"It's the unlock code for the door. Now give me your other hand. This belongs to you."

Rupa opened her hand and stared at the tiny memory slip Lin had placed there. "My diary!"

"Yes. I'm sorry I took it. But I put something else on there, too. Information about Le Birman—and Reuben Faro."

"What?"

"Listen to me. The drug Le Birman told you about—it hurt Sabine, it can hurt other women. Read all of what I've written quickly, right now. Tell the others. If you're in any danger—any of you—use the information to bargain with Reuben. Don't back down until he gives you everything you need to get away from here."

"I don't understand," Rupa said, her mouth open in shock. Lin could see her beautiful white teeth and the small, delicate tip of her tongue. Under different circumstances, Reuben might have taken her as his Wife, as part of the spoils. He was certainly capable of working it that way, and sending the rest of them to other good households. The rich men of Green City would be clamoring to lay claim to the sudden influx of extra women: even a half dozen was a shower of abundance for them. After their punishment and their reeducation, of course. But Lin would make sure that they'd never have to submit to the Agency or the Bureau again.

"There's more, too, about the Panah. All my notes, all Ilona's notes. If he doesn't help you get out of here, tell him you'll send it all to the Agency. They'll know what to do with it." She pulled Rupa close to her in one last embrace, kissed her on the cheek. "Now go, Rupa. And take the others with you."

"I'm not leaving without you!"

"Don't worry about me," Lin said softly. "I'm going to find Sabine." She pushed Rupa away and out the door, then slammed it shut behind her and locked it.

When she was certain Rupa wouldn't return, Lin lit the match and gazed reverentially at the flame until it nearly burned down to her fingers. With a quick flick of her wrist, she tossed it on to the pile and watched the clothes ignite, then the wood, and the other trinkets that could burn first, and easily.

The acrid smoke filled the room, and the flames spread around and into the pile, penetrating deep into its heart. The room danced and glowed with orange light, transforming the melting devices into gleaming magma. It was the measure of her life's work, and Ilona's before her. She was glad to destroy it all. She had no regrets, except for the biggest one: that she could not set Sabine free along with the others. Death had beaten her to it.

She took out the vial of Sleep from her pocket, opened it, and spilled the pills into her hand. With one swift motion, she put them in her mouth, lifted her neck like a swan, and swallowed.

Lin's last thought was not a question, but a prayer that they'd meet again, she and Sabine, once the fire had reduced her body to ash and burned all the pain out of her bones.

BOUTHAIN

He suspected they'd be outside waiting: Reuben Faro, standing in front of a phalanx of Security, guns raised and pointed at them. Bouthain prayed his drug had been effective, that it had paralyzed Sabine's vocal cords so that not even a whimper could betray her to them.

But the looming figures existed only in his imagination. The elevator doors opened to blank space and the empty corridor beyond, a wormhole for them to slip into and make their escape from Shifana. Bouthain tried to control the tremor that seized his hands as he held onto Sabine's gurney. He and Mañalac carefully wheeled first Sabine, then Julien, into the low-lit corridor. A cool draft brought out drops of condensation on the heated polymer cocoons that swathed the two sleepers, hiding them from sight.

Mañalac was explaining the quickest way to the ambulance bay. "Mortuary's nearby," he said, pointing ahead. "But we go straight to the bay. I have an ambulance waiting. Arrangements all done."

"Did you use any official portal?" Bouthain asked.

"No, sir." Mañalac explained how he'd duplicated records from the last patient in quarantine. Nobody checked carefully anymore since there were so few patients left. "Should be easy for you to go straight back after we leave and fix things."

"Oh, I'm coming with you," Bouthain said casually.

Mañalac reared back: "No, sir! Too dangerous!"

"Really? I'll have you know, Mañalac, that I was at the front lines during the insurgency. I saw men bombed and blown up, and usually I was the one who had to sew them back together. A little drive to the border in a sandstorm shouldn't be too hard in comparison. Is there anything else you'd like to warn me about?"

Bouthain couldn't hear Mañalac's whispered reply, but the

nurse probably wished he were lying in a body bag along with Julien and Sabine. The whole hospital feared Bouthain's dry anger, a reputation that he cultivated carefully so that most of them would leave him alone unless absolutely necessary.

Bouthain chuckled to himself, recalling how Julien could never get used to his way of speaking about the most serious things as if they barely mattered at all. If the young doctor were awake, he'd jump up from the gurney in protest, but Julien, sufficiently drugged, lay still as an abandoned shell.

As they crept along the subterranean passageway, Bouthain could only mark their progress by the lights that ran along the ceiling at regular intervals. Eight hours to go until they woke up. In Bouthain's mind, the man who raped and impregnated Sabine was another dark figure in the invasion of Reuben Faro and his Agency foot soldiers. Who had done this to her—a Client, or someone else? Bouthain had seen many rapes in his career, treated many victims of sexual assault in Green City, even young boys. What else did they expect when they repressed the normal urges and behaviors in human beings? What was shamed into submission was bound to erupt, cruelly and unnaturally, somewhere else. But his clinical assessment of a societal problem at large distanced him from the reality of a woman who had been victimized in such a cowardly way. He was surprised at how much anger there was inside him at the hard facts of her violation, the injustice at its root, and the trauma that had manifested so bizarrely that he, too, was swept up in its aftermath.

"Almost there, boss," muttered Mañalac. Hating to be called "boss," Bouthain only grunted in reply.

The corridor widened into a larger foyer, immediately bringing with it a change in air pressure. Beyond two sets of doors, brightness beckoned, promising warmth and safety. Mañalac went up to the door display and pressed his hand on it, then tapped in a code. The display glowed red, and another red light flickered to life on the other side of the door. "Quarantine, quarantine, quarantine," a robotic voice affirmed. "Commencing quarantine procedures now."

"They'll clear the bay for us," said Mañalac.

"I know." Bouthain was tired; Mañalac's detailed explanations were wearing him out. If Mañalac was talking out loud for Julien's benefit, he was wasting his breath: Julien could not hear him through the chemical-induced sleep and the insulation of the pod. The nurse wouldn't be the first person to try to talk to the dead, but Sabine and Julien wouldn't be the only ones to die if it all went wrong.

Bouthain wished Julien were awake so he could observe everything with his intelligent blue eyes and take the pressure off his mentor by giving directions to all those around him: instructions about the quarantine rules, or an explanation for some little-understood aspect of hospital statutes. Bouthain had taught him well. But the silence from the gurney behind them was complete, emanating the truth that the connections between people were only temporary. At best they could psychically visit one another from time to time, but they would always remain mysteriously out of reach to one another. Death was feared, Bouthain knew, because it changed those distances from temporary illusion to irreversible permanence.

As they passed through the double doors, the red light glowed on the surfaces of their faces and the bodies behind them. They stopped the gurneys there; Mañalac stepped on a small lever near the front wheels, and they locked into place. There was a slippery sound of parting plastic, and then a rush of fresh air over Bouthain's skin that made all his pores tingle. Everything suddenly seemed brighter, more hopeful. For the first time, he started to wonder if this insane plot might just succeed.

The antechamber was deserted, as part of quarantine procedure. Protocols had been developed to prevent exposing any more people than necessary to the hideousness of the Virus. Even Bouthain's colleagues lowered their voices whenever discussing it. Bouthain had taken for granted their squeamishness about all things having to do with women and their bodies. He had often spoken of the need to erase the stigma surrounding the disease and its victims. But this general disdain would be useful to them now, and the quarantine protocols would help them to get away without being detected.

Mañalac patted Sabine's shoulder though the bag. Bouthain wondered if she would be cold or warm to his touch; there was no time for him to see for himself. He went to a closet and rummaged around inside for a set of green scrubs that he quickly slipped on: a gown, a mask, boots, gloves. Mañalac followed suit: they were both now two anonymous hospital workers dealing with a dangerous biological situation.

"We have to close the transport cases now," said Mañalac.

"Is the ambulance ready?"

"Waiting in the bay," Mañalac replied, with some pride. Julien had always said this nurse got things done even before Julien asked for them, anticipating what was needed and figuring out how to do it without having to be consulted. Bouthain would make a note of it and find a way to recommend a promotion for the man after this was all over.

"Let's do it, then."

Their conversation faded as the gurney rose on its hydraulics, lifting the pods up into the air. Then forward movement again: they passed through the second set of doors, out into the ambulance bay. An insistent droning drowned out most sound: the sandstorm was still raging outside the hospital. Bouthain didn't know how they were going to get through the storm, despite his earlier nonchalance.

The new space was filled with incandescent white light.

From darkness into light, stage by stage: the place they were going purer than the one they were leaving behind.

A slight bump and then a jerk, as Sabine's gurney clicked into place with the back doors of the ambulance. It tilted slightly, raising her head higher than her legs. The plastic surrounding had been designed to make it easy for a body to slide down the angled surface of the gurney. Bouthain hated seeing bodies treated like offal, flung onto heaps before being cremated: the same in war and the Virus epidemic. He made sure to guide her pod with gentle, respectful hands into the mouth of the ambulance. Then he and Mañalac did the same for Julien.

Mañalac quickly leaned into the ambulance. "Not long now. Little more patience, you'll be safe soon," he murmured, just before he closed the doors. It sounded like a benediction to Bouthain's ears. If Mañalac was religious, he'd better keep praying that they made it to the border without Reuben Faro catching them.

Mañalac took the driver's seat, switching on the ambulance lights and testing the wheel; Bouthain climbed into the passenger seat and buckled himself in. Mañalac tapped a code into the ambulance dashboard display, and the door of the bay began to lift onto a solid yellow wall that was already blowing sheets of dust into the bay.

Mañalac lowered his mask for a moment and glanced over at Bouthain. "Ready, boss?" They weren't technically supposed to call him boss, or chief, or anything else besides his title. But "boss" was an ironic term of respect among the working class of Green City: a subtle sign that signaled not Bouthain's superiority, but Mañalac's total trust in him, no matter what the consequences.

Bouthain nodded tersely. "Let's go." Mañalac pulled up his mask again, pressed down on the accelerator, and swung the ambulance into the maelstrom outside.

Almost as soon as they'd left the bay, the winds, blowing in all directions, began to buffet the ambulance, restricting them to a stop-start crawl through the streets. Driving through the city was usually an easy task, with the city laid out in a grid that driverless cars could navigate. But sandstorms were weather phenomena that reduced visibility to zero and confounded even the most capable navigation system, so Mañalac had to use his own sense of direction to get them out of Green City heading toward the border, a four-hour drive away from Green City. In the sandstorm it would take them much longer to get there. They'd be in Semitia by nightfall, if they were granted a miracle.

Everything around them was a sickening orange haze. At times Mañalac could hardly see two feet in front of him; the flashing lights of the few vehicles on the road made small bright pinpoints that he followed carefully, but not too closely. At other times the wind and sand lifted a little, so Bouthain could see familiar landmarks turned into darkened shadows, palm trees oscillating like windmills, as if possessed. The buildings that normally looked so solid in normal weather seemed to tremble in the onslaught, and lights were going out in windows like eyes closing, one after the other.

The ambulance's air system filtered out the worst of the sand, but Bouthain was glad for the mask he wore: it added an extra layer of protection. The elderly and the weak often died in the days after this kind of storm, from asthma attacks or inhalation-induced pneumonia. Usually Bouthain counted himself among the invincible, but he knew that the sand, if it got into his lungs, could kill him, too.

They drove for an hour in this way, speeding up a little, slowing down, the wheels of the ambulance underneath them grinding noisily into the sand on the road. The sound of sand beating against the windows and roaring wind was a constant hum in their ears. Every once in a while the gears of the ambulance would slip and the engine emitted an angry groan, but above his surgical mask Mañalac's squinting eyes never wavered from the road. Bouthain felt grateful for the nurse's steadfastness; his heart was beating fast and hard, and he doubted he'd have the stamina to drive for this long in such dire conditions. It was more frightening than he had anticipated. These kinds of sandstorms were not frequent, but twice or thrice a summer the shamal wind blew in from the north and devilishly whipped up the desert sand and dust into towering, massive clouds. The dry lands created by the destruction of the Final War had made the storms much worse over the last several decades: you could drive for hours and still not travel the circumference of one. Bouthain had never before driven straight into the belly; the best bet for survival was to hunker down indoors, or better yet, underground, to avoid being hit by flying debris or crushed by the buildings that collapsed in the storm's path. He felt suffocated, and a panicked thought arose before he beat it back down: what if they were buried alive in all these tons of sand?

They made steady progress, however. Here and there a lone figure struggled to walk against the wind: traffic guards, wearing protective gear with masks and hoods, patrolling to make sure everyone was safely indoors. There were fewer and fewer cars on the streets, most of them abandoned on the side of the road, doors open and lights flashing. Already being covered up in sand, by tomorrow morning, when the storm died down, they'd be hulks, their paintwork and engines ruined by the grinding torrents that stripped them as if every inch had been sandpapered. The ambulance was equipped with special filters so it wouldn't choke like the cars did. They were built like tanks, these ambulances, equipped with everything necessary to save lives short of a full operating theater; so much better than the rickety, ill-equipped vehicles they'd had during the War. But the roads could become impassable if the sand piled up too quickly.

They were silent: Mañalac concentrated while Bouthain listened for any sound from the back of the ambulance. He'd have gone to the back and checked on his patients, but he was strapped into his seat and it was too dangerous to move.

"Little more patience," said Mañalac, sensing his agitation, even though Bouthain could have sworn he hadn't moved a muscle. "Try to nap."

"I don't need any rest," sniffed Bouthain, stung by the suggestion that he couldn't keep up the pace. But against his will he found himself lulled by the soft rocking of the ambulance. Eventually his eyelids closed and he slipped gently into a light, blank sleep.

Bouthain woke up with a start when his ears popped, but he knew exactly where he was. No need to rub his eyes or groggily reorient himself: he saw that they'd managed to leave the city and were now climbing up into the mountains, ascending slowly and, yard by yard, making painstaking progress through the western pass, halfway to Semitia. Sometimes they skidded this way or that, but Mañalac regained control quickly each time the ambulance lost traction.

"Good morning, boss," said Mañalac.

Bouthain smiled for the first time. "Was I out for long?"

"Only a few hours. You kept talking in your sleep. Not like those two in back. They haven't made a sound."

The windows of the ambulance were coated in layers of dust, but when he craned his neck to look back, Bouthain could see the orange mass of the dust storm had completely enveloped Green City behind them. He breathed out in relief. Nobody could come after them now: Reuben Faro would be stuck there until the next day. With a clear road and open skies ahead of them, they could be in Semitia by evening.

"What did I say?" asked Bouthain curiously.

"Don't know, boss. Strange things. About the war, a man with no leg. Your patient?"

"I saw many men without legs, Mañalac," said Bouthain. "And arms. War's got a strange way of making you lose your limbs for no reason."

Mañalac knew better than to say anything. He drove on in silence while Bouthain continued to observe the road closely. He'd often come here for picnics with his family as a child. His parents brought food and drink, and they perched themselves on the edge of the cliff, legs dangling, watching the mountain hawks circling higher and higher through thin, dry air, the sky separated into bands of blue, bluer, bluest strips in the fine, crisp light, the sun shining through the peaks, stinging his eyes.

He'd loved these mountain passes and higher elevations, savored cooler weather in the hot summer months. The barren rocks dotted with scrub brush and the occasional sturdy date tree had drawn him in with their wild stubborn beauty, as had the endless pulsing skies and the deep gorges into which you could throw a shout and a hundred echoes would come back to you. Even as a young boy he'd recognized the mountains as a place where a man knew who he was, without having to be told by anyone whom to obey or what to believe.

It was strange to no longer hear that howling wind, or strain to see what was in front of them. The road was open, the ambulance engine humming powerfully. Soon, Bouthain thought it might even be safe enough to stop the vehicle so he could check on Sabine and Julien. He had no real way of calculating exactly when they might wake—the drug worked differently on everyone—but he wanted to take their vitals and at least make sure they were not in any respiratory distress.

Mañalac slowed the ambulance down, then brought it to a halt. Bouthain cocked his head quizzically; had the man read his mind? But he could see that something was wrong, very wrong. Mañalac wasn't looking at him, but at the display on the dashboard, where the rear camera showed two black cars stopped behind them, and a group of men standing in the road, holding guns.

Bouthain waited for shouting, pounding on the doors, or a volley of gunfire. If they were dragged out, a single gunshot would put an end to any misery for himself and Mañalac. But what would happen to Julien and Sabine?

"I'm sorry, Mañalac," he breathed, as his door was wrenched open with a clatter.

"Come on out, Rami."

Bouthain recognized the voice before he saw Reuben Faro: a low baritone, rumbling with a mix of authority and displeasure. The other men, Reuben's guards, stood at a distance; only Faro waited nearby as they slowly emerged from the ambulance. Bouthain's knees almost gave way but he refused to stumble in front of Faro, or to hold on to the door to steady himself. His leg muscles spasmed and ached as they came back to life after the long hours of cramping in his seat.

"Reuben Faro."

Faro said, "It's been a long time, Rami." He was bigger and more menacing than Bouthain remembered him. He'd put on weight and muscle; he was in exceptionally good shape for a man his age. He'd grown a beard, and there was white in it and in his hair, but he was still a man in his prime, stronger and faster and younger than Bouthain.

"Indeed," said Bouthain. "Is all of this really necessary?" He nodded at the guards, the vehicles, the guns. "You could just let us go."

"You know I can't do that. Come on, open up. I want to see who you're hiding in there."

Bouthain nodded at Mañalac, who was trembling beside him, his eyes glued to the raised guns held by Reuben's guards. Mañalac walked slowly to the back of the ambulance, fumbling with the doors. Faro didn't prod him, or shout at him to hurry, as Bouthain might have expected. He stood easily; there was no use running, or trying to fight him. No point, either, in pretending that neither of them knew what cargo was contained within the ambulance.

Finally Mañalac unlocked and opened the doors, and they slid open easily on their tracks, showing the two bodies entombed within.

Bouthain spoke calmly: "She died early in the morning."

"Why is she in full quarantine?"

"She was Virus positive. We found out when we did her blood tests. She was entering the acute phase, which triggered the organ failure. It happens like that: they go down fast. Even the young ones. And the strong ones. It's an ugly way to go. We have to mop up the floors afterwards, there's that much blood." Bouthain spun out his tale for the man, adding unnecessary details. Ordinary men were terrified of the Virus, but Reuben hardly blinked.

"And who's in the second pod? Another one? Get them both open. You, Bouthain, not him."

Bouthain climbed up into the ambulance, opened the first pod, then the second. He beckoned Faro to follow him inside. When Faro crouched beside him, Bouthain gently moved aside the wrapping over Sabine's face, not knowing what he would see, terrified that it would divulge all.

To his profound relief, she was still and pale, frozen still, not a hair moving, not even an eyelash. Bouthain could hear Faro exhaling harshly in the semidarkness. Without waiting for a response, he uncovered Julien's face more quickly. "It's Dr. Asfour."

"Dr. Asfour? *Julien* Asfour?" Bouthain could hear Faro's heavy, ragged breathing. "What happened to him?"

"He committed suicide. We found his body inside his office." Bouthain's voice was dry as tonic water.

Reuben looked puzzled. "Why did he do it?"

Bouthain thought fast; he had to make the explanation as plausible as possible. "Shifana doesn't really like it when staff members kill themselves. Orders are to dispose of their bodies as quickly as possible. Between you and me, I think he got too close to the girl. He wanted to help her. Love-struck. The poor fool." He thinned his lips disapprovingly, hoping his words and demeanor were convincing Faro. "Then he realized he'd made the wrong choice, and the consequences for his career. . . well, he was a driven man. He couldn't handle the idea that he'd engineered his own failure, I suppose."

"Pity," said Faro. "I liked him. Oh well. Sometimes they crack under pressure. It wouldn't be the first time. So how did he do it?"

"Poison," was Bouthain's laconic reply.

"Messy. Does his family know?"

"They'll be told it was an accident. Something happened in the lab, something that necessitated quarantine for him, too. We don't want to underscore his weakness, do we?" Bouthain was gambling now that Faro wouldn't ask too many questions about the medical side of things. He knew that Faro had reached a breaking point, that he could no longer keep up the elaborate ruse of his secret alliance with the Panah. He'd want to move things along quickly. But when men broke, the results were ugly; they would destroy anything around them as they came undone.

"Wait, wait, Reuben, what are you doing?"

It wasn't easy for the larger man to maneuver around inside the tight confines of the ambulance, but Bouthain had no space himself to reach forward and prevent him from thrusting his face near Sabine to peer closely at her body.

"Faro, be careful. . ." said Bouthain. "The Virus is not a joke. You wouldn't want to become a carrier."

"I'll take my chances," said Reuben Faro.

If Sabine were awake, she'd tremble violently at the nearness of the man. Bouthain had noticed her doing it whenever they touched her at Shifana—trauma, no doubt, from her bad experiences with the men she'd encountered. He watched Reuben pondering her body, fearing that something would give her away, a twitch of her lips, the involuntary creasing of her forehead, a moan. He'd have to distract him somehow. "Faro. This isn't protocol. It's not safe. Leave it alone, now. Even if you don't care about your own health, I'm responsible for it. I'll have to answer for it if you end up infected."

Faro chuckled, a soft, low sound: Bouthain and his protocols were of no importance to him. He reached inside the pod and pulled apart the rest of the polymer covering, then unfolded the cotton cloth around Sabine, exposing her entire body to his examination.

Reuben held his hand over Sabine's mouth and nose. "She's not breathing."

"Have you forgotten the rules of science? They may no longer apply to you, but they still apply to other people," Bouthain said with surprising harshness. "The dead don't breathe. No, Faro, don't touch her."

But Faro's fingers were already touching her face, strong and firm, finding coldness where he was expecting warmth. Then he lowered his fingers to her neck, pressing her throat in search of her pulse. Bouthain knew it would be too thready for anyone but an experienced physician to detect.

"Sabine? Are you awake?" said Faro. He turned back to Bouthain.

Bouthain glanced at his watch. "It's been six hours. Rigor mortis has come and gone. In another hour, she'll start to decompose. We have to get her to crematorium before that happens. You, on the other hand, must go straight to quarantine; you'll infect other people if you don't."

But Faro ignored him, murmuring to her in a voice that

was soft yet urgent. "Wake up, Sabine. Wake up!" His fingers were still lying lightly on Sabine's neck. Would he reach around with both hands until they encircled her throat, and squeeze tight? Bouthain felt himself go numb.

At last Faro removed his fingers from Sabine's throat. He took out his device, turned on the camera, and aimed it at Sabine's face. The device let out a small beep, and then he was backing away, straightening himself with caution, as if moving too fast caused him pain. Finally at some distance, Faro rested his hands on his hips, arms bent sharply at his elbows, shoulders squared. His eyes, dark and watchful, looked wet and he was blinking hard. Bouthain pitied him. Faro was no monster; he was a man trapped in a life that promised him absolute power but in return had stripped him of everything good and honorable. The Agency had taken a man who might have been a kind husband, a loving father, and turned everyone who might have loved him into his enemy. Maybe this was just the moment to appeal to his better sense. Or his mercy, if he had any left. "So if everything's in order, we'll be on our way," said Bouthain. "All right, Faro? Mañalac, let's go."

Faro pursed his lips and shook his head. "Not so fast."

"What's the problem?"

Faro's eyes had hardened; his glance was a sharp knife. "Tell me, Rami. Why have you come all the way here with two corpses and a nurse, in a quarantine ambulance? Don't you have more important things to do at the hospital right now?"

"Well, I. . ." Bouthain spoke carefully, slowly, as if testing each word for its viability before releasing it. He dared not look at Mañalac now. "Well, to tell you the truth, this is a very personal journey for me."

"How so?"

"Dr. Asfour. . . Julien. I was very fond of him. And wanted to see him off myself."

"So he was your friend?" Faro's voice was gentle with understanding. Then it grew brutal. "Or was it something more between the two of you?" The insinuation that there was something illicit between Bouthain and Julien hung in the air like the dust motes surrounding them, the remnants of the storm's passage from the mountains down to Green City, miles away. The rules of Green City were equally far from them; distance made its diktats appear weak and watered-down.

"I'm too old for that sort of thing, Reuben. That might be hard for you to imagine. But he was my star pupil. He had so much promise. And now he's dead. So can you give him some dignity here?"

"I wish I could do that," said Faro. "But I can't. My superiors already know a woman has broken cover, emerged from underground. She's dead now, so there's nothing to be done about that. But someone has to answer for everything that happened at the hospital. Frankly, about Dr. Asfour's suicide, well, your explanation sounds flimsy. I'm sure there's a better one you can give me instead. I wish you'd called me, Rami, I really do. I could have helped. We could at least have saved Dr. Asfour, you and I. Anyway, this is the end for you. You won't go any farther."

"But what about their bodies?" said Bouthain. "We can't just leave them here." His voice cracked. He had finally run out of ideas.

"Why not?" said Reuben Faro. In his voice Bouthain heard a shrugging of shoulders, a spread of hands upturned to indicate his vast indifference to their fate. Of course he and Mañalac were already dead to Faro. If he'd seen through their ruse, leaving Sabine and Julien in the middle of this wilderness would be a fitting punishment for their crime. Either way, they'd die here soon enough, unable to move towards food or water, no one to care for them as they came out of their drug-induced stupor. Faro could pretend to find their bodies later and denounce them, posthumously, as traitors.

Mañalac darted forward suddenly, turning and running for cover behind the ambulance. A shot rang out from the distance and Mañalac dropped onto his hands and knees, blood trickling from his neck onto the ground. Before Bouthain could realize what had happened, the guards were swarming over Mañalac's body, lifting it up and taking it back to their vehicles.

By instinct Bouthain began to walk, moving quickly, leading Faro away from the ambulance. There was no time to waste: nearly eight hours had passed since they'd left Shifana, and Sabine and Julien could wake at any moment. His own fate meant little now. Bouthain was a son of Green City; he knew what was going to happen to him as surely as he knew his own name. The Leaders had always made it clear how they dealt with disobedience: quickly, brutally, and without hesitation. So what if Faro was saving him for an underground cell in the Agency? Bouthain was not afraid; he had a pill in his pocket. He could swallow it at any time and put an end to all his struggles. As he walked away with Reuben Faro, there was nothing happening inside him, only a growing sense of calm, as if he were moving in a dream.

"Where do you think you're going, Bouthain?" shouted Reuben Faro.

SABINE

My body is loose and amorphous. I have no sense of where I begin or end; I'm as pliant as seaweed floating in a gentle current. But something is touching me, stroking my neck. I'm tingling where the sensation moves, left and right, up and down. It's ticklish. I want to giggle, yet I can't make a sound.

"Sabine? Are you awake?"

The voice comes from far away, as if I'm underwater and someone's calling me back to the surface. I can see ripples, spreading out in circles from where each syllable has dropped into the darkness. Then the words sink down to the bottom where I am, drifting, drifting. . .

"She's blue. . ."

"It's been. . . six hours. . .crematorium. . . quarantine. . ."

Someone's fingers are digging into my throat. Someone is breathing into my face. It's a man's scent. Cigarettes and cologne.

The fingers lift from my throat. The words that come next are clearer, spoke in a soft whisper: "You were beautiful."

I sense where I am a split second before my mind perceives it, just long enough to send a current of adrenaline into every inch of my skin, electrifying every nerve and cell. The covering over my face has been torn apart. The light against my eyelids is a warm red glow, after all these hours of being so tightly enclosed in the dark. My eyes won't open.

There's a sigh, and then a moment later, a little beep.

I can only tell he's receded by the lessening of an invisible pressure near me, like clouds lifting after heavy rain. Space has opened up around me, but still I dare not peek into it, in case he's still close and looking at me. Sensation returns to me, little by little, as I hear a shifting around and shuffling footsteps: the sound of someone, or two people, maneuvering themselves out.

I lie completely still, unsure if I'm still being watched. The voices that ensue are muffled but in a different way now: beyond a physical barrier, not a psychic one. Have they moved further away? They're not fighting or arguing, but they sound tense and annoyed. Only now do I become aware that my back is drenched in sweat and that there's an intense itching in my hands and feet.

The itching intensifies into a burning as I hear a popping sound, a metallic crack I've never heard before. There are frenzied footsteps falling, lots of them, and barked commands to *move, move, move*. Then a loud, hoarse shout:

"Where do you think you're going, Bouthain?"

I start to tremble. I force myself to hold still until I can hear the sound of engines starting. I hang on until the vehicles have pulled away and everything has become quiet again, except for the soft whimpering that comes from somewhere deep and low inside me. My throat's opened up enough to let sound out; does that mean Bouthain's drug is wearing off now? Is it safe enough to get up from this position?

I use my hands to pull my legs over the side of the pod. When I try to stand in the narrow confines of the ambulance, I tumble over. I push back up to a low crouch, shivering, and reach out to the compact shelves lining the ambulance walls stacked with medications and bandages. My scrabbling fingers find a packet of cooling gel for burns: I tear it open and pour it all over my face and neck. Only when the searing sensation under my skin has calmed down do I realize that the ambulance isn't moving anymore.

"Dr. Bouthain? Mañalac?" I call out. My voice quavers. There's no answer. A glance at their empty seats in the front of the ambulance confirms my fears. Julien and I are alone.

I drag myself over to Julien. He's lying motionless in his pod, face slack, skin a strange, other-worldly tint of blue. I try to shake him awake, but he's unresponsive.

The back doors of the ambulance are hanging open, letting in gentle light and a cool, sweet breeze filled with the clean scent of mountain air and the dry, fine dust of a wadi somewhere in a valley. The gray and brown cliffs in the near distance tell me that we're in one of the rocky passes on the way to the border. I don't know which one; I've never left Green City before today. When I look beyond the edge of the road, I see a long drop to what I recognize from screen images: a dry creek bed below.

I ease myself out of the ambulance. There are footprints on the ground, a lot of them. Where are Bouthain and Mañalac: what's happened to them? How could they abandon us here? Maybe the engine stalled and they went to look for help. But wouldn't one of them stay behind to watch over us? There's nobody around us now, not even their ghosts.

I look down and shudder when I see drops of blood in the dust, and a trail of more blood leading a few feet away. Something terrible has happened. There's no other explanation for their disappearance. There's nobody else here, except for the mountains and the sky and the clouds ringing the tops of the mountains.

I press my forehead against the door, letting its coolness soothe the aching in my head. I need time to resurface, to make sense of everything. My thoughts are skittering around like marbles in my head. And the fear is still there, even though I know I'm fully awake.

When Bouthain injected me with the drug, I kept waiting for the dying to begin, as if it was an event that would somehow announce itself to me, with darkness or light, heaviness or a feeling of becoming lighter than air. I kept guessing what death would look like. Would death be ugly like Reuben Faro? Or kind and benevolent, like Bouthain? Or would my mind conjure up my mother's lovely face up for me as my brain began to go out in phases?

I barely remember lying in the pod, cool and dark, the case lined with a soft, downy material that moved and whispered all around me, as if I were floating on water. I was safely hidden away, a fetus nestling in the womb, my twin Julien in the pod next to me. With Bouthain and Mañalac in charge, there was nothing more to need, to strive for, to desire.

Then I sank into those hours of death-not-death, and the howling wind, shaking and shifting us around as we lay dead to the world. I was aware of snippets of muffled conversation, voices I couldn't quite recognize. But it was nothing like sleep.

I look at Julien's still face, wondering if was easier for him to surrender to Bouthain's drug? Or could he actually be dead, the result of too much of the drug?

Sabine, are you awake? It's a refrain that won't leave my mind now. That deep growl that spoke to me in my stupor has embedded itself in my brain.

Out here, I'm the only woman left in the world.

When I've regained some of the strength in my arms and legs, I lean on the back door of the ambulance to close it. It's not likely that anyone will pass us by on this deserted patch of road, but I don't want them to see the pods with one of the lids lifted open. The buzzing in my head grows with each step and my legs groan and complain as if every blood vessel in them has burst, but at least I'm out of the prison of the pod. The cocoon couldn't shield me from what I have to face now.

I walk around the ambulance, examining it in its entirety, a sleek yellow bullet checkered with green and black squares and the logo of Shifana Hospital. How long will it be before an air patrol drone spots us and sends an Agency car to check: before or after we die of dehydration and starvation? We didn't take any food or water with us, we were in too much of a hurry to leave, and we were hoping to be across the border today, even with the sandstorm.

The billowing orange cloud hangs over the skyline of the

City, the sandstorm still relentlessly battering the streets and buildings of the place I've always called my home. But from this distance—a hundred miles, at least—it's a phenomenon I'm observing on a distant planet through a powerful telescope. I can't believe we actually drove through that. I'm glad I was unconscious for most of it.

It's actually better to be in the Panah when there's a sandstorm of such magnitude. Sometimes I see the start of it when I'm coming back from a Client, the dust blowing in low clouds that I'd mistake for mist or fog if I didn't hear the eerie hissing as it scratches against the roads. When we're safely back home, we cluster together in frightened twos and threes, listening as the wind moans overhead and the warehouse creaks and complains like an old ship forced against an ocean gale it can't withstand. We always expect to emerge from the Panah and see that the warehouse has been blown away, but somehow, it's still standing, all but buried in dust and debris.

My mother was always terrified of the sandstorms but my father would laugh them off with a bravado that thrilled me when I was small. "Come on, Sabine, let's go chase it!" he'd exclaim, as soon as news came through that a sandstorm was gathering at the edge of Green City. My mother would scream at him that he was mad, but I'd already be at his side, running for the car. We'd get in and rush towards the outer suburbs to watch the storm approach.

We'd stop at the side of the road and get out of the car, bandanas tied around our faces. I couldn't believe anything could be that big. The sandstorm was bigger than a building, than an airplane, than an entire shopping mall. It seemed to have no beginning and no end, it seemed to have always existed. A towering yellow mass of boiling sand and dust, turning in on itself over and over again, heavy with its own momentum and orbit. The storm stretched from one end of the horizon to the other, and went on as far as the eye could see. And the deafening noise: the hooves of a thousand angry horses striking the ground at the same time.

The winds preceding its arrival rose and fell in pitch, whipping our clothes around our bodies and nearly choking us with dust. Still, we were rooted to the ground; we'd stand there and hold hands, fascinated by its fury, bigger and more overwhelming than any human force. We'd turn around and rush home just in time before the roads closed and the curfew alarms sounded, exhilarated by our daring, ignoring my mother's angry shouts when we returned.

As I examine the bleak landscape and the road Julien and I have already traveled, I strain to feel some of that old exhilaration, that distant feeling that nothing could touch me as long as I was holding my father's hand. A slim stretch of road disappears around a blind curve a hundred yards away—the path we've yet to take. How far are we from the border? Or are we hopelessly lost? I tighten my grip on the ambulance's door. I call out again for Bouthain and for Mañalac. I know something has happened to them, and I have no other choice. "I'm going to get us out of here, Julien," I say out loud.

My hand slowly pulls open the door wide enough for me to get inside. The seat is high; I have to climb up to get into it. I pull myself up and awkwardly heft myself into the cab, hips first, then one foot, then the other. Leaning over, I pull the passenger side's door closed. The jerking wrenches the incision on my stomach, but the pain's overshadowed by a mixture of nervousness and daring at what I'm about to do.

I close my own door, then stare down at the controls, wondering which switch turns the engine on. I've never driven a car before; I've always been driven from the Panah to Clients' houses, floating inside my head on a cloud of fatigue and relief that the night's over and I can be taken home in peace and solitude. How hard can it be, though? Even cars drive themselves.

I reach out and press a button. A loud horn sounds, making me jump in my seat. That isn't right.

Are you awake, Sabine? Again the words, but the voice sounds different, an older echo this time.

Shut up, I tell myself. I won't be distracted by shadows now. I press every button on the dashboard in front of me, wave my hands in front of panels, look frantically above and below for pedals or a stick, anything that might give me control of the ambulance.

A closer examination of the steering wheel reveals what I'm looking for: grooves in the back of the wheel that I can fit my fingers into, one for the accelerator and the other for the brake. At last the ambulance wakes up, its engines coughing and spitting, then roaring into life. I stare, astonished, at the panels lighting up; a raw, raucous laugh escapes my lips.

The control buttons are very sensitive to my touch: the slightest pressure makes the ambulance lurch out of its tracks and move forward with a jolt, or stop so suddenly that I'm thrown forward in my seat, nearly banging my head on the wheel. Julien's pod slides back and forth noisily behind me. "Sorry, sorry," I call out, even though I presume he can't hear me.

I ease the ambulance out onto the road, following the blind curve, which leads to a steady downhill slope. It takes me only a few minutes to get used to driving the car: it's easy to direct it down the empty road. A gentle nudge of the navigator steers us to the left or right, and as my fingers press down in the grooves, I begin to enjoy the scenery going past, the dun-colored mountain walls, little ledges dotted with small trees and scrub brush, an occasional gecko dashing across the road. Here and there the ambulance skids clumsily, and I have to hold the wheel tight to negotiate between the accelerator and the brake.

We climb down for about fifteen or twenty minutes. Soon the road levels out, and we're in desert flatlands once more.

The porcelain blue sky meets the horizon in a line as straight as a ruler. The sandstorm is far behind us, and so is Green City. I'll have to drive for I don't know how long to reach the border. I have no way of knowing distances, and the ambulance's navigation system is still a mystery to me.

To pass the time, I imagine conversations with all the women of the Panah: Rupa, Diyah, Su-Yin, Mariya, Aleyna. How would I tell them everything that's happened to me? They'd be amazed, horrified, curious. They'd tease me about Julien; their hearts would thrill at how we lay together that night in the hospital. They'd cry with me, for me, for the assault on my body and the loss of the pregnancy, no matter how unformed and unknown the clump of cells. They'd hate my attacker, whoever he was, applaud my courage at taking Bouthain's drug and using death to cheat Reuben Faro.

Maybe they wouldn't understand how I could trust an unknown man and his untested medicine. I'd tell them that I'd trusted Bouthain because of his regard for Julien. I know Bouthain wouldn't voluntarily leave either of us until we're safe. I know he did all of this for his star pupil. You'd have to be blind not to recognize, in Bouthain's loyalty, the finest of love, the purest of compassion, wrapped up in his grouchy exterior.

As I keep my finger on the accelerator, driving down the never-ending tunnel of sand, I long to hear Bouthain's raspy voice one more time. His dedication to his job gives shelter to anyone who suffers. What he did for me goes far beyond the extent of any job. I wonder if Bouthain and Mañalac are still alive. They are probably dead by now. Or will be soon. There is no mercy in Green City.

But when it comes to imagining how I'd explain things to Lin, my imagination comes to a stop. A mixture of guilt, shame, and fear rises in me as I picture her listening to my tale. I've ruined everything by exposing the Panah to Reuben Faro's wrath.

I stop thinking for a while and concentrate on the road. I drive for so long that I'm no longer sure whether I'm asleep or awake. "Julien, please wake up," I say, turning my head a little to the side so that the words can reach him. "Please. I don't know how much longer I can do this."

My mind drifts back to a moment with Joseph, a half-memory, a flash of something. Instead of darkness, I can see the gray of an early morning, the streets of Green City, the faint light and a soft drizzle lathering the sky through a bedroom window.

All of a sudden I'm back in the bed with the black silk sheets, the black champagne glass on the side table. If I turn my head to the side, I can see the fizzy bubbles breaking on the surface of the liquid. *Sabine? Are you awake?*

It's Joseph's voice. Joseph's hands. Joseph's body bearing down on mine. I suddenly remember it all: his weight and pressure, my subdued acquiescence. The fear underneath all the grogginess.

The desert is a sea in front of me; the mountains behind are a wall between past and present that I've just traveled through. I could dismiss all of this as fantasies, as nightmares, as vivid imaginings. But insomnia is not what caused those blank spaces in my mind. The soreness in my belly and my thighs I'd felt in the Panah were not just cramps or an upset stomach. I was violated, on the first night Joseph gave me the black champagne, six weeks ago.

Sabine? Are you awake? is what Joseph whispered to me before he began to touch me, while I was unconscious in his bed. He was the father of that unborn, unwanted child, nothing more than an embryo, nothing less than an earthquake in my life.

It's too much. I let go of the steering wheel, which sounds a violent alarm as we go spinning off the road and bounce onto the soft shoulder. Julien's pod knocks against the ambulance walls, shifting violently from one side to the other. I bang my head on the door. The ambulance comes to a stop at a disjointed angle, half off and half on the road. The engine is still running erratically, a loud ticking sound filling the cab. I press my fingers to my head and they come away sticky with blood.

As we sit there, I begin to shake. I put my arms onto the steering wheel and lean my head against them. I want to cry, to fill the air with apologies. To my parents. To Lin. To the Panah. To Bouthain and Mañalac. And to Julien. I want my last word to be *sorry*. I have broken every rule, transgressed every limit. Maybe this is what I deserve. Maybe I should just die right here.

But as my trembling subsides and the sobs dry up, as the sun starts its descent towards the horizon, I ask myself why I should die for Green City. It's stolen everything from me: my parents, my home, my future. My body, my sanctity, my friends from the Panah. Lin. Why should I give it the last thing I have left: my life?

I slot my fingers into the steering wheel, turn the ambulance back on. Push the accelerator button and carefully, slowly, back up on the road. Now straighten it out. Switch on the lights, it's starting to get dark. That's it. That's good. Now drive, Sabine. There will be time, later, to take account of everything, to reconcile what I know with what I've learned. But now, I have to drive for my life.

And we're off, the engine growling. I'm leaning forward in my seat, pushing the steering wheel as if I can make the ambulance move faster with physical effort. The sun begins to disappear and twilight spreads from the east, the moon a full yellow circle above me. Soon in the distance I can make out the border fence: a crooked horizontal line that glimmers with a low-voltage electric charge. The closer we get, the more defined it becomes, like the bars of a cage. I lower my head and clench my teeth, and press hard on the accelerator. I've had enough of cages.

There's a roar and a bang as we crash into the fence, larger and stronger than I imagined, a steel alloy, designed for resistance. But the ambulance tears a bullet-shaped hole into it and we pierce through it to the other side.

We skid to a halt twenty yards after the fence; the ambulance gears whir and grind, but the wheels won't obey anymore. I hear rapid footsteps and cries of alarm all around me. I stay in my seat, breathing hard, as they open the doors, both front and back. Gentle hands tug at my shoulder. A man and a woman in the olive green uniforms of the Semitia Border Guards peer at me, in shock and concern. There's astonished curiosity all over their faces, as if I've dropped in from another planet. But no guns. There are no guns pointed at me.

"Are you all right?" says the woman. She's young, my age. Maybe even younger. Red-haired, hazel-eyed, and sharp-faced, she looks just a bit like Lin. Surprise shines in her eyes, as if she's practiced for this moment but never really expected it to happen. Am I the first woman from Green City that she's ever seen?

She squares her jaw, smoothes her features into an expression that's professional and reassuring. "Nobody's going to hurt you. You're safe now." She's probably been trained to say it; it's exactly what I need to hear. I lean to the side, rest my head on the door of the ambulance, and exhale slowly. I didn't even know I was holding my breath.

And then, from the back, a thin voice, like the first cry of a child entering the world.

"What's happening? Sabine, where are you?"

"Julien," I say, "I'm right here."

ACKNOWLEDGMENTS

Thank you:

Simon Kristensen published the short story on which *Before She Sleeps*'s first chapter is based and invited me to Copenhagen to read it out loud. Warsan Shire heard me there and told me to turn it into a novel; I've written this book expressly on her urging. Claire Chambers, who has always been a friend and huge source of encouragement, introduced me to the work of Susan Watkins, who gave generous feedback on an early draft of the book and information about the vast field of dystopian feminist fiction. Sunny Hundal's *India Dishonoured: Behind a Nation's War on Women* helped me gain a deep understanding of the devastating effects of gender selection on Indian society. Monica Byrne's *The Girl in the Road* helped me figure out a contemporary-sounding voice for a futuristic tale. Shandana Minhas shared her impressive knowledge of science fiction and cheered me on when I was ready to give up. Wellesley friends Susan Gies Conley, Edris Goolsby, and Anna Balogh kept urging me to persist, reminding me that if I could survive four years at W, then I could write this book. Writer friends Christopher Merrill, Aamer Hussein, Rachel McCormack, and Peter H. Fogtdal offered support as I sweated through months of writing and rewriting. Rick Slettenhaar was a brother-in-arms and a shoulder to lean on during the terrible time after Sabeen Mahmud's death. Syma Khalid and Alina Hasanain Shah helped me with the medical and scientific aspects of Julien's work and research. MacGregor Rucker offered me helpful feedback on crucial scenes in the book. The music of Chilly

Gonzales, especially the song "Gentle Threat," helped me develop the noir atmosphere of Green City.

Special thanks go to my agents Jessica Woollard and Clare Israel for believing in this novel, as well as my publisher Lori Milken for her valuable input. And reserving the best for last: my editor and friend Joseph Olshan, with whom working on this book together has been one of the most difficult and most rewarding experiences of my life.